DEATH OF A LOBSTER LOVER

Hayley plodded along the beach, falling a distance behind Liddy as sand made its way inside her shoes making her more and more uncomfortable and causing her to slow down her pace.

As she rounded the bend and caught up with Liddy, Hayley found her friend standing in the sand, frozen in place, staring at something.

Hayley followed her gaze over to the smoldering fire, the last tiny embers crackling and flying up into a cloud of smoke.

There was a body lying in the sand.

The head was turned slightly so Hayley was able to recognize the face.

It was Jackson Young.

And next to him tipped over in the sand was a pot, somehow knocked off the wire grate placed over the fire, the sand having absorbed the boiling water, as three lobsters, lucky enough to still be alive, crawled slowly back towards the ocean in a daring desperate bid for freedom . . .

Books by Lee Hollis

DEATH OF A KITCHEN DIVA

DEATH OF A COUNTRY FRIED REDNECK

DEATH OF A COUPON CLIPPER

DEATH OF A CHOCOHOLIC

DEATH OF A CHRISTMAS CATERER

DEATH OF A CUPCAKE QUEEN

DEATH OF A BACON HEIRESS

DEATH OF A PUMPKIN CARVER

DEATH OF A LOBSTER LOVER

EGGNOG MURDER
(with Leslie Meier and Barbara Ross)

Published by Kensington Publishing Corporation

A Hayley Powell
Food & Cocktails Mystery

DEATH OF A LOBSTER LOVER

LEE HOLLIS

KENSINGTON PUBLISHING CORP.

http://www.kensingtonbooks.com

KENSINGTON BOOKS are published by

Kensington Publishing Corp.
119 West 40th Street
New York, NY 10018

ISBN-13: 978-1-4967-0256-2
ISBN-10: 1-4967-0256-5
First Kensington Mass Market Edition: July 2017

eISBN-13: 978-1-4967-0257-9
eISBN-10: 1-4967-0257-3
First Kensington Electronic Edition: July 2017

10 9 8 7 6 5 4 3 2 1

Printed in the United States of America

Chapter 1

Crunch, crunch, crunch.

"Mona Barnes, please tell me you are not eating food in my car!" Liddy barked, eyeing her suspiciously through the rearview mirror of her brand-spanking-new black Mercedes E-Class Sedan.

"Nope," Mona said from the backseat, waiting for Liddy to avert her eyes back to the road before shoving her hand into a crinkled bag of Lay's Cheddar & Sour Cream potato chips again that was sitting in her lap, and shoveling out a generous handful of chips.

She quickly stuffed them into her mouth.

Crunch, crunch, crunch.

"Mona!"

"What?" Mona sighed, swallowing and then licking her greasy fingertips.

"You just lied to my face!"

"No, I didn't! I lied to the back of your head."

"It's a figure of speech! The point is you lied! You are clearly snacking back there and probably getting crumbs all over my new leather upholstery!"

"Hey, you were the one who insisted we drive in your fancy new car," Mona said, crumpling the now-empty bag of chips and tossing the trash in the empty seat next to her.

"That's because Hayley's car wouldn't have made the two-hour trip and the only other alternative was for all of us to squeeze into the front of your dilapidated old wreck of a truck!"

Hayley, who was wearing earbuds and listening to an audiobook version of a Jo Nesbø crime thriller on her smartphone, yanked the buds out of her ears and swiveled around in the passenger's seat to address her BFFs. "What kind of girls' weekend are we going to have if you two are fighting the whole time?"

"I had one request, just one request before agreeing to drive us, and that was *no* eating in my new car. So what does Mona do? She scarfs down a bag of chips even before we've crossed the Trenton Bridge and left the island!"

"Well, you were the one who said we couldn't stop at McDonald's on the way. I was afraid I'd starve!" Mona growled.

"I said no fast food. I'm totally open to lunch at a quaint, tasteful little side-of-the-road restaurant," Liddy huffed.

"There are no quaint, tasteful little side-of-the-road restaurants on the way to Calais, Liddy," Hayley said, smiling.

"I rest my case," Mona said before reaching into the pocket of her gray sweatshirt and pulling out a Snickers bar, which she noisily unwrapped.

Liddy's blood boiled as she whipped her head around to glare at Mona, whose lips were smudged with chocolate as she chewed on a generous hunk of the candy bar.

"Liddy!" Hayley yelled. "Watch out!"

The Mercedes swerved back across the yellow line as

Liddy jerked the wheel to the right, narrowly missing a blue Ford truck approaching fast from the opposite direction.

The driver pressed angrily on the horn.

"Can you *please* pay attention? I'd like to live long enough to at least see Salmon Cove," Hayley said, exhaling a sigh of relief now that the car was back to moving in a forward straight line.

Salmon Cove, Maine, was a small remote fishing village located in the farthest reaches of Down East Maine near the town of Calais. When the three of them had initially discussed going on a weekend getaway during Bar Harbor's busiest time of year, in mid-July, the last place on their minds was Salmon Cove. Liddy pushed hard for them to go to Martha's Vineyard, but that was a bit pricey for her more frugal friends. Hayley's suggestion of going on a simple shopping trip to Portland was met with bored yawns. They had already done that two times this year alone.

Finally, it was Mona who came up with Salmon Cove. She had gone there practically every summer when she was a kid. Her family owned a cabin in the woods near the scenic waterfront. The family would go fishing and swimming and play games for two whole weeks. Mona even learned her lobstering skills from a local boy whose family had a boat and a small business nearby. By the time she graduated from high school, Mona was already ready to set up her own shop in Bar Harbor.

Mona's uncle Cecil still owned the cabin to this day. Mona's father had sold it to his younger brother after suffering a stroke. Traveling to Salmon Cove just wasn't as easy as it had been for the family so they were happy to get rid of it. Mona hadn't been back since.

Mona had recently heard through relatives that her

uncle Cecil was currently visiting an old Army buddy in Arizona, and so the place was just sitting there empty. She e-mailed Cecil, and he quickly wrote back and told her that he would be happy to offer his cabin to Mona and her friends for a few days. Hayley honestly loved the idea of not having to split a hotel room. That would leave an ample amount of spending money for decadent seafood banquets and plenty of strong cocktails at the local watering hole.

Liddy wasn't sold on the idea of a weekend in the boonies, and even tried to bow out of the trip altogether at one point, but then circumstances changed.

She split up with her boyfriend, Sonny Rivers, a local attorney.

Or they were just taking a break.

That actually was the official story from Liddy.

But according to Sonny, it was definitely over.

He was done.

And Liddy had yet to accept that cold hard fact.

But suddenly the idea of getting out of town had much more appeal to her and she jumped on board at the last minute, insisting on driving them all to Salmon Cove in her new Mercedes that she had recently purchased in Bangor, which many in town believed was her way of trying to cheer herself up.

Hayley had pulled Mona aside before they left and made her promise not to mention the breakup during their vacation and Mona, who loved toying with and relentlessly teasing Liddy, begrudgingly agreed.

That lasted about twenty minutes into the trip.

"What you need, Liddy, is to find a new boyfriend so he can help you get that big ole stick out of your butt," Mona said from the backseat.

"I don't need a new boyfriend because Sonny and I

have not broken up. Like I've said over and over again, we're just taking a break."

"You can say it until you're blue in the face, but nobody's going to believe you," Mona said, popping the remainder of the candy bar in her mouth, and then scrunching the wrapper into her fist before stuffing it in the seat pocket in front of her. "Why do you think he dumped you? Was it the age difference?"

Hayley wanted to fling open the car door and jump out.

Liddy cringed. "No, Mona. Age had nothing to do with our decision to *take a break*!"

"Come on! It's like Maggie Smith dating the kid who played Harry Potter!" Mona howled.

Liddy gripped the wheel, her knuckles white, gritting her teeth, ready to burst a blood vessel.

"Can we *please* change the subject?" Hayley begged.

Mona shrugged, and wiped the chocolate off her face with the arm of her sweatshirt.

"Go ahead and eat all the snacks you smuggled into my car, Mona. I have no problem with that."

"Seriously? Okay! What suddenly changed your mind?" Mona asked, curious.

"I'm hoping even you have enough good manners not to talk with your mouth full," Liddy sniffed.

"Don't bet on it," Hayley said, turning to see Mona tearing open a package of beef jerky.

Luckily, by the time they reached Machais on Coastal Route 1, Mona had passed out and was snoring loud enough that Liddy felt the need to crank up the volume on her radio and blast '90s classics the rest of the way to Calais.

Hayley and Liddy bopped up and down in their seats, singing along to their favorite Spice Girls song crooning to their imaginary boyfriends to just tell them what they want, what they really, really want!

The cabin was just fifteen minutes outside of Calais, and when they reached the town they had to wake Mona up from her peaceful slumber to guide them the rest of the way. Mona was grumpy and groggy, but she managed to get them there, with the help of Liddy's Waze app on her phone, and when they finally pulled up to the cabin that was at the end of a gravel road and tucked into a secluded wooded area, Hayley's and Liddy's mouths dropped open in shock.

It was a dump.

The whole structure tilted to one side as if it was ready to collapse.

A tarp had been hastily thrown over the entire roof, undoubtedly to cover up some holes where rainfall or snow might leak inside.

There were empty beer cans littering the property.

A rusted-out Volkswagen bus with no tires in the back.

A pitiful pile of wood stacked up against the side of a wall.

"We're here!" Mona said, jumping out of the car. "Pop open the trunk, Liddy, and I'll take our bags inside."

Hayley turned to Liddy, who sat frozen in the driver's seat of her Mercedes, unable to move. "I know it's not the Ritz-Carlton. But it's not so bad. It has a certain charm."

Liddy didn't respond.

She just stared at the cabin, mouth agape.

Mona, bogged down with her duffel bag and one of Liddy's Louis Vuitton carry-ons, trudged over to the front door and tried pushing her way through, but it was obviously jammed.

After a few tries banging into it with her shoulder, it

gave way and creaked open, and she disappeared inside with the bags.

"Maybe it looks completely different on the inside," Hayley said brightly, trying her best to be encouraging.

She persuaded Liddy to get out of the car and reserve judgment, at least until they had a chance to go inside and see what they were up against.

They joined Mona in the cabin.

Liddy looked around. "You're right, Hayley. It is completely different . . . it's worse!"

In all honesty, it wasn't that bad.

The whole place had been recently swept and there was a full bed with clean sheets in one corner and bunk beds in another corner. The tiny kitchen at least appeared clean. No dirty dishes in the sink. And there was a small refrigerator where they could store food.

But it was small.

And calling the place no-frills was being generous.

There would be no five-star reviews on TripAdvisor.

"This sure brings back a lot of happy memories," Mona said, beaming.

Liddy, in a rare show of restraint, refrained from commenting.

She just kept walking around, taking it all in, and sizing it up.

She suddenly stopped and turned to Mona. "Where's the bathroom?"

"There isn't one," Mona said casually.

"What do you mean there isn't a bathroom?" Liddy asked, aghast.

"I mean there isn't one. There's an outhouse out back!"

That's when Liddy completely lost it.

She grabbed her Louis Vuitton carry-on that Mona had deposited next to the door and stormed out. "I did not sign up for a *Little House on the Prairie* weekend! We are not Laura Ingalls Wilder and her two dirt-poor sisters!"

"Not you, that's for sure. You're more like that spoiled brat Nellie Oleson!" Mona bellowed as Liddy slammed out the door and marched back to her Mercedes.

"Hurry up! Let's go! We're checking into a hotel!" Liddy screamed from outside.

Hayley didn't want to side with Liddy and hurt Mona's feelings, but she too couldn't imagine actually using a creaky old smelly outhouse.

And she definitely couldn't imagine in that moment that using an outhouse for four days would soon be the least of their troubles.

Chapter 2

"Fully booked? You can't be serious!" Liddy gasped, eyes blinking.

The hotel's roly-poly desk clerk, surprised by this rather pint-size force of nature questioning his command of the hotel's reservation system, struck a defensive posture, but couldn't help but glance back down at his computer screen to double-check his assertion. After a quick scroll down, he regained his confidence and raised his weary eyes back up to meet Liddy's.

"Yes, I'm afraid so. Fully booked."

"Who on earth would *intentionally* come to this backwater town and actually want to *stay* here?" Liddy remarked, her face a mix of disgust and wonder. "I mean, I would understand if someone's GPS got all screwed up and they drove here by mistake, but to actually *plan* a trip here? I don't think so!"

"*We* did," Mona barked.

"Yes, but that's because I've never set foot here until today so I didn't know any better," Liddy said, before turning back to the clerk behind the desk. "I doubt you have a lot of repeat business."

"As a matter of fact, we have many visitors who adore Salmon Cove and return here every summer for their vacation," the clerk sniffed, his jowly cheeks swinging like a basset hound's, as his rotund body tensed and the few strands of hair on top of his head seemed to stand on end. He pushed them back with his hand.

"Well, we're from Bar Harbor so you can understand why we're not impressed with Salmon Cove," Liddy said, every last word dripping with disdain.

The desk clerk had pretty much had enough. He cleared his throat and summoned up as much indignation as his portly frame could manage. "Well, we may not be as glamorous as *Bar Harbor* or boast a national park, or have anything as majestic as Cadillac Mountain or Thunder Hole to behold, but Salmon Cove does have its charms."

"I think it's a beautiful little town," Hayley offered weakly, trying to tamp down the situation as she noticed the red-faced desk clerk curling his pudgy fingers into a hammy fist, spoiling for a fight.

"And no, you won't spot anyone as famous as the Obamas showing up at a local ice cream shop or Martha Stewart walking her dogs along Sand Beach, but we do have our share of famous visitors every year," the desk clerk blurted out, determined to defend his beloved hometown.

"Like who?" Liddy asked, folding her arms.

The desk clerk froze for a moment, not expecting anyone to actually challenge him by asking for a specific celebrity. He foolishly thought that this odious harpy, who had ruined his afternoon by bursting through the door and throwing around an abundance of attitude, would just trust him and let it go.

But no.

She stood there, arms folded, waiting.

"Tracey Gold," the desk clerk stammered.

"Who?" Mona asked, dumbfounded.

"Tracey Gold," the desk clerk said again, feeling smaller and smaller by the moment.

"Who the hell is that?" Mona demanded to know.

"The actress from *Growing Pains*," Hayley said softly.

"That show from the eighties with Kirk something or other, who used to be cute but is now creepy and weird and judging everybody because they're not as religious as he is?" Mona asked, struggling to remember.

"Yes," Hayley said, nodding.

"So Tracey Silver played the mother? I thought that was Jody Lighthouse or something," Mona said, scratching her head.

"You're thinking of the mother. The mother was played by Judith Light," the desk clerk jumped in, unable to restrain himself any longer.

"No, she wasn't! Judith Light was in *Who's the Boss?*, the one with Tony Danza!" Hayley quietly offered.

The affronted desk clerk glared at her, bemused by the fact she was joining her friends in ganging up on him.

"Then who played the mother on *Growing Pains*?" Mona asked.

"I don't know!" the desk clerk sputtered. "But I do know Tracey *Gold* played the sister!"

"Oh, yeah. Now I remember. Didn't she get sick or something?" Mona asked, as the desk clerk sighed, having thought the discussion was finally coming to a merciful end.

"She battled bulimia," Liddy said, finally chiming in and adding her two cents. "I read about it in *People* magazine a while back."

"She was here and she had Ebola?" Mona gasped, spinning her head around, eyes bulging as if she would suddenly be able to spot some insidious airborne virus.

"Not Ebola, Mona! Bulimia!" Hayley cried. "It doesn't matter! The man was just trying to make a point."

"Well, he didn't exactly do a bang-up job of it now, did he?" Liddy laughed. "Comparing some washed-up eighties sitcom actress to Martha Stewart to impress us? It's sad, really."

The desk clerk appeared as if he was going to hurl his massive bulk over the counter and strangle Liddy, but he held himself, and repeated one last time to the three women, with more than a hint of relief, "Like I said, we're *fully* booked."

At that moment, as if a gift from the heavens, a family of four arrived to check in and the desk clerk was finally freed from his torturous interaction with Liddy and her pals, who huddled in a corner to debate their next move.

"I say we suck it up and go back to the cabin and spend the night, and then we can drive back in the morning," Hayley suggested, tired from the long drive and anxious for a plan.

"I have absolutely no intention of spending one night in that rat-infested hovel. Do you hear me? I say we drive back tonight," Liddy insisted.

"I didn't haul butt all the way down here to stay just one night! I want to enjoy the whole long weekend! Like we planned!" Mona wailed.

"Well, we came in my car and my car is leaving in two

minutes!" Liddy hollered, turning for support to Hayley, who labored to stay neutral.

"How will I get home?" Mona barked.

"Take a bus!" Liddy said.

"Greyhound doesn't come all the way down to Salmon Cove!" Mona countered.

"Then hitchhike for all I care, Mona! I'm leaving right now!" Liddy screamed as she swiveled around to march dramatically out the front door.

Before she took a step, a man appeared out of nowhere flashing them all a warm smile as he walked past them and up to the desk clerk, who was finishing up with the family of vacationers.

"Just wanted to see if I could get another room key card. I can't seem to find the one you gave me when I checked in," he said.

"Of course," the desk clerk said. "Just give me a minute."

"No hurry. I'm off for a hike. I can just pick it up when I get back," he said.

He was strikingly handsome, not tall, almost Tom Cruise short, thin and wiry in a tight-fitting T-shirt, wearing khaki shorts that showed off his sturdy hairy legs, and L.L.Bean hiking boots.

The desk clerk smiled. "Have a nice time, Mr. Young."

The man spun back around and finally noticed Hayley, Liddy, and Mona, all of whom couldn't help but stare at him, taking in his obvious attractiveness.

He flashed that winning smile. "You here visiting, ladies?"

Liddy quickly stepped forward, like some Jane Austen character determined to leave her sisters in waiting behind as she seized her moment to engage the moneyed and eligible and swoon-worthy bachelor in the remote English village. "Yes, we're from Bar Harbor."

"Nice place. But it's much too crowded with tourists this time of year, to be perfectly honest. I like the tranquility of Salmon Cove."

"Me too," Liddy said, unconcerned with her stunning contradiction from just a few moments before in front of everyone in the hotel lobby.

Mona chuckled.

Hayley couldn't stop watching the desk clerk, who was so astounded by Liddy's brazen turn, he was struck speechless.

"Where are you from?" Liddy asked, almost singing the words like an animated Disney princess.

"Boston. I'm a writer. The name is Jackson Young. Maybe you've seen my byline? I do mostly puff pieces for travel magazines. But it pays the bills and allows me to come up here and get away from it all, work on my novel which I'll never finish, and gorge on lobster."

"Yeah, that's why we came too," Mona said. "Except the novel part. I hate reading books. Don't have the patience for it."

"He's talking about writing a novel, not reading one, Mona," Hayley said softly, shaking her head.

"I especially needed to get away," Liddy continued, her voice cracking just a bit, batting her eyes for effect. "You see, I recently broke up with my boyfriend and thought some quality time away with my two best friends would be the tonic I need."

"You said you and Sonny were just taking a break!" Mona howled.

"No, it's definitely over. Sonny and I are finished. Kaput. Finito!" Liddy said in Mona's direction before adding, "The end."

"Are you married, Jackson?" Hayley asked.

"Me? Oh, no, mostly a wandering spirit, I guess you have to be to be a travel writer. But hey, I've been doing this job for a long time and there are days when I think I might want to settle down, but . . . man, I should just shut up. Too much information!"

"Not at all! I'm riveted," Liddy cooed, not a hint of sarcasm in her voice.

"Well, I don't want to keep you ladies from your bonding time," Jackson said, nodding to the three of them before turning to leave.

"I love lobster too!" Liddy blurted out.

This stopped Jackson in his tracks.

He took another look at Liddy and smiled.

God, the man certainly possessed a hypnotic smile.

Their eyes locked and they drank each other in for a moment.

"Good to know," he said with a wink.

"What are you talking about?" Mona interjected, oblivious to the burgeoning love connection unfolding right in front of her. "You hate eating lobster. Especially tearing off the claws and cracking the shell. You told me it's like dissecting an animal in biology class and the whole process makes you want to hurl!"

There was an awkward silence before Liddy said evenly, "But I love the taste of lobster meat in a nice pasta dish, Mona. Let's leave it at that."

"Hope to see you ladies around," Jackson said, though he was looking right at Liddy.

And then he disappeared out the door.

Liddy watched him go, and then slowly turned to Hayley and Mona, her mind racing.

"You know what? I'm too tired to drive back to Bar Harbor tonight. Why don't we just suck it up and at least stay one night in the cabin before we head out tomorrow," she said as if it had been her idea.

"I'm getting whiplash from you constantly changing your mind!" Mona said, shaking her head as they trudged back out the door to the car.

Chapter 3

The Starfish Lounge, located just across the street from the one hotel in town, was the local watering hole that served as the social center in Salmon Cove. It was narrow and musty and a bit claustrophobic, and there was a distinct fishy smell emanating from the harbor outside, but there was something quaint and familiar about the place, and Hayley felt right at home upon entering with Liddy and Mona.

It was early, just after eight in the evening, but the place was packed and a Tim McGraw classic played on the old-fashioned jukebox in the corner. Mona managed to stare down a couple of fishermen who were finishing their mugs of beer until they got up and offered their table to the trio of female strangers who had just arrived.

"Thank you," Mona said sweetly, as if relinquishing their table had totally been their idea.

"What do you gals want to drink?" Liddy said, snapping open her purse and fishing around for some cash.

"Just a club soda with lime," Hayley said, resigned to her role of designated driver for the evening.

"I'll take a beer. Nothing fancy. Whatever's on tap," Mona said.

"Well, I'm going to need something a lot stronger," Liddy said. "It's imperative that I dull my senses if I'm going to spend the night in that crumbling rat trap in the woods."

"You know, you're really starting to tick me off, Liddy," Mona barked. "Quit putting down my family's vacation home."

"Forgive me, Mona," Liddy said, every word dripping with sarcasm. "I didn't realize you thought of your little getaway destination as Balmoral Castle where the Queen spends her summer days traipsing across the grounds with her corgis!"

"Was that an insult?" Mona asked Hayley.

Hayley nodded.

"Can you just get me a friggin' beer? Is that too much to ask, Liddy?" Mona growled.

Liddy crossed to the bar and ordered a round from the statuesque, sturdy, busty bartender with flat blond hair and a weathered face that had probably been stunning years ago when she was a sprightly young woman. But years of hard living had undoubtedly taken its toll, and now in her fifties, though still attractive, there was a hardness that had calcified her once soft features. Only when she smiled after Liddy made a joke could you see the roughness fade and a hint of that long-lost beauty return.

Suddenly a white dish rag in a hammy fist appeared in front of Hayley's face, and she sat back in her chair, startled. It was the young bar back, nineteen or twenty years old, and he vigorously, almost violently, wiped down the table. He was a big lug, over six feet, a flat nose and big lips, matted brown hair, his body a mix of muscles and fat. He wore a tight-fitting Starfish Lounge T-shirt and scrubbed the table until it rocked back and forth, at one point nearly tipping over.

Once he was done, he stuffed the rag inside the left hip pocket of his faded ragged blue jeans and noticed Hayley and Mona for the first time.

"You're new here. I haven't seen you before," he said in a gruff, not quite welcoming voice.

"We're just visiting," Hayley said, smiling.

He didn't smile back. "What are you doing here?"

"Are you deaf? We're visiting! Like she said! We don't live here!" Mona yelled, not inclined to receive the third degree from a bar back who didn't seem to boast a lot of brainpower.

In fact, as he stared at them, eyes blinking, a vacant look on his face, it struck Hayley that he almost seemed a bit slow, if not outright mentally challenged.

"Where are you from?" the boy asked, fingering his dirty dish rag that slung down his side from his back pocket.

"Outer space. We're aliens. We've been sent here to suck the brains out of all earthlings in Salmon Cove!" Mona said, shaking her head in frustration.

The boy's eyes widened as he digested this information.

It was almost as if he actually believed Mona.

Hayley decided to put his mind at ease.

"We're from Bar Harbor. And I assure you we're one hundred percent human," Hayley said. "I'm Hayley and this is Mona. What's your name?"

"Boyd," the boy said, eyeing them suspiciously. But then he was distracted by the door opening and a young girl entering the bar. She was a petite thing, roughly the same age as Boyd, maybe twenty or twenty-one, her tiny head and limbs sticking out of an oversize sundress with a lobster print. She wore thick glasses and appeared shy and demure, almost waiflike. Boyd stared at her as she approached the bar to speak with the owner.

By this time, Liddy had walked back over from the bar carrying a bottle of beer, a cosmo, and Hayley's club soda in her hands.

Boyd blocked her way.

"Excuse me," Liddy said politely.

Boyd didn't budge.

He was too busy staring at the tiny girl who was still struggling to get the bartender's attention.

"Hey! Beanstalk! Step aside so my friend can sit down!" Mona snapped.

Boyd glanced down at Mona, gawking at her as if he still believed her joke of being an alien from another planet, and then moved off, still clutching his dish rag like it was a security blanket as he slowly moved toward the girl at the bar and said hello. The girl turned and smiled at him and they started a conversation that was drowned out by Tim McGraw's singing from the jukebox.

Liddy set the drinks on the table and then plopped down to join her two friends. "The bartender owns the place. Her name is Sue and she's quite a character. By the way, she knows all about your family's cabin, Mona, and she agreed with me that it should be condemned. I liked her instantly."

Mona grabbed her beer and chugged it down, ignoring Liddy.

Just as Hayley lifted her club soda to take a sip, someone slammed into her chair from behind. She dropped the glass and the soda spilled all over the table. Then two hands glommed on to her shoulders. She cranked her head around and up to see an elderly man, pushing eighty, a Red Sox baseball cap pulled down over his head, white stubble covering his face, using Hayley to balance himself. Everyone at the table could smell the bourbon on his breath.

Sue the owner scooted out from behind the bar and raced over to help. "I'm so sorry, ladies. He's been a bit over-served. Here, Rufus, let me help you back to the bar."

Rufus slapped her hand away, and bellowed in a slurred voice. "I'm fine, Sue. I just slipped on your wet floor on my way back from the john. You shouldn't mop it so much."

Hayley glanced down at the floor, which looked like it hadn't been mopped or swept in a decade.

"Stop making excuses, you old drunk. You can hardly stand upright! Ellie, get over here and help me with your grandfather!"

The young ragamuffin in her lobster sundress that was nearly swallowing her up whole broke away from her conversation with the slow-witted bar back Boyd and scampered over to Sue, taking old man Rufus by the arm, coaxing him away from the table.

"Come on, Grandpa, it's after eight. Time to go home."

"I don't want to go home, Ellie! I just got here!"

"You've been here since we opened at noon, you old coot! Now get out of here! We'll see you tomorrow," Sue said, signaling Boyd, who was only too happy to rush over and assist his little crush, whose name apparently was Ellie, with her grandfather.

They quickly ushered him out of the bar.

Sue turned back to Hayley, Liddy, and Mona. "Again, I'm sorry for the commotion, ladies. Your next round is on me."

Mona lit up. "Thank you, Sue!"

"Rufus is here every night drinking too much. But he's been here for years. Part of the local charm, I guess," Sue said with a resigned smile. "Everyone comes in here expecting to see him so I put up with it."

"We have plenty of our own Rufuses back in Bar Harbor," Hayley said, laughing.

"I believe it," Sue said, grinning, before lumbering back behind the bar to attend to her other customers.

Despite Liddy's misgivings, Salmon Cove did share certain similarities with Bar Harbor. There was the small town coastal laid-back ambience, the eccentric, colorful locals, and more than likely, the hidden dark secrets that always seemed to surface eventually.

Chapter 4

Sue returned shortly with the free round she had so kindly offered on a tray and set the drinks down in front of Hayley, Liddy, and Mona.

"Enjoy, ladies," Sue said.

"Thank you, Sue. This is very nice of you," Hayley said, reaching into her pocket and pulling out a five-dollar bill. She dropped it on the now empty tray as a tip.

"Appreciate it," Sue said just as the door to the bar swung open and Ellie returned, Boyd on her heels like a loyal basset hound.

"What'd you forget?"

"My car keys," Ellie said, looking around. "We got Grandpa all strapped in, but I can't seem to find my keys."

They all began a quick search of the bar area until Boyd spotted something shiny on the floor and scooped up the keys in his big fleshy hand. He gently handed them to Ellie.

"There you go, Miss Ellie," Boyd said, smiling shyly.

"Thank you, Boyd. You're a peach," Ellie said, averting her eyes because she was embarrassed the big oaf was gazing at her so wide-eyed and lovingly, drool practically spilling out of his mouth.

"Would you like me to ride home with you just to make sure you get your grandad home safely?"

"No, Boyd, I don't want to bother you."

"It's no bother, really."

"But how would you get back to the bar to finish your shift?"

"I can walk."

"It's four miles."

"I don't mind."

"No, really, I'll be fine. But thank you."

There was a long, interminable silence.

Neither of them knew what to say next.

Finally, unable to handle the awkwardness of the situation, Ellie blurted out a fast "good night" and hightailed it out of the bar.

"When are you going to ask that girl out on a date, Boyd?" Sue asked as she mixed a cocktail for a sleepy-eyed woman at the far end of the bar.

"What? I don't know what you mean . . . What?" Boyd stammered.

"Give me a break, Boyd. It's obvious to everyone in town you're crushing on that girl big-time," Sue said, chuckling.

Boyd's face turned five shades of red.

"She's just a friend," Boyd said, wrenching the dirty dish rag from his waist and wiping down the already clean table next to Hayley, Liddy, and Mona.

"Any man who says a girl is just a friend always wants more," Sue said, setting the cocktail down in front of the woman at the end of the bar, who nodded as she knocked it back. "What you need to do is get your nose out of those silly comic books you're always reading and do something about it."

Boyd finished cleaning the table and desperately searched for another chore to embark on that would help him escape from this excruciatingly uncomfortable conversation.

"Boyd, you're a good kid. You deserve to have a nice girlfriend. Someone to go to the movies with, have dinner with, a companion you can talk to and confide in," Sue said, coming out from behind the bar and walking up behind him.

Boyd spun around, shaking his head vehemently.

"Stop it, Sue. Ellie doesn't like me that way."

"I think she does," Sue said. She turned to Hayley, Liddy, and Mona, who sat eavesdropping at the table behind her. "Am I right, ladies?"

"It was pretty clear to me," Liddy said, sipping her drink. "The shy body language, the sweet smile, the eyes that seemed to say, 'I'm fragile but I trust you not to break me.' That girl was definitely working it."

"She was not that calculating, Liddy. Stop projecting," Hayley said. "But I agree that she likes you, Boyd. I just think you're going to have to make the first move."

Sue turned to Mona, who was sucking down her beer, bored. "What about you?"

"Me? I think all this gooey matchmaking crap is a waste of time. This isn't a friggin' chick flick. Let the two of them work it out without all of you fluttering around like a bunch of annoying overgrown cupids."

And with that, Mona slammed her beer down on the table and stood up. "Now if you'll excuse me, I've got a hankering to hear some classic Garth Brooks."

She marched over to the jukebox, fished some change

out of her pocket, and began flipping through the songbook underneath the glass using the dials on the side.

A shaggy-haired man, around the same age as Mona, tall, lean, handsome, wearing a ragged T-shirt, ripped jeans, and boots, sat at a table near the jukebox, nursing a beer. A beautiful golden retriever lay at his feet quietly, looking like she was sleeping, but her eyes were open and occasionally blinking.

The shaggy-haired man stared at Mona.

She didn't notice him.

He put down his beer and leaned forward, his eyes fixed on Mona, who was punching in a number on the jukebox.

Both Hayley and Liddy were intrigued by this good-looking man who seemed to be so captivated by Mona.

They exchanged curious looks.

Finally, the man leaned down, patted his dog on the head, and then stood up and marched up behind Mona.

"Excuse me," he said.

"Wait your turn. I'm not done," Mona barked, dropping a few more coins into the jukebox.

"Mona? Mona Butler?"

Mona's whole body froze.

Suddenly she recognized the voice.

A smile crept across her lips.

She wheeled around and gasped. "Corey! Corey Guildford! What the hell are you doing here?"

"What do you mean? I live here! What are you doing here? I couldn't believe it when I saw you. Mona Butler! Back in Salmon Cove!"

"It's Barnes now."

"So you finally got hitched?"

"Worst mistake of my life. He's a total loser. But he's my loser, I guess."

"How long has it been?"

"About twenty years, something like that. The summer after my high school graduation, I think," Mona said, smiling.

Yes, Mona was smiling.

This must have been a *very* close friend.

Corey hugged Mona, drawing her into him, holding her tightly.

And Mona hugged back.

They held each other for what seemed like forever.

Mona gently rested her head on Corey's shoulder.

Corey's hand dropped dangerously close to Mona's buttocks.

Neither was ready or willing to let the other go.

This unexpected reunion was borderline romantic.

Definitely sweet and rather touching.

Hayley and Liddy watched this unbelievably rare scene, for Mona anyway, with mouths agape.

Finally, Liddy couldn't stand it anymore.

"Mona, don't you want to introduce us to your friend?"

Mona finally pulled away from Corey.

"Not really," she said flatly.

"Corey Guildford," he said, stepping over to their table with an extended hand, which both Hayley and Liddy eagerly shook. "Old friend of Mona's from years back."

"I see," Liddy said, shifting in her seat, enjoying the moment. "I'm surprised she never mentioned you."

"You *never* mentioned me? I'm crushed, Mona," Corey said, playfully.

"We just hung out when we were kids. Stealing beers from his parents' cooler and skinny-dipping at Rocky Point," Mona said, her eyes narrowing, warning Liddy to lay off.

But Liddy had no intention of letting this delicious

conversation fall by the wayside. She relished witnessing Mona twisted up in knots.

"Skinny-dipping? How wild and uninhibited! That's certainly not the Mona we know. What other little secrets have you been keeping from us, Mona?"

"I got plenty of secrets when it comes to Mona," Corey said with a devilish smile. "Want to hear one?"

"Corey . . ." Mona said, her face pleading with him to stop.

"Yes, please!" Liddy squealed. "We want to hear everything!"

"Well, for one thing," Corey said. "I taught her everything she knows about lobstering."

Liddy sat back in her chair, resoundingly disappointed. "That's it?"

Mona sighed with relief.

"Is that true, Mona?" Hayley asked. "This is the boy you told us about?"

"Damn straight," she said, nodding. "Corey's family has been lobstering in Salmon Cove for generations. He taught me all the basics about hauling traps. It's because of him I got such a successful business back home in Bar Harbor."

Corey's golden retriever didn't like being left alone at the table so she stood up from the floor, stretched out, and ambled over to the group to rub up against Mona, who reached down and scratched her head affectionately.

"Beautiful dog," Mona said, flapping the dog's ear.

"That's Sadie," Corey said. "I think she likes you."

Hayley watched Corey as he stared at Mona, a big, wide, happy grin on his face.

Sadie wasn't the only one who seemed to adore Mona.

Chapter 5

"Honestly, I can't watch Mona make a spectacle of herself anymore," Liddy said, shaking her head in disgust.

"What are you talking about?" Hayley asked, cranking her head around to see Mona and Corey immersed in a heated game of pool. "They're just playing pool."

Mona was on a roll and beating him soundly. She was about to sink the last ball in the corner pocket.

"I mean, she's a married woman. She shouldn't be carrying on like this," Liddy said, scowling.

"You know what I think? I think you're jealous," Hayley said, sipping the last of her club soda through a straw.

"Me? Jealous? Of Mona? That is utterly ridiculous. What could I possibly be jealous of?"

"You're feeling insecure about being dumped by Sonny, and suddenly a good-looking man is paying attention to Mona and not to you."

"How dare you psychoanalyze me, especially while we're on vacation!"

"That isn't exactly a denial," Hayley said.

Liddy downed her cocktail in a huff.

Across the room, Mona drove the last ball into the left corner pocket and then whooped and hollered as she raised her pool cue over her head in victory.

Corey bowed to her superiority, and then wrapped his big arms around her in a tight hug, which again, he held for far longer than just a "friend" normally would.

Mona didn't seem to mind and made no move to extricate herself.

"They're *just* friends," Hayley said weakly as she and Liddy watched Mona and Corey casually grope each other with their hands.

Liddy picked up her bag off the floor and dropped it down on the table. "I'm ready to go back to the cabin."

"*Now*? But you said you wanted to get blindingly drunk so you wouldn't be consciously aware that you were sleeping in that dump tonight."

"I changed my mind. I'm done. Let's go," Liddy said.

As the designated driver for the evening, Hayley didn't have much of a choice. She waved at Mona, who ambled over with Corey close behind her, barely any shade between them.

"Liddy wants to leave," Hayley said.

"Back to the cabin? Really?" Mona asked, eyes wide, genuinely surprised.

"Yes, I'd like to get an early start in the morning, and I want to get a full eight hours of shut-eye so I'm fresh for the drive," Liddy said, fishing around in her bag for a mint.

Mona shrugged. "Okay."

Corey touched her arm. "You can't leave yet. I want a chance to redeem myself and show you I actually can play pool. How about two out of three?"

"I'm sorry, Corey, but Liddy's tired," Mona sighed.

Hayley knew Mona wanted to stay and spend time with Corey, but Mona was first and foremost a loyal friend, and if her friend was ready to leave, then she was going to abide by her wishes.

Even if it was Liddy.

"Then let your friends go back to the cabin now and I'll drive you home later myself," Corey said.

"I don't know . . ." Mona said, torn.

"Please, Mona. I haven't seen you in years and you're leaving tomorrow so this is my only chance to spend some time with you," he said, almost pleading.

"It's already coming up on midnight now . . ." Mona said.

"So you're just going to take off and leave me standing here with a glass slipper?" Corey asked.

"Now that was *really* corny," Liddy said, rolling her eyes.

Hayley turned to her. "If he had said it to you, you would've thought it was the most romantic thing you'd ever heard."

Liddy couldn't argue with that because she knew Hayley was right.

"Okay," Mona said hesitantly.

"Did you hear that, Sadie? She's staying!" Corey yelped happily.

Hearing her name, Sadie instinctively stood up off the floor again, shook her fur out, and then trotted over for some loving attention from her master, who rubbed her head.

"It was nice meeting you, Corey," Hayley said, sticking her hand out to shake.

"A pleasure, Hayley, but I'm a hugger," Corey said, ignoring her hand and enveloping her in his arms.

He then let go and stepped back to face Liddy, arms outstretched.

"I'm good, thank you," Liddy said. "It was nice meeting you. Let's go, Hayley."

"Leaving so soon? I just got here," a man's voice said from behind them. They all turned to see Jackson Young, looking sexy in an open tight-fitting plaid button-down shirt that highlighted some impressive pecs and some equally tight blue jeans that accentuated his muscular legs and round bubble butt. The man had definitely been on a lot of strenuous hikes to get in that kind of shape.

Liddy stood gazing at him, speechless.

"I was hoping you would let me buy you a drink," he said, eyes twinkling.

"Liddy is tired so we're calling it a night," Hayley said.

"It's not *that* late, Hayley," Liddy scoffed. "What's the harm in staying a little while longer? What do you think will happen? My Donna Karan dress will turn into an off-the-rack rag from Kmart and my Mercedes will turn into a pumpkin?"

Corey turned to Mona. "You know, she's right. The whole Cinderella theme *is* kind of corny."

"Yeah, but she stole it from you and is running with it," Mona said, chuckling.

Ignoring them, Liddy turned and smiled at Jackson. "I would love for you to buy me a drink."

"Then I guess it's my lucky night," Jackson said, taking her by the arm and leading her over to the bar.

Hayley couldn't believe it.

"I swear she told me she was tired," Hayley said, turning to Mona and Corey, both of whom had already wandered back to the pool table and were setting up for their next game.

Hayley plopped back down at the table alone and

signaled Sue for another club soda. She knew she was in for a long night.

Hayley sat by herself for the next hour until last call.

She didn't mind.

It was nice to see Liddy and Mona both having such a good time.

Still, she could barely keep her eyes open and couldn't suppress her yawns any longer. She just wanted to go to bed. Even if it was on a lumpy mattress in the upper bunk at Mona's dilapidated family cabin.

Liddy suddenly hustled over to her as the bar began clearing out and whispered excitedly in her ear, "You'll never guess what just happened! Jackson has asked me to be his date at the lobster bake on Sunday!"

"What lobster bake?"

"It's like an annual thing that just happens to fall on this weekend. The whole town comes out for it. Jackson says we can't miss it!"

"But we're leaving tomorrow," Hayley said.

"That's what I want to talk to you about. I say we suck it up and just deal with staying at the cabin. I mean, come on, Hayley, how bad can it be?"

"But you were so adamant—"

"You know me, Hayley, sometimes I just need time to process and adjust. And that's what I've done. I have processed the situation and adjusted. And now I want to stay."

Mona sauntered over to them as Corey hung their pool cues back on the wall rack.

"You're not going to believe this, Mona, but Liddy wants to stay the whole weekend," Hayley said.

"Seriously?"

"Jackson wants me to be his date at the lobster bake," Liddy gushed breathlessly as if they were back in high school discussing the prom in excited whispers during study hall.

"That's great news," Mona said, beaming, before she twisted around and called out to Corey. "Hey! We're staying! So I can be your date to the lobster bake on Sunday!"

Corey gave her an enthusiastic thumbs-up. If he had been wearing a cowboy hat he would have tossed it in the air in jubilation with a "yee-haw!"

Hayley was happy her friends had dates to this big lobster bake she had heard nothing about until now.

And she would find some way to make the most of her fifth wheel status.

Really.

She didn't mind.

Much.

As she stood up and fumbled around in her coat pocket for the car keys, she saw Jackson sidle up next to Liddy and casually press a hotel room key card in her hand.

She heard him whisper in her ear, "I found the key card I lost earlier today so now I have an extra. In case you need it."

Liddy shivered with delight and gave him a peck on the cheek.

"Good night, you devil," Liddy cooed.

Jackson touched his cheek where she had planted the kiss and feigned swooning, and then he backed away, lingering by the door, stealing one last glance at Liddy, delighted.

And then he slipped out the door and was gone.

Liddy noticed Hayley eyeing the key card in the palm of her hand. "Don't judge me, Hayley."

"I would never—" Hayley protested.

"It's not like I'm going to use it!"

"I believe you," Hayley said.

"Yet."

And then Liddy burst out in a fit of girlish giggles, euphoric to be back in the game, an object of desire.

It was sweet.

But there was something about Jackson Young that wasn't quite right.

Hayley couldn't put her finger on it.

She had only had the briefest of exchanges, and on the surface he seemed quite nice, but there was something odd about his behavior and demeanor.

Like he was trying too hard.

Perhaps to cover something up about his true personality.

She certainly didn't have the same feeling about Corey.

He seemed perfectly relaxed and normal.

But there was definitely something off about Jackson.

He was too forced and too eager.

She couldn't tell Liddy because she feared she would just come off as merely jealous and petty.

And besides, Liddy was so smitten at this point there was very little chance she would even listen to her reservations or take them seriously.

So for once Hayley held her tongue.

And hoped she was wrong.

Island Food & Spirits
by
Hayley Powell

Part One

Who doesn't love summer vacation?

My brother, Randy, and I sure did when we were kids, and we would meet up on the last day of school, and walk home together, talking about all our fun and exciting plans for the lazy days of summer with our friends.

I'll never forget one year as we strolled home from school in the waning days of spring just before my eighth-grade graduation. Randy and I were in high spirits when we arrived home, and burst through the back door into the kitchen to raid the cookie jar before dinnertime. We suddenly stopped dead in our tracks, assaulted by a pungent, all too familiar aroma that filled the entire house, which immediately struck fear in our hearts.

Both of us knew our mother, Sheila, had been boiling lobsters in the big black steel pot steamer on top of the stove, and was now sitting at the kitchen table cracking lobster claws and tails and filling a large bowl with the sweet lobster meat.

Randy was already looking a little green because he hated lobster with a passion! The smell of it, the taste of it, the sight of live lobsters crawling around in the meat bin in the refrigerator before suffering a horrific, violent death thrashing around in bubbly boiling water, the whole idea of it made him sick.

He turned to face me. We both knew the sight of our mother humming a romantic Beatles song and tearing a fully cooked lobster apart while perusing her arsenal of lobster recipes from her card file could only mean one thing!

Mom had a new beau!

And by the time Mom made a big deal of ringing the dinner bell, which she must have bought that day because she had never before rung a dinner bell, our worst fears were confirmed. We were joined by a big, weathered, rugged-looking man with arms that looked like large barrels to me. I'll call him Mr. C since many of Mom's former boyfriends still live in town, and probably prefer not to be mentioned in the local paper as one of her many exes.

Mr. C was one of the team of lumberjacks

in the Great Maine Lumberjack Show that they held in the summers off island, across the bridge in the town of Trenton. That would explain his huge arms and bushy beard.

We all sat down at the dining room table, which had been perfectly set with our grandmother's antique dishware that Mom only used for special occasions.

Mom waltzed into the dining room, carrying a large platter in her hands piled high with her perfectly toasted, overstuffed Maine lobster rolls. She giggled coquettishly as she set it down in front of Mr. C, who made a big display of smelling them and complimenting Mom on how delicious they looked before he scooped one up and tossed it in his mouth, followed by a fistful of potato chips. He had barely swallowed it when he grabbed another lobster roll, and then another, and another, scarfing them down in record time as if he was focused on winning some kind of lobster roll eating contest!

Between bites, Mr. C informed us that he was a master woodcutter and could start a fire with two sticks, cut down a tree in three minutes flat, and so on and so on, clearly on a mission to impress his new gal pal's children.

Randy and I just sat there praying he would run out of steam and this meal would soon come to a merciful end, but each time there was a pause in the conversation, and we pushed back our chairs to make a mad dash for our bedrooms, he grabbed another lobster roll and popped it in his mouth and told us another story about his favorite subject—himself!

All I could focus on were the dollops of white mayo and bits of celery that were caught in his beard.

Finally, Mr. C grabbed his belly and jiggled it. His stomach was at long last full! Randy and I exchanged a quick glance. We were seconds away from a fast escape. Free! Free at last!

But then Mom spoke up and said, "Guess what, kids? Roger is taking us camping this weekend!"

Roger, of course, not being his real name.

This was crazy! Our mother *hated* camping. There was no logical reason for us to ever go camping! But the motive was crystal clear. Mom was hell-bent on us bonding with her new beau, and the idea of a weekend in nature with a real live lumberjack was like the plot from one of those Harlequin romances she devoured especially during the summer.

By now, Mr. C had gotten a second wind (especially after Mom served him another one of her world-famous—her words, not mine—Blueberry Lemonade Cocktails) and was prattling on about what an expert camper, hunter, and fisherman he was, and how there was nobody else you would want to be out in the woods with than him. Randy and I just slumped back in our chairs, visions of watching ABC's TGIF lineup of sitcoms on TV in our rooms quickly dissipating.

A few days later when the weekend arrived, we left the comfort of our cozy little home, and drove miles and miles out of town listening to the same stories again from Mr. C. Expert camper, yes, expert fisherman, yes, expert hunter, yes, we get it! Thank God it wasn't hunting season!

After what seemed like days, we finally pulled up to an old, ramshackle, abandoned cabin with dirt-covered windows, weeds, and bushes growing wild all around it. There was a small cut path that led to the front porch with one lonely looking old rocking chair and above the front door a very scary and disturbing skeleton of a deer head complete with antlers that seemed to be staring right at us, daring us to go inside.

I was about to turn to my mother and tell her I absolutely refused to stay one night at this place because everything about the area reminded me of that movie *Deliverance*, which I stayed up late watching on TV one night when I was supposed to be asleep. I never got over it! I was already hearing the banjos playing in my head!

Suddenly the door to the cabin creaked open and I spotted a dirty, long white beard poking out. Then, in the blink of an eye, all hell broke loose! A crazed man sprinted out the door, jumped off the old porch, and ran straight toward the driver's side of Mr. C's truck! Mom let out a little screech! Mr. C flung open the driver's-side door, sprang out, and ran at the screaming old coot, all the while yelling at the top of his lungs.

We watched in horror as they both took a flying leap and collided in midair, crashing to the ground with a thud.

As the two men punched each other and rolled around we sat frozen in our seats until suddenly they stopped and began laughing and clapping each other on the back while helping the other up off the ground.

Apparently, in all of Mr. C's long-winded stories, he forgot to mention that his old buddy Goober from his Army days worked at this campground site, and they hadn't seen each other in years, and he thought it would be nice to stop and say hello before heading to our campsite. I could see my mother's tight smile as she was introduced to the old codger, which was not a good sign. She didn't like surprises. So Mr. C quickly lost a point.

After all the introductions were over, Goober ticked off his list of instructions, all the wildlife dos and don'ts like never feed the wild animals, especially the bears, and most importantly, always clean up after our meals and lock our food away so those greedy, nosy bears won't be tempted by any yummy smells. Mr. C reminded Goober he was an expert camper and there was no need for him to worry.

When we finally arrived at our remote campsite near a picturesque lake, Randy and I were tasked with collecting small sticks and wood for the fire pit at our site. When we returned, Mr. C was giving Mom a lesson on the proper way to erect a tent. We could tell from her face that she was over her whole lumberjack fantasy *big*-time. It was going to be a long weekend.

As Mr. C unrolled the tent and hauled the poles out of his truck, I couldn't help but notice that the flimsy, faded, patched green tent didn't look too sturdy. It was probably old enough to have been with him during his Army days with Goober. But I had no choice. That tent was going to be our home for the next few days.

It took longer than expected for Mr. C to finish putting up the tent. There were a lot of four-letter words along the way, especially when he accidentally jammed one of the poles into his fingers. After that, he got busy building the fire, telling us he was one-fourth Native American so starting a fire was second nature to him. He rubbed two sticks between his hands for what seemed like an hour, all the while mumbling and cursing. Randy and I had to stifle our giggles. Mom was losing patience. Finally, she stood up with a loud sigh, reached into her pocket, and hauled out a pack of matches. She grabbed a couple of paper napkins and lit the kindling and logs until a nice fire was crackling and roaring, and then sat back down with a huff.

Mr. C looked a bit miffed, and announced he was going to go fishing for our supper, but our mother held up her hand and said he had done quite enough work for one day. She crossed to one of the two coolers we brought, and pulled out three neatly wrapped, you guessed it, lobster rolls! And one peanut butter sandwich for Randy.

After dinner Mom asked Mr. C to lock away the cooler in the truck, and then with all of us yawning, we crawled into the tent for the night. Mr. C wanted to tell ghost stories, but I fell sound asleep before he could decide on which one to tell.

I don't know how long I was out before I was awakened by Randy thrashing around in his sleeping bag beside me. I tried to turn to see what was wrong, but I couldn't because there seemed to be a heavy weight holding me down! I could hear my mother yelling at Mr. C, screaming that he had put the tent up wrong because it had collapsed on us in the middle of the night! I tried desperately to lift the tangled mass off me, but it was useless. Finally, Mr. C managed to bunch up enough of the material and yank it off us. Now we were lying in our sleeping bags looking up at the night sky. There were no stars, which meant, yes, the clouds were hiding them, because it was about to rain! And it did. Buckets of it came pouring down on us. Mom begged Mr. C to get the tent back up, but in the dark and with all the rain, he managed to fix enough of it to allow only three of us to squeeze back inside. By then, the rain was subsiding so Randy volunteered to sleep outside on the wet ground in his Justice League of America sleeping bag.

I tried falling back to sleep, but after all the excitement, I just couldn't. After what seemed like hours, my eyes finally got heavy, and I was about to close them and forget about this whole horrific first day of camping when I heard Randy whimpering outside the tent. Curious, I crawled out to ask him what was wrong, and that's when I saw him, sitting up, with one hand over his mouth, trying to muffle his screams. His other hand pointed at a very large Maine black bear, not more than twenty feet away! The bear had apparently opened the cooler and was digging through it! Yes, the one Mr. C was supposed to have locked up tight and put in his truck. He forgot! The bear was using his paws to shovel leftover lobster rolls into his giant mouth!

I let out a tiny scream of surprise, and then caught myself, but it was too late! The bear stopped and slowly stood up on his hind legs, staring in our direction, and let out a thunderous growl. I felt my heart stop!

To Be Continued

Sheila's Perfectly Tasty Maine Lobster Rolls

<u>Ingredients</u>
4 1¼-pound lobsters steamed

1 celery stalk, finely chopped
2 tablespoons fresh lemon juice
2 to 3 tablespoons real mayonnaise
Fresh ground pepper

6 New England–style hot dog buns
2 tablespoons butter, room temperature

Fill a large pot with enough water to equal an inch deep; bring to a boil and add a good amount of kosher salt. Add your lobster, cover, and cook 8 to 10 minutes, until bright red. Transfer lobsters to a pan and let cool.

Crack your lobster shells and pick the meat from the claws and the tails, and cut into one-inch pieces. In a bowl, mix lobster, celery, lemon juice, and 2 tablespoons of mayonnaise; season with salt and pepper and add more mayonnaise as you need it.

Heat a large skillet over medium heat. Butter both flat sides of the hot dog rolls and toast until golden brown. Fill with a generous amount of the lobster mixture, serve and enjoy!

You can also serve this refreshing summer cocktail with your lobster rolls!

Blueberry Lemonade Cocktail

<u>Ingredients</u>
1 ounce blueberry vodka
1 ounce lemon vodka
5 ounces lemonade
Splash of blueberry syrup
Blueberries for garnish (optional)

In a glass filled with ice add all the ingredients, give it a stir, and there you have a tasty, fruity summertime cocktail.

Chapter 6

Hayley was up early the next morning and tiptoed around quietly, although the deafening sound of Mona's snoring obliterated any chance anyone might hear her walking across the creaky floor. Liddy was curled up on the couch, a comforter pulled up over her head and just a few strands of her curly hair visible. She had refused to sleep in either the double bed or one of the bunk beds because she had decided, with no proof whatsoever, that all the mattresses were riddled with bedbugs. Mona was flat on her back on the floor because she could never sleep comfortably on any kind of soft mattress. Her arms and legs were outstretched as if she were trying to make snow angels, her mouth wide open, a cacophony of snorts and grunts flying out of it at an unsettling pace.

Hayley pulled on some shorts and a loose T-shirt, slipped into a pair of sandals, grabbed the car keys, and left her buddies to their peaceful slumber. She drove into town in Liddy's Mercedes to the local coffee shop to pick up some coffee and pastries for when her friends finally woke up.

It was still early, not yet eight on a Saturday morning. She found a parking spot right in front of the diner, and when she walked in the door the place was bustling with business. Three harried waitresses buzzed around with coffeepots and balancing breakfast plates on their arms while a seasoned cook in a white stained T-shirt and with hairy arms fried up strips of bacon and slabs of ham on the grill in the open kitchen. On another grill he was sizzling six rows of perfectly round pancake batter, flipping a few over with his spatula while glancing up only occasionally to check the green order slips hanging in front of him. The booths and tables were packed with bleary-eyed locals and a few fresh-faced tourists filling up their tummies before setting out for a day of hiking and sight-seeing.

Hayley walked up to the glass case next to the register and perused the assortment of fresh baked goods, eyeing some strawberry scones, blueberry muffins, and glazed doughnuts. Hayley had thought of stopping in the small grocery store on the corner for some fresh fruit, but after drinking at the local bar until last call the night before, she was confident her friends would prefer sugary comfort food to ease the pain of their inevitable hangovers.

After making her selections, the wiry, half-asleep young man behind the counter informed her it would be about ten minutes before he could bag up her pastries and pour her takeaway coffees, so Hayley took a seat on a stool at the counter and ordered a black coffee while she waited. That's when she noticed Ellie sitting right next to her, focused on a plate of scrambled eggs and sausage in front of her.

"Did you get your grandfather home safely last night?" Hayley asked with a smile.

Ellie turned to her, only a hint of recognition on her face.

She nodded. "Yes, I did. Thank you. I'm sorry, I don't remember your name."

"That's because we didn't officially meet. I'm Hayley Powell," Hayley said, extending her hand for Ellie to shake. "My friends and I are just here for the weekend. We were at the bar last night when you came in."

"Nice to meet you, Hayley," Ellie said, taking her hand. "Yes. Grandpa can be a handful, but I managed to get him home."

"Boyd seems like a very nice man," Hayley said, unable to resist.

"Who? Oh, Boyd! Yes, I suppose so," Ellie said as casually as she possibly could.

"Sweet," Hayley added.

Ellie stabbed at her sausage with a fork and raised it to her mouth, biting off a hunk before nodding in agreement. Her mouth was full so she only managed to say "Uh-huh" as a reply.

"Are you two . . . ?"

Hayley drew it out. She wasn't sure why she was putting this poor girl on the spot. She just thought Ellie seemed like a well-meaning, kind girl and she was curious to know more about her.

"Oh, no!" Ellie said, shaking her head. "I mean, we've known each other forever, since grade school, but we ran around in different circles and have hardly ever spent any time together. I just see him at the bar when I come to fetch Grandpa."

"Well, that's too bad," Hayley said, sipping her coffee.

"Why do you say that?"

"Well, it's clear to me he harbors a big crush on you."

"He does?" Ellie asked, straightening herself up on the stool, genuinely surprised.

"You haven't noticed?"

"No, not at all," she said, a titter escaping her lips.

"Well, it was obvious to everyone at the bar."

"It was? Oh, Lord! Now I'm embarrassed!" she wailed, dropping the forkful of sausage back down on her plate and covering her face with her hands.

"Why would you be embarrassed?"

"Just the idea of anyone in town talking about me! I've always been a very private person."

Hayley was thoroughly enjoying this conversation. Maybe she could help with a bona fide love match and jump-start this budding romance between the lumbering, simple-minded boy and the soft-spoken, doe-eyed, shy, insecure wisp of a girl.

"Well, are you seeing anyone at the moment?" Hayley asked, leaning in, curious.

"Gosh, no! I've never really had a boyfriend. I mean, to be honest there were a couple of boys in high school I pined after, but they never looked at me twice or anything."

"Why not? You're a lovely, attractive young woman."

She buried her face in her hands again. "Stop it."

"I'm serious, Ellie," Hayley said. "Why on earth don't you have a boyfriend?"

She stared at her eggs for a moment, pondering, and then she shrugged. "I don't know. I guess I've had trouble getting close to anyone after my father died."

Damn.

Hayley had really stepped in it now.

The last thing she wanted to do was upset the poor girl.

"I'm so sorry," Hayley said. "We can change the subject if you want."

Ellie instinctively put a hand out and touched Hayley's arm. "No, it's all right. It was a while ago. He died in a plane crash."

"Oh my God, how awful," Hayley said, now regretting her insistence on getting this timid girl to open up.

But Ellie remained sitting on her stool, upright, strong. The touchy topic of her father's tragic death wasn't causing her to crumble. "He was a really handsome man. Here, I have a photo of him."

Ellie reached into her bag and pulled out her wallet. She flipped it open and showed Hayley a picture of her father, who was striking, reminiscent of an old movie star like Cary Grant.

"Oh, my . . ."

"Yes, he was quite popular with the ladies in his day, you know, before . . ." Her voice trailed off for a moment, and it looked like she might tear up, but instead she gathered herself, cleared her throat, and continued. "My mom was never around so my granddaddy raised me. Or as Sue says, I raised *him*," she said, chuckling. "Sue's kind of been like a mother figure for me since I was a little girl. She's always telling me I can't hide from life forever and I need to get out there."

"Sue seems like a very wise woman," Hayley said gently.

"Did she pay you to say that?" Ellie asked, grinning.

She had a beautiful, warm smile.

There was no reason in the world this cute, prepossessing girl should be hiding from anything.

The young, sleepy-eyed man behind the counter arrived with a paper bag of pastries and two coffees in a cardboard takeout carton. He rang the order up on the register. Hayley reached for her bag and counted out some bills.

"Well, I think Sue is right. And for what it's worth, I also think you should go out on a date with Boyd."

"A date? Really? I don't know," she squealed, her cheeks flushed with red, totally flustered.

"Go on. Give him a chance," Hayley said, scooping up her bag and carton of coffees. "It was nice chatting with you, Ellie. Hope to see you around."

"Bye," Ellie said, beaming, as Hayley walked out the door.

Chapter 7

As Hayley fumbled her way out of the coffee shop, balancing the paper bag of pastries and carton of coffees, a woman appeared to hold open the door for her.

"Thank you so much," Hayley said, smiling gratefully.

The woman watched her glide across the sidewalk toward her car and instead of walking inside the restaurant she followed behind her.

"Excuse me, Hayley Powell?" the woman asked.

Hayley spun around to face the woman. She was probably in her mid-forties, short-cropped silver hair, slender, athletic body, tanned fresh face with very few signs of age. She was in a turquoise T-shirt and gray yoga pants, her feet slipped comfortably in a pair of deck shoes and a matching fanny pack around her waist, both of which matched her T-shirt.

"Yes, I'm Hayley," she said quizzically.

"I hope I didn't startle you. I'm Polly Roper," the woman said.

Hayley instinctively moved to shake the woman's hand, but realized both of her hands were full, one with the bag, the other with the carton of coffees.

"Here, let me help you with those," Polly said, reaching out with a thin, bony hand, the fingernails painted with turquoise nail polish, to take the paper bag of baked goods.

Polly certainly was a fan of turquoise.

Now with a free hand, Hayley shook Polly's hand.

"I'm a friend of Sue's, who owns the bar around the corner you were at last night. She told me all about you, how you write a food and cocktails column for your local paper in Bar Harbor," Polly said.

"Yes," Hayley said, amazed at how fast word got around in Salmon Cove.

"I'm sorry, I don't usually make a habit of having to know every last detail about every stranger who comes to town, but Sue thought I would be interested because I'm essentially your counterpart here in town. I write a cooking column myself for the *Salmon Cove Journal.*"

"I see," Hayley said, a bit relieved she wasn't on some kind of terrorist watch list or anything like that.

"I must confess, I am guilty of a bit of online stalking. I looked up your paper and read a few of your columns. That's why I recognized you," she said. "From your very pretty picture next to the byline. Your recipes look delicious, by the way."

"Well, I look forward to stalking you as well," Hayley said brightly, her head swelling from Polly's gushing compliments.

"How long are you in town for?"

"Just a few days, I'm afraid."

"That's too bad," Polly said with a slight pout. "I was hoping we might be able to get together, exchange a couple of recipes, engage in a little shop talk."

"Well, I'm here with two friends, but I suspect I may have plenty of free time," Hayley said, certain Liddy and

Mona would be otherwise engaged with their respective paramours for the duration of their stay.

"That would be marvelous," Polly cooed, reaching into her fanny pack for a business card and handing it to Hayley. "That's my cell phone number and e-mail address."

"I'll be in touch," Hayley said before noticing someone hovering near her car. She glanced over to see a female uniformed police officer, big-boned, tall, thick brown hair pulled back in a severe bun, a stern, serious face, typing the license plate number of Liddy's Mercedes into an electronic reader.

Hayley twisted her head back to Polly, who was now frowning. "I better go deal with this."

"That's Sheriff Wilkes," Polly practically spit out. "She's a real ballbuster but don't let her bully you!"

"Thanks for the advice," Hayley said, warily. Just the sheriff's intimidating height and dour face was making Hayley's stomach turn with nerves.

"Have a great day," Polly sang as she handed the bag of pastries back to her and pranced off down the street.

Hayley slowly, cautiously approached Sheriff Wilkes, who had yet to notice her. Hayley waited a beat, but the sheriff was too fixated on her electronic ticket gadget thingy. It spit out a ticket the size of a gas receipt, which she stuffed in a small envelope and then leaned forward and slipped it underneath the windshield wiper of Liddy's car.

Hayley cleared her throat loudly.

Finally, Sheriff Wilkes leisurely stood upright, adjusted her sunglasses, and turned to Hayley.

"Good morning," Hayley said, forcing a smile.

Sheriff Wilkes never cracked a smile. She remained stone-faced except for a barely perceptible nod. At least

Hayley thought it was a nod. Maybe it was the fly that buzzed past her face, which caused it to move forward slightly.

"This is my friend's car, and I . . . I just came into town to pick up some breakfast . . ." Hayley stammered. "Well, I was just curious to know why I'm getting a ticket."

There was a long, agonizing pause.

Hayley cleared her throat again.

Why, she didn't know.

It wasn't as if she had to clear her throat.

This towering woman in uniform was just making her extremely nervous.

Finally, mercifully, after what seemed like a full two minutes of tense silence but was probably just a few seconds, Sheriff Wilkes responded, "You're parked too far from the curb."

Hayley looked down at the tires and raised an eyebrow. There was barely an inch between both tires and the curb. "What? No, I'm not. Look, the tires are practically touching the side. Look!"

But Sheriff Wilkes didn't look.

She just stared at Hayley behind those terrifying dark sunglasses on her face.

Hayley stupidly tried again. "Look!"

"I already did when you were inside the diner and guess what, they're too far from the curb," Sheriff Wilkes said in a low growl. "You broke the law. If you disagree, you can always fight it in court. But you're not talking yourself out of a ticket."

Sheriff Wilkes glared at Hayley for a few seconds longer, and then turned and marched off down the street toward her squad car, which was parked near the corner.

Hayley was rattled as she snatched the ticket out from underneath the wiper and got into the driver's seat of the

Mercedes. She ripped open the envelope and studied the ticket. Sure enough, it was a parking citation. And it was going to cost her sixty-eight dollars. It was signed by Daphne Wilkes, Sheriff of Salmon Cove, and in Hayley's opinion, a world class b-word.

Oh, what the hell, she was on vacation.

She was feeling a little wild.

Why not just say it?

"Sheriff Daphne Wilkes is a world-class bitch!" she shouted.

And then, noticing the driver's-side window was open slightly, Hayley suddenly felt guilty and looked around to make sure no passersby had heard her.

Chapter 8

If Hayley thought that attending the Salmon Cove Lobster Bake the next day was going to be a relaxed and peaceful Sunday afternoon, she was sadly mistaken. The stress kicked in almost immediately, before they had even left the cabin, when Liddy was stood up by her date, the dashing Boston-based travel writer Jackson Young.

She was, to say the least, apoplectic.

"This is absolutely outrageous! Nobody has ever stood me up before!" she wailed, gripping her phone tightly, her knuckles a ghostly white, and texting him yet another angry message. "He confirmed last night and now suddenly he's a no-show? What the hell is going on? Should I call him again?"

"You've already left four messages on his voice mail already," Hayley said, trying to reason with her.

"And about a hundred and fifty texts," Mona added, checking her watch, sighing. "Listen, can we leave? Corey is already there waiting for me."

"That is so typical of you, Mona, rubbing my face in the fact that *your* date has been in constant contact with you all morning and my date has given me nothing but radio silence!"

"Corey is *not* my date! We are just two old friends meeting up to hang out together and eat some lobster and corn on the cob. That's all it is! I'm a married woman, Liddy!" Mona barked defensively.

"You're an *unhappily* married woman, and that's a big difference," Liddy spit out, madly tapping numbers into her phone and then clamping it to her ear before instantly shifting her tone to calm and unconcerned. "Hello, Jackson, this is Liddy again. I've still heard nothing from you so I am just going to assume we are no longer going to the lobster bake together today. This is the last message I will be leaving as my friends are begging me to accompany them, and I certainly don't want to keep them waiting any longer. I hope this finds you well, and that you have the opportunity to enjoy some of the delicious seafood they have here in Salmon Cove. It was a pleasure meeting you, and I wish you a safe trip back to Boston. Bye now."

She tapped the phone to end the call and then instantly returned to her high-pitched screeching.

"That bastard! I will kill him if I ever see him again!"

"*Please*! Can we just go?" Mona begged.

"Fine. I'll drive," Liddy said, scooping the car keys off the kitchen counter that Hayley had scrubbed and wiped down the night before because there was a thick film of dirt covering it.

Hayley snatched the keys out of her hand. "You are in no condition. I will drive."

"Fine. But promise me if you see Jackson walking along the side of the road, you hit the accelerator and run him down."

"No," Hayley answered emphatically, heading out the door.

"I'm not suggesting you kill him. Just cause some long-lasting damage. I want him to suffer for his sins."

"No!" Hayley called back from outside.

"I just thought I'd put it out there," Liddy sniffed, following her.

Mona brought up the rear, shaking her head.

When they arrived at the Salmon Cove Lobster Bake, which was held in a town park near the waterfront, there was already a massive crowd milling about at all the food stands that were lined up in three different rows that cut through the middle of the park.

Parking was impossible so Hayley had to backtrack almost half a mile to find a space for Liddy's Mercedes. After squeezing into a spot along the side of the road, they trudged back toward the park, Liddy complaining the entire way and Mona shouting at her to please shut up. Hayley was already tired of their constant bickering and needed a respite.

Corey Guildford came to her rescue. He swooped in from out of nowhere. He had been waiting for them patiently near the entrance, like his loyal golden retriever Sadie probably did by the front door of his house waiting for him to come every night. Sadie was at his side as Corey leaned in to kiss Mona. She jerked her head away and scrunched up her face, as if it was agony having to receive an innocent hello kiss from this sweet, personable, good-looking guy.

It just made Liddy even more irritable.

Where was her hello kiss from Jackson?

"You're looking lovely today, Mona," Corey said shyly. "Doesn't she, Sadie?"

He looked down at his dog, who was hugging his pant leg, smiling and panting.

"If your friends don't mind, Mona, I'd like to show you around, and introduce you to a few of my friends," Corey said, glancing over at Hayley and Liddy to make sure it was okay with them.

"Why?" Mona asked.

"Why?" he asked, puzzled. "I don't know. I think they'll like you."

"Seems awfully forward of you, introducing me to your friends. What are you trying to do here?" Mona asked accusingly.

"For Pete's sake, Mona! Stop trying to scare him off and just go with him and enjoy yourself! Is that so hard?" Liddy said.

"I'm not trying to scare him off!" Mona yelled, mortified, a defensive tone in her voice.

"Wouldn't matter even if she was. I don't scare easily," Corey said with a wink.

Hayley really liked this guy.

"Come on, Mona," Corey said firmly, reaching out and taking her hand.

Mona jumped, as if someone had just hit her, and wrenched her hand free from his grip. "What the hell are you trying to do now?"

"I was just holding your hand, Mona, I promise I wasn't going to slip a ring on it," Corey said, laughing. "Let's go. You can lead."

Mona eyed him warily and then marched off in a huff.

"I can tell she likes me," Corey said, smiling.

And then he followed her off.

"Why is Mona being so mean to that poor man?" Liddy asked, watching Corey run to catch up to Mona. "He's just trying to be nice to her."

"Because she likes him more than she's willing to admit. And you know how she is. She's already married to Dennis, and even though he's a deadbeat useless loser, those are her words *not* mine, she still feels loyal to him, so she's terrified of getting emotionally attached to another man," Hayley said.

She noticed Liddy staring at her.

"I watch a lot of Dr. Phil," she explained.

"I need a drink," Liddy said, not listening to a word she had just said. "There is something to eat every which way you turn so I would assume there has to be a bar around here somewhere too if there is a God!"

Liddy wandered off, leaving Hayley on her own.

Chapter 9

Hayley weaved through the crowd following the puffs of steam rising high in the air from the boiling seafood pots located in the center of the park. Since she was smack-dab in the middle of a local lobster bake, then by God, she was going to splurge on a lobster. She lined up behind a crowd of people stretching back a good twenty yards to wait her turn.

Right up near the front of the line she spotted Ellie and Boyd. They were giggling over something, and Ellie had her hand placed gently on Boyd's fleshy forearm. She looked lovely in a sleeveless cobalt print sundress and stretch wedge sandals, while he rocked a striped polo shirt that stretched over his belly, along with shorts and deck shoes. Hayley noted both looked very fashionable for a simple lobster bake.

Boyd's face was lit up and happy.

He couldn't take his eyes off his date.

Yes, Hayley realized, the two of them were actually on an honest-to-goodness date.

Ellie and Boyd.

Just like she'd hoped.

Apparently, Ellie had taken her advice to heart and decided to give Boyd a chance. Hayley thought about walking up to them and saying hello, but she decided to leave them alone. It was probably best not to interrupt them especially since the date appeared to be going very well.

As a man lifted a lobster, which had two rubber bands tied around each of its claws, and dropped it into the boiling water before quickly covering the pot with a lid, Ellie squealed and hid her face in Boyd's broad chest. Boiling lobsters was always a rather violent and heartless task. Most people opted not to think about how their favorite shellfish was actually prepared, and instead, focused on the mouth-watering taste once they had been fully cooked and their limbs had been so mercilessly torn apart.

Boyd eagerly wrapped his arms around Ellie protectively, relishing the moment.

Embarrassed by her silly reaction to the lobster being dropped in the pot, she looked up at him in mock horror.

Boyd couldn't stop beaming.

Suddenly Hayley felt someone tugging on her arm.

"Hayley! Am I glad to see you!"

Hayley turned to see Polly Roper, in a pink blouse with a bulky white apron tied around her waist, and a harried look on her face.

"Polly, how nice to see you," Hayley said before taking stock of Polly's panic-stricken expression. "Is there something wrong?"

"Yes, I have a bit of an emergency," she said, wiping sweat from her brow with a perfectly manicured hand that today was painted a bright pink to match her blouse. "I have a booth over there where I'm selling my blueberry pies."

Hayley glanced over to see a small gaggle of people hovered around an unmanned booth stacked with white boxes.

"We've been busy all morning, because, well, at the risk of boasting, my pies are the best damn pies in Down East Maine!" Polly said, clearly boasting.

"They sound yummy," Hayley said, not quite sure where this was going. "I'll be sure to buy one."

"I hired a local boy, Danny McMillan, to help me man the booth and move the pies, worst mistake of my life, and he snuck three pies while I was out buying paper plates and plastic forks, and ate every damn one!"

"Without paying for them?"

"That's not the point," Polly said, shaking her head vigorously.

Hayley chose to keep quiet from this moment on and just let poor Polly talk.

"I promised him three pies for helping me out. I just didn't expect him to eat them all before we even opened the booth for business," she declared, worry frowns now lining her forehead. "And now he's gone home with a tummy ache!"

Hayley finally had a sense of where this was going, and felt safe enough to speak again. "So now you're without a helper!"

"Yes!"

"Well, don't worry, I would be happy to help you sell your pies," Hayley said, gently taking the frazzled Polly by the arm and leading her back over to her booth. Her lobster feast was just going to have to wait.

Hayley had a friend, albeit a very new friend, in need.

And she couldn't leave her in the lurch. She just prayed there would still be a few lobsters left at the end of the day.

For the next three hours, Hayley and Polly worked nonstop handing out pies and collecting money and chatting with the locals, who were downright enamored of these apparently highly addictive blueberry pies. It was a credit to Polly's obvious baking talent. In fact, Hayley was so worried the pies would sell out, she grabbed one off the table and set it to the side so she could buy it later for herself.

By the time Polly pocketed the last ten-dollar bill and handed off the last boxed pie, it was almost four in the afternoon.

Hayley dropped down in a folding chair, exhausted.

"I don't know how to thank you," Polly said, smiling gratefully. "I couldn't have gotten through this without you."

"Well, I confess, I stole one of your pies, so consider us even," Hayley said, pointing to the box she had set aside during the mad rush.

"Oh, no, I insist on giving you a cut of the sales," Polly said, counting out the cash she had stuffed in the pocket of her apron.

"I wouldn't hear of it. Your friendship is payment enough," Hayley said, nervously checking out the lobster vendors, who were pouring water out of their lobster pots and cleaning up their spaces.

As Hayley feared, it was nearing the end of the day and it looked like everyone was fresh out of lobsters.

"Don't stress out," Polly said, noticing her new buddy's alarmed expression. "There is another vendor down by the beach who has plenty of lobsters to last until well after sundown."

"I wasn't worried," Hayley lied.

"I tell you what. Let me buy you a lobster dinner. It's the least I can do," Polly said.

"All right, I won't argue," Hayley said, standing up. "Because I am starving."

As Hayley and Polly made their way down toward the beach, watching families pile into their cars to head home, Hayley glanced around for any sign of Liddy, or Mona and Corey, but didn't spot them. She wasn't too concerned. She assumed Liddy was at the local watering hole drowning her sorrows. As for Mona and Corey, well, she was brimming with curiosity about what went on between them today, but would have to wait to get any answers out of the reliably recalcitrant Mona Barnes.

Just as Polly had promised, an older couple in their late sixties, in psychedelic T-shirts, wearing white aprons like Polly, the husband with long hair and a bushy beard, his wife with a frizzy mop on top of her head and adorned with beaded necklaces and bracelets, probably Grateful Dead hippies from a time long past, boiled lobsters in a pot on an open fire, with plates and utensils on a table made of birch wood behind them.

Hayley excitedly ordered a lobster with extra butter and all the fixings, and then stepped back to let Polly place her own order. That is when she noticed two people a long distance down the beach. They seemed to be arguing. Hayley squinted to get a better look and immediately recognized Sue, the owner of the Starfish Lounge. Her face was contorted in rage and she wagged a finger in a man's face. His back was to Hayley, but he seemed somewhat familiar.

As Sue stepped forward, getting closer to him, almost in a threatening manner, the man took a step back away from her. He apparently had heard enough from this woman and didn't want to listen to her anymore. The man whirled around to walk away from her, and Hayley was finally able to get a good look at his face.

It was Jackson Young.

Chapter 10

After finishing her lobster and bidding adieu to Polly, Hayley hiked back from the town park to the Mercedes. There she found Liddy leaning against the driver's-side door. She appeared calm, serene, almost at peace.

Hayley approached her cautiously. "I hope you haven't been waiting too long."

"No, I've actually had a lovely time. I was entertained by two drunks at the bar, local lobstermen I presumed. They both had a strange odor about them, a mixture of bourbon and fish bait. Aside from that, they were quite amiable."

"I'm sorry, Liddy, I know this whole weekend has been one big disappointment for you," Hayley said.

"I've come to the realization that I am a victim of my own high expectations," she said with a confirming nod.

"Come again?"

"I had a whole picture in my mind of how this week-end was going to be. I envisioned the three of us staying in a quaint, lovely cabin resplendent with charm," she said wistfully. "And when we got there, I was just wish-ing for a bathroom indoors."

"I agree Mona could have prepared us a little better about what to expect," Hayley said, giving her that one.

"And then there was Jackson. After meeting him, I let my expectations once again get the best of me. In my mind, I cast him in the role of my handsome suitor, usually played in my dreams by George Clooney. This suave, down-to-earth, most perfect man, unattainable in reality, to be honest. And when he failed to live up to that image in my mind, it sent me into a tailspin," Liddy said, chuckling at the absurdity of it all.

"Well, don't beat yourself up," Hayley said, smiling. "None of us knew Jackson was going to turn out to be a lying cad."

"But do we really know that for sure? Actually, we know very little about him. He may have received an emergency call from Boston, and then had to rush back for all we know," Liddy said, trying to convince herself.

"Yes, but he could've called or texted you to let you know," Hayley said.

"I suppose. But I'm too tired to be mad anymore," Liddy sighed. "I'm completely over it."

Hayley decided not to mention that she had just seen Jackson Young down by the beach with Sue the bar owner. Liddy seemed to be in a good place right now, and she was not going to risk getting her worked up all over again.

Mona trudged up to them, scarfing down a lobster roll. She finished it off, and licked some mayonnaise off her fingertips. With her mouth half full, she said, "I'm going to catch a ride home with Corey. He went to go get his truck."

"Fine. We'll meet you back at the cabin," Liddy said, pressing a button on her key to unlock the Mercedes.

"Hey, sorry you got stood up, Liddy. For what it's worth, Corey got a weird vibe from that Jackson guy the other night at the bar so you probably dodged a bullet."

"Well, tell Corey I appreciate his concern," Liddy said, annoyed. "But I am highly skeptical that he has some reliable sixth sense about Jackson, a man he literally knows nothing about."

"The guy stood you up," Mona argued. "That proves Corey's suspicions were dead-on."

"We are not one hundred percent certain he stood me up on purpose. I was just saying to Hayley it is quite possible he was called away for some emergency . . ."

"He stood you up!" Mona insisted. "Corey and I saw him at the lobster bake with our own eyes!"

Liddy dropped her car keys and they clattered to the ground. "What?"

"He was heading down toward the beach alone," Mona said.

"He was *alone*? Because when I saw him he was with—" Hayley stopped herself. The second the words spilled out of her mouth she desperately wanted to suck them back in, but it was too late.

Liddy whipped around. "*You* saw Jackson too?"

There was no denying it now.

Hayley nodded, pinching her nose and pursing her lips.

She knew a tsunami-size meltdown was about to hit.

And Liddy did not disappoint.

"How dare that two-faced revolting creep show his face after leaving me high and dry! I have never been so insulted, so publicly humiliated in all my life!"

She was spiraling fast.

Hayley knew she had to quickly intervene to minimize the damage.

"I wouldn't go so far as to say you were publicly humiliated," Hayley said, trying to calm the situation. "I mean, nobody in town even knows who you are, let alone that Jackson stood you up!"

"Why were you trying to keep this from me, Hayley? To protect him? How could you be more concerned with *his* emotional well-being than with mine?"

"All I was thinking about was *your* emotional well-being because I thought it was in your best interest to avoid this breakdown!"

"Breakdown? This isn't a breakdown! Believe me, you will know when I'm actually having a breakdown! Now finish what you were saying!"

"What do you mean?"

"You said you saw him with someone! Who was it?"

"I don't see how this helps . . ."

"Who was he with, Hayley?" Liddy demanded to know.

Hayley sighed. "Sue, the owner of the Starfish Lounge."

"I thought she was a lesbian," Liddy said, surprised.

"What made you think that?" Mona asked.

"Well, she seemed so smitten with me at the bar," Liddy said dramatically. "Gay women love me."

"I don't think Sue is a lesbian," Hayley said, before quickly adding, "But that doesn't mean she's involved with Jackson. In fact, when I saw them, they were arguing."

"Well, I think there is one way to get to the bottom of this. Take me back to where you saw them," Liddy said, bending down to pick up her car keys and pressing the button to lock the doors again.

"I don't see how that's going to solve anything . . ."

"I do. It will make me feel much better to get some closure on this horrible, disastrous day."

"You told me you were over it," Hayley said quietly.

"I was lying!" Liddy shouted.

While Mona waited by the Mercedes for Corey to arrive in his truck, Hayley reluctantly led Liddy back to the town park, passing a few stragglers chatting as the last of the vendors loaded up and drove away. When they reached the beach, there were no signs of anyone around. The tide was slowly coming in and the crashing waves were washing up close to the rocky shore where the sand ended.

The hippie couple who had fed Hayley her lobster dinner had packed up and gone as well.

Down the beach and around the bend, they spotted smoke rising from a fire.

Liddy gave Hayley a quick, knowing nod and marched down the beach with the firm belief she would find Jackson Young, possibly in the warm embrace of another woman.

At least that was probably the image playing on repeat in her mind.

Hayley plodded along, falling a distance behind Liddy as sand worked its way inside her shoes, making her more and more uncomfortable and causing her to slow her pace.

As she rounded the bend and caught up with Liddy, Hayley found her friend standing in the sand, frozen in place, staring at something.

Hayley followed her gaze over to the smoldering fire, the last tiny embers crackling and flying up into a cloud of smoke.

There was a body lying in the sand.

The head was turned slightly so Hayley was able to recognize the face.

It was Jackson Young.

And next to him, tipped over in the sand, was a pot, somehow knocked off the wire grate placed over the fire, the sand having absorbed the boiling water, as three lobsters, lucky enough to still be alive, crawled slowly back toward the ocean in a daring, desperate bid for freedom.

Island Food & Spirits
by
Hayley Powell

Part Two

I let out a tiny scream of surprise, and then caught myself, but it was too late! The bear stopped and slowly stood up on his hind legs, staring in our direction, and let out a thunderous growl. I felt my heart stop!

Behind me, I could hear Mom and Mr. C scrambling to get out of the tent to find out what was going on. Both froze on the spot at the sight of the gigantic bear just a few feet from Randy! My mother gasped and clutched my arm, squeezing me tight and pulling me closer to her. Mr. C had this shocked expression on his face, like he couldn't believe what he was seeing, and then, without warning, he turned around and hightailed it out of there, screaming like a little girl straight into a thicket of trees and disappearing into the woods, leaving me, Mom, and Randy to deal with the angry, growling Maine black bear staring us down!

Well, you should know one thing about our mother. She can be a bear in her own right when it comes down to protecting her cubs! Suddenly Mom took off in a dead run full tilt straight past Randy, heading right for the big, growling bear, all the while waving her arms over her head and screaming, "Get away from those lobster rolls, you mangy beast!"

I guess the poor bear didn't expect to see such a petite woman with bright red hair sticking up all over her head running and yelling, and causing such a scene. The bear at that point decided, after a tasty meal of lobster rolls, it was probably time to depart, so he dropped down on all fours and lumbered out of the campsite.

As he disappeared into the night, Mom stopped in her tracks, and then dropped to her knees, shaking at the realization that if the bear hadn't run off, she didn't have a Plan B!

Randy and I raced over, clapped her on the back with our hands, and told her she was a hero. But she just gathered herself and waved us off, and told us to help her put the empty cooler away in the back of the truck. As we walked back to the half-erect tent to hopefully get a few more hours of sleep before daylight, a sheepish Mr. C emerged from the woods from where he had been obviously hiding, and rambled on about how he went to get help, but couldn't find any in the vicinity, so he rushed back as quick as he could to dispatch the bear himself.

We could see the veins popping in our mother's neck, which always happened when she was trying to stay calm and not blow her top! She quietly told us it was time to get some much needed shut-eye, and steered us into the tent. I looked back to see Mr. C trying to follow us, but one death stare from Mom and he knew he wasn't welcome, so he retreated to Randy's sleeping bag and burrowed his way inside.

The next morning, I woke up to the intoxicating smell of bacon and eggs that sizzled on the open fire. Luckily, the bear hadn't busted into the second cooler we brought with our breakfast supplies. I had high hopes that after we ate, we would be heading home. Mom was completely one hundred percent over Mr. C, which was abundantly clear when he complained that his eggs were overdone and she shoved them at him anyway and told him to shut up and eat them. Randy, however, was the first to burst my bubble. He had awakened earlier and heard Mom and Mr. C discussing the events hours earlier. Mr. C apologized profusely for his cowardly behavior, and begged her to give him one more chance. My mom, being a fair-minded woman, reluctantly agreed, so we were officially stuck out here for at least one more day.

After breakfast, Mr. C excitedly unlatched his small fishing boat from the trailer attached to the back of his truck, and with Randy's help, carried it down to the lake's edge. My heart sank. I hated fishing! And so did Randy. Well, to be honest, Randy hated most outdoor activities, actually most activities that didn't involve watching television.

All four of us climbed into the boat with our poles and smelly bait. We packed for lunch, and after snapping on our life jackets, set out to catch some fish for dinner. Mr. C waved off wearing a life vest because, according to him, he was an expert swimmer. It went downhill pretty fast from there! Mr. C spent the next half hour guiding the boat out into the open lake, and bragging about his high school swim team years, and how he nearly qualified for the Olympics his senior year.

After what seemed like hours, but in reality was probably another ten minutes, Mr. C was still going on about his swimming glory days when suddenly I felt a tug on my line.

I turned to Mr. C and said, "I think I've caught a fish!"

Well, you would have thought I told him there was a free lobster buffet at the Hollywood Slots! He jumped to his feet, rocking the boat violently, practically throwing his own fishing pole overboard as he tried to step over me to wrest control of my pole!

The heavy end of his own pole whacked Mom in the back of the head, and she let out a painful yelp! Mr. C ignored it as he frantically tried to reel the fish in. Mom was furious. She stood up and demanded an apology, but when he ordered her to sit back down and be quiet, that was the final straw. Nobody puts Mommy in a corner! She screamed that she wasn't about to be his "little woman" who just did what she was told, and gave him a shove. It was a gentle shove, not too hard, but it was enough to cause Mr. C to lose his balance and topple over the side of the boat straight into the water, but not before grabbing Randy and dragging the poor kid along with him to use as a human life vest.

Mom screamed at Mr. C to swim with Randy back to the boat, which was slowly drifting away, but Mr. C was in a full panic, splashing around, clutching Randy, who bobbed up and down in the water afloat from his life vest to save himself!

"I can't swim!" he wailed, crying like a baby.

Mom sprang into action and managed to get the motor going, and then guided the small craft over alongside a terrified Mr. C and Randy, who was sputtering and coughing out water. Mom and I reached down and pried poor Randy loose from Mr. C's grasp, and then we hauled him back into the boat. Mom then tossed Mr. C a rope, which was tied to the inside of the boat, but before he could use it to climb aboard, she gunned the motor and the boat sped back to shore, dragging a bumping and spinning Mr. C in the water behind us.

Once we were safely back on land, we all silently packed up to leave and securely fastened the boat to the trailer. Mom was finally, much to our relief and delight, ready to go home! Mr. C knew he was in the doghouse so he refrained from making conversation most of the way except to ask if we wanted to stop for lunch somewhere.

Mom very quickly and sternly replied, "No."

When Mr. C pulled up in front of our house, Mom barely allowed the truck to come to a complete stop before she jumped out, and ordered Randy and me to grab our knapsacks and go inside the house. We loitered just a bit by the front door because we were dying to hear what Mom was going to say to Mr. C.

Mr. C, oblivious to Mom's building rage, casually put his truck in park and shut off the engine. He jumped out, and made a move to come inside the house with us.

"Hey, since we didn't stop for lunch, how about you whip up some of that Lobster in Spicy Tomato Sauce dish you were telling me about the other night?"

We could see her just staring at him, her face beet red and her eyes blazing with fire. She calmly reached down and opened the cooler she had just pulled out of the back of his truck. Then she grabbed a plastic bag of lobster rolls that we never had a chance to eat on our fishing trip.

"You want lunch? Here is your lunch!" she hollered as she hurled the rolls at Mr. C, a string of curse words escaping her lips, words I had no idea she even knew!

Mr. C threw his hands up to protect his face from the flying lobster meat covered in mayonnaise, and ran to the safety of his truck, wiping dollops of mayo off his face as he sped away. Mom chased after him half a block, still throwing what few lobster rolls were left at the truck like a Hall of Famer baseball pitcher!

Later that evening, Mom ended up following Mr. C's advice and making that delicious Lobster in Spicy Tomato Sauce for us (Randy of course happily munched on a peanut butter sandwich), and she promised us we would never have to lay eyes on Mr. C ever again. And then she sat back and enjoyed a Whiskey Peach Cocktail to relax herself after our exciting summer camping adventure.

Whiskey Peach Cocktail

Ingredients
4 basil leaves
½ ounce agave
3 ounces of whiskey
4 ounces of peach puree
Club soda

In a tall glass muddle your basil and agave until aromatic.

In a shaker filled with ice add your whiskey and puree and shake until blended.

Fill your glass halfway with ice. Pour the whiskey peach mixture over the basil. Then finish off with club soda.

Sheila's Lobster in Spicy Tomato Sauce

Ingredients
1 pound boxed spaghetti
2 tablespoons olive oil
2 tablespoons butter
1 large shallot, finely chopped
1 tablespoon crushed red pepper flakes
1 pound grape tomatoes
1 to 1½ pounds cooked lobster meat
(if you prefer shrimp, go for it)

Lemon wedges for serving
Cook your spaghetti according to the directions until al dente.

Heat your oil and butter in a large skillet on medium-high heat and cook the shallots and red pepper flakes for two minutes or until shallots are soft. Add the grape tomatoes, and cook until they are soft and juicy, about 5 to 6 minutes.

Add your lobster meat and mix well.

Now add your drained pasta and half of the reserved pasta water, and simmer to thicken, coating all the pasta. Add more water as needed.

Top the pasta with the lemon zest. Serve with lemon wedges for added lemon flavor if desired.

Despite what my brother Randy might tell you, this dish beats a peanut butter sandwich any day!

Chapter 11

Liddy screamed at the top of her lungs, and a couple of seagulls who were peacefully balancing on top of a floating buoy several hundred feet out from shore shot up into the air, wings flapping madly, spooked by the sudden sharp sound.

Hayley took Liddy, who was still screaming, by the arms and shook her violently. "Liddy, calm down! I don't want to have to slap you, but I will!"

Liddy struggled to regain her composure, taking deep breaths, but then she would glance down at the dead body and start hyperventilating again.

Hayley immediately called 911 on her cell phone and reported what they had found, and within minutes, they heard sirens approaching in the near distance.

"Are you absolutely sure he's dead?" Liddy panted, her hand on her chest.

Hayley stepped closer to Jackson and knelt, examining him. "He's definitely dead."

She knew better than to touch the body, but she got down on her hands and knees to get a good look at him and study his face. His mouth was contorted into a silent scream, his lifeless blood-red eyes open and staring up at her. She shuddered, and then noticed some discoloration, purple bruising on Jackson's neck.

"Now, that's interesting," Hayley said, curious enough to lean in even closer to study them.

"What is it? What do you see?" Liddy asked breathlessly as the sirens stopped, and from the edge of the beach, they could hear car doors opening and slamming shut.

"He's got bruises on his neck and the red in his eyes means blood was forced up in the whites of his eyes," Hayley said.

"What does that mean?"

"It means he probably died from strangulation."

"You think he was murdered?" Liddy gasped.

"I'm pretty sure of it," Hayley said.

"Step away from the body right now," a loud voice demanded.

Hayley looked up to see Sheriff Daphne Wilkes, flanked by two officers, a small, wiry, wide-eyed, shaking, nervous male who had obviously never seen a dead body before, and a heavy, tall, serious, Mack Truck of a woman, charging down the beach toward them.

"Somebody strangled him," Hayley offered.

"How do you know? Do you have training as a criminologist?"

"No, I just watch a lot of shows on Investigation Discovery."

"You are compromising a crime scene," Sheriff Daphne bellowed. "Now, I won't tell you again. Get away from the body!"

Hayley sighed, annoyed, and crawled to her feet. "I didn't touch anything."

"Officer Caribou, escort these ladies over there where they won't be in the way, and keep an eye on them. And I don't want them going anywhere until I've had a chance to question them," Sheriff Daphne ordered.

"Yes, ma'am," the heavyset female officer said, and then lumbered over and roughly grabbed Hayley and Liddy by the arms. "Come with me this way, ladies."

Hayley and Liddy were shunted off to the side while Sheriff Daphne circled the body a couple of times before kneeling and examining it closely, no doubt arriving at the same conclusion as Hayley. Sheriff Daphne then stood up and quietly confirmed to her officer that she believed Jackson Young had indeed been strangled.

Duh.

Hayley was hardly a fan of the sour, ill-tempered sheriff, who gleefully wrote unfair parking tickets and spoke down to her as if she was a petulant child.

Liddy grabbed her cell phone and called Mona. "Mona, what are you doing? Where are you?"

She paused as Mona spoke.

"Well, have Corey drive you back! This is an emergency! Hayley and I found Jackson Young on the beach!"

Hayley caught Sheriff Daphne stealing a few glances back in their direction. She began to fear she might wind up on the suspect list if she wasn't careful. Certainly, if anyone overheard Liddy's loud and hysterical threats promising to do Jackson Young serious bodily harm for so callously standing her up, her name most definitely would be on the top of the list.

"He's dead, Mona! Dead! Somebody killed him!"

Liddy paused, and gasped. "No, of course it wasn't me! Don't be ridiculous!"

She cupped her hand over the face of the phone and turned to Hayley. "She's on her way back."

Sheriff Daphne whispered something to her male officer before trudging over to where her female officer was holding Hayley and Liddy at bay. She nodded to the stone-faced Officer Caribou, who walked back over to the crime scene to join her partner.

"When did you discover the body?" Sheriff Daphne asked, a grave tone in her voice.

"Just a few minutes ago," Hayley said. "We called 911 right away."

"The strange thing was, we were out here looking for him," Liddy spilled out nervously. "Hayley had seen him down here earlier so we walked here to try to find him."

"Why were you looking for him?" Sheriff Daphne asked, curious.

"I wanted to kill him," Liddy said matter-of-factly, before the realization of what she had just admitted hit her. "I mean, not literally! Figuratively! I wanted to give him a piece of my mind, that's all!"

"He stood her up," Hayley said, trying to be helpful. "They were supposed to meet at the cabin where we are staying and come to the lobster bake together but he never showed up."

"I see," Sheriff Daphne said, her words brimming with subtext as she stared at Liddy, her eyes full of suspicion.

Sheriff Daphne stood there silently for an interminable amount of time before turning to Hayley. "And after you called 911, instead of waiting for the police to arrive, you took it upon yourself to poke and prod the body to see if you could figure out what happened?"

Hayley reacted, arching her back defiantly. "No! I told you, I never touched the body. I just noticed the marks on his neck and the blood in his eyes. I did not compromise the crime scene in any way!"

"So, when you saw Mr. Young earlier, was he with someone?" Sheriff Daphne asked, her eyes boring into

Hayley, causing her to shift her body to one side. The sheriff was making her feel supremely uncomfortable.

"Yes," Hayley answered. "He was with Sue."

"The owner of the Starfish Lounge?"

"Yes," Hayley said, nodding. "They were arguing."

"About what?"

"I wasn't close enough to hear."

"Okay," Sheriff Daphne said. "I would appreciate it if you stick around for a few days. I'm sure I will have more questions."

"But that's impossible," Liddy piped in, upset. "We are going to drive back to Bar Harbor first thing in the morning."

Sheriff Daphne glared at them and then said quietly and evenly, "Again, I would appreciate your cooperation. It would go a long way in showing me you are actually a help to this investigation and not a hindrance."

Meaning if you blow town, you will be suspects.

"We'll do whatever is necessary," Hayley said, squeezing Liddy's hand, a firm signal that she should just keep her mouth shut.

"Ladies, I'll be in touch," Sheriff Daphne said, giving them a dead stare for a moment longer, a blatant attempt to intimidate them, before turning her back on them and walking over to Jackson Young's corpse.

Liddy was shaking. "I just want to go home."

"I think it's important we do what she says," Hayley said, catching Sheriff Daphne once again peeking over at them.

"She's not exactly a breath of fresh air, is she?" Liddy scoffed.

"No, she obviously doesn't like us, which is weird," Hayley said. "She doesn't even know us. But I think it's probably in our best interest not to give her any more reasons to hate us."

By the time Hayley and Liddy walked back up from the beach, Mona and Corey were pulling up in Corey's truck.

Sadie was in the back, tail wagging excitedly.

As Mona jumped out of the passenger's side, Liddy hurled herself into the arms of Mona, who stiffened and scrunched up her face.

"It's horrible, Mona. Poor Jackson is gone. I still can't believe it," Liddy wailed. "Such a handsome, sweet man, in his prime! How could this happen?"

Mona shook her head. "Just this morning you were saying he was a horrible monster and you wished terrible things would happen to him!"

Liddy pushed away from Mona and snapped, "For your information, you are *terrible* in a crisis."

Mona shrugged, unconcerned. This wasn't anything that was going to keep her up at night.

Corey slid over and leaned out the passenger-side window. "I'd be happy to give you gals a lift back to your car but you'll have to ride in the back with Sadie."

Liddy threw up her hands, and then climbed into the cargo bed of Corey's pickup truck, and was greeted by sloppy wet kisses from Sadie.

"This day just keeps getting better and better," she groaned.

Hayley's stomach was tied up in knots. She was still dealing with the trauma of discovering a dead body on the beach.

And now she had the sickening feeling her troubles with Sheriff Daphne Wilkes were just beginning.

Chapter 12

"We've waited around all day for that sheriff to call, and she hasn't bothered to so I say it is time we pack up and go home," Liddy declared, zipping up her suitcase.

"I know you are upset about Jackson, and you just want to get out of here, but we were always scheduled to stay through Tuesday, and I've already taken the time off from the paper, so I think we should stay put for at least one more day just in case the sheriff has any further questions, and then we can leave," Hayley said.

She was a little nervous about ticking off the surly, rude sheriff with a presumably personal vendetta against them.

"I agree with Hayley," Mona said, chugging down the last of her bottle of beer at the rickety old kitchen table.

"Of course you agree with Hayley. Staying in Salmon Cove means more precious lovey-dovey moments with your handsome, sweet-natured lumberjack and his adorable and equally sweet-natured dog," Liddy said, annoyed.

"Corey is not a lumberjack. He's a lobster man," Mona barked.

"What is the difference? He's gorgeous and an outdoors-man, who looks like he just stepped off the pages of an

L.L.Bean catalog," Liddy said, scowling. "Who would want to leave that behind?"

"I'm a married woman," Mona said.

"You keep saying that, Mona, and every time you do, it is with far less conviction," Liddy said.

Mona slammed down her empty beer bottle and stood up from the flimsy table. "I've heard just about enough."

"Would you two please stop bickering? I can't take it anymore. This was supposed to be a fun girls' weekend, and it's been nothing but agony ever since we got here," Hayley moaned.

"Well, it's not our fault a dead body turned up to put a damper on things, Hayley. You should be a bit more sympathetic to what I'm going through. Jackson and I shared a very deep, very real connection."

"You met in the lobby of a hotel for two seconds and then had one drunken conversation at a bar!" Mona howled.

"Hayley, please help me here. Mona just doesn't get it," Liddy pleaded.

"I'm sorry, Liddy, but Mona has a point. You and Jackson were not exactly a longtime couple like David Beckham and Posh Spice," Hayley said quietly. "You had just met before he—"

"Was brutally strangled to death!" Liddy screamed. "That's the other reason we should hit the road as soon as possible. Do either of you care that there is a mad killer on the loose? Who knows where he could be lurking about? He might be right outside our door at this very moment waiting to strike!"

Mona stared at something on the wall of the cabin.

Liddy noticed and huffed, "Mona, are you even listening to a word I'm saying?"

Mona pointed at a gray lump in the upper corner of the wall near the kitchen. "What is *that*?"

"What is what?" Hayley asked, turning around to get a better look at what had suddenly gotten her attention.

"Is that a bat?" Mona asked, stepping closer.

"A bat? Like a real flapping, black-eyed rat with wings?" Liddy screamed. "Where? Where?"

"Up there! It looks like he is sleeping," Mona said.

"Well, for the love of God, Mona, don't wake it up!" Liddy shrieked.

But it was too late.

Mona had already picked up a broom, and with the handle, gently nudged the gray balled-up mass.

Suddenly without warning, the bat jolted awake and, with extended wings, flew from its spot on the wall and swooped around the room. As it fluttered around Mona, she swung at it with the broom handle, driving it over to Liddy, who screamed at the top of her lungs and frantically waved her arms around. The bat squeaked loudly as it landed in Liddy's nest of curly hair and got caught.

"Get it off me! Get it off me!" Liddy bawled, crying and screaming.

Hayley rushed forward to physically yank the bat's claws out of Liddy's hair, but before she could reach her, Liddy, in a panic, bolted for the door, shaking her head violently and swatting frantically with her hands at the bat nestled in her hair.

Liddy whipped open the door, and ran out straight into the chest of a tall man hovering outside.

Liddy, assuming it was the killer she feared might be lurking about, let loose with a deafening and sustained high-pitched shriek and pounded her fists hard against the man's chest in a lame attempt to defend herself. The startled man grabbed Liddy's wrists, desperately trying to get her wild, hysterical onslaught under control.

It was Corey Guildford.

He instantly noticed the bat scratching and flapping on

top of her head, released his grip on her, and with a meaty hand, yanked the bat out of her hair and hurled it into the night sky.

Liddy wiped tears away from her face and stared at Corey for a moment, before collapsing in his arms, simpering. "Corey, you need to take me to the hospital immediately. I need to be checked for rabies."

"Did the bat bite you?" Hayley asked, concerned.

"No, but you never know," Liddy said. "Better safe than sorry."

"You don't have rabies!" Mona bellowed, leaning the broom up against the kitchen sink.

"You must know a lot about nature, Corey, being a rugged outdoorsman and all. Do you think I'm in any danger of contracting rabies?" Liddy asked, still helpless in his arms.

"I'm pretty sure you're okay," he said, suppressing a smile and winking at Hayley and Mona. "But I'm guessing you could sure use a drink right about now."

"Yes, I think that's the smart choice," Hayley said. "You need something to calm your nerves."

"I need something to dull my senses so I'm not reliving this nightmare over and over again," Liddy said, pulling away from Corey.

"Then allow me to escort you ladies into town and buy you all a drink. This may be my last chance, since Mona tells me you're all leaving tomorrow," he said.

"That's very kind of you, Corey, thank you," Hayley said, grabbing her bag.

"Yes, let's get as far away as possible from this vermin-infested hole," Liddy said before spinning around and glaring at Mona. "I swear, you intentionally swung that broom handle around to drive that rat with wings right in my direction."

Hayley pushed Liddy out the door.

"Mona did no such thing," Hayley said, pushing Liddy in the direction of Corey's truck where Sadie waited in the flatbed, tail wagging. She turned back to Mona. "Right, Mona?"

"No, I totally did," Mona said as a smile crept across her lips.

Corey stifled a laugh, and then put his arm around Mona as they walked toward the truck. Hayley noticed Mona shift uncomfortably as Corey gently lowered his open hand, resting the palm on the small of her back, but then Mona couldn't help but relax into it. She obviously enjoyed his touch. And it was clear to Hayley at that moment, that despite her full-throated protestations and denials, Mona Barnes was falling for this guy.

Big-time.

Chapter 13

"Yeah, we argued. I won't deny it. The guy really pissed me off," Sue said from behind the bar at the Starfish Lounge.

"What did he do?" Hayley asked, nursing a Jack and Coke as she sat atop a high chair near the service station where Sue was washing glasses.

"He was just real nosy, always poking around and asking questions, about me and my customers, ever since he blew into town. I finally told him to knock it off at the lobster bake!"

"He told us when we met him that he was a travel writer. Just part of the job, I guess," Hayley shrugged.

Sue was having none of it.

"A travel writer talks about what's the nicest hotel to stay at, or the best restaurant to order fried clams, or which hiking trails have the most scenic views. Jackson's questions were far more personal and they just rubbed me the wrong way," Sue said, scowling.

She finished washing the glasses and then poured a mug of beer for a scraggly faced, big, burly fisherman wearing a dated "Make America Great Again" ball cap.

Hayley stirred her drink with a straw and casually

glanced back up at Sue. "At the risk of ticking you off again, just how personal did his questions get?"

Sue sighed and leaned down on the bar in front of Hayley. "Look, I'll be honest with you, Hayley. I've had a few troubles in the past. I went through some pretty rough times back when I was serving in Afghanistan. And as proud as I am of my days in the military, there's also a lot of stuff that went down there I'd rather not talk about."

"I understand completely," Hayley said, determined not to upset this large, imposing woman with an obvious short fuse.

"I got into a few scrapes with the law when I came home to Salmon Cove after two tours. Mostly related to my PTSD," Sue said, eyes downcast, her voice barely audible over the crooning of Toby Keith coming from the jukebox.

PTSD.

Post-traumatic stress disorder.

A very common affliction for soldiers returning from combat.

"Here's the thing," Sue said. "Other than my family, my doctor, and Sheriff Wilkes, nobody knew about those incidents. I didn't tell a soul. And Sheriff Wilkes was kind enough not to leak them to the local paper. But then Jackson Young comes in here and starts asking me all about them."

"Maybe he somehow got his hands on the police report."

"Yes, I suppose it is possible, sure, but why would a travel writer even care about *my* secrets? How do you square digging up my personal problems with writing a simple travel article? I mean, it doesn't make any sense."

Hayley nodded. Sue was right. Jackson Young's insatiable curiosity went far beyond a fluffy puff piece on a quaint, out-of-the-way Maine tourist destination.

"And he didn't stop there," Sue said. "He wanted to know intimate details about my customers, everyone who hangs out here. I tried to be polite at first because he was in here spending money every night he was in town, but then I caught him asking Boyd and Ellie personal questions about me at the lobster bake and that was the last straw. So I dragged him down to the beach and had it out with him."

"What did he say when you told him to stop asking so many questions?"

"He rattled on about how he was just trying to paint a colorful portrait of the Salmon Cove locals for his article, but I could tell he was lying, which just made me madder than a wet hornet!"

"Was there any kind of physical altercation between you two?"

Sue eyed Hayley warily. "I may have jabbed a finger in his chest when I was yelling at him to lay off with all the questions, but when I left him at the beach, trust me, he was still very much alive. I didn't even know he had been killed until one of my customers told me later that night at the bar."

"Do you have any idea who might have strangled him?"

"We have a pretty tight community here. I've known a lot of these people all my life and I can't imagine any of them going off the handle like that and murdering a man. I think it was an outsider, someone not from around here, maybe a random mugging or something."

"In Salmon Cove?" Hayley asked, incredulously.

"I know it sounds far-fetched, but what other explanation is there?"

Sue wandered off to the other side of the bar to wait on a customer who had just walked in. Hayley glanced around the bar. Mona and Corey were engaged in a heated game of pool near the back where it looked like Mona was kicking Corey's butt again and loving every minute of it. She also spotted Liddy, who had left Hayley ten minutes earlier to freshen up in the bathroom. She was standing a few feet from the restroom, immersed in a conversation with a young couple sitting at a table near the window. Hayley could tell from Liddy's pursed lips that she was annoyed, and from her eyes darting back and forth, it was clear she was eager to find some means of escape. But the couple, who were in their mid- to late twenties and both very attractive, were oblivious to her body language and continued talking her ear off and making it very difficult for her to make a graceful exit.

Hayley's eyes then fell on Boyd, hunkered down at a table near the jukebox, his face buried in a comic book.

Hayley slid off the high chair at the bar and ambled over to him.

"Hi, Boyd, I'm Hayley. We met the other night."

"I know," Boyd said, never raising his eyes from his comic book.

"What are you reading?"

"*The Third Coming*," Boyd said, in a flat, listless tone. "It's about aliens who are coming to Earth to enslave us, and how they are sending down some of their top soldiers in human form to study our habits and customs and to also learn our weaknesses in order to make the invasion go faster and easier."

"Sounds exciting," Hayley said.

Boyd looked up at her with a mix of surprise and disgust. "It is *not* exciting. It's scary. This is happening. This is real."

"Okay," Hayley said, trying hard to react in a way that would not offend him. "I'll try to be prepared."

"You better be," Boyd said, looking up from his

comic and staring at her with a dead-serious expression. "Because when they arrive, it's going to be a bloodbath."

"Good to know," Hayley said, biting her lip. "Sorry to bother you, Boyd. I just saw you and Ellie at the lobster bake, and I was curious to know how your date went."

Boyd's sober face slowly gave way to a slight smile. His cheeks turned beet red and his eyes quickly averted back to his comic book.

"It was nice," he said in a whisper.

"That's so great to hear," Hayley said.

Suddenly Liddy was at her side, clawing at Hayley's arm. "I thought I would never get away from those two!"

"Excuse us, Boyd," Hayley said. "It was lovely to talk to you. I'll let you get back to your comic book."

Boyd stared at Liddy, eyes wide as saucers, and then back at his comic book. He flipped the page around and showed a drawing of a female alien in a steel bustier and with curly black hair and Medusa-like snakes slithering out of the top of her head.

"I didn't notice it before when I first saw her, but she looks just like the alien queen!"

Liddy glanced down at the comic and gasped. "How could you say that? I look nothing like her! I don't have snakes coming out of the top of my head!"

Hayley grabbed Liddy by the arm and steered her back over to the bar.

"I look nothing like that! If there is any comic book character I resemble it's Veronica from the *Archie* comics. She may have been a bitch, but she had so much poise and style."

"Boyd's a little off. I wouldn't worry about it too much," Hayley said, chuckling.

"Can we go now, please? I don't want to get stuck talking to those two over there again," Liddy said.

"I don't want to leave just yet. It looks like Mona's having a good time and I don't want to cut it short," Hayley said.

"Fine," Liddy said, sighing. "But if those two come over here, *you* talk to them."

"Who are they?"

"A couple of tourists from Ohio, Dayton or Cleveland, I think, but who really cares? They snagged me on my way back from the bathroom and wouldn't stop chattering about how much they loved Salmon Cove, and how they sold their house and all of their possessions and bought an RV and have been driving around this great nation for the past two years seeing the sights and meeting all kinds of interesting people our country has to offer, and all I wanted to say was, 'Wake up! You are not two of those interesting people!'"

"I think it's admirable they've decided to treat life like one big adventure," Hayley said, glancing over at them.

They both smiled and waved at them.

"Stop drawing their attention. I swear, if you get stuck in a conversation, you'll never get rid of them," Liddy warned.

Suddenly something slammed into Liddy's back and she was thrown to the ground. It was the fisherman in the "Make America Great Again" cap. He was swaying back and forth, bleary-eyed, blisteringly drunk. He pounded his empty beer mug on the bar for another round.

Hayley bent down, took Liddy by the arm, and helped her crawl back up to her feet. "Are you all right?"

"Yes, just a little shocked. I didn't see that coming," Liddy said breathlessly. "That's one of the fishermen who kept me company when I hung out here during the lobster bake. He's even more soused now than he was then!"

"Hey!" Sue bellowed, charging toward them from the

other end of the bar. "You just knocked that poor woman off her feet, Lewis! You need to apologize."

"I ain't apologizing for nothing, Sue, just pour me another beer," the fisherman mumbled, as he squinted at Liddy and sneered. "Hey! Have we met?"

"You've had enough, Lewis. I think it is time for you to go home," Sue said.

"Don't you dare tell me when I should go home. I'll go home when I'm damn good and ready. Now are you going to pour me another beer or do I have to come back there and do it myself?" the drunken fisherman slurred.

That was all Sue needed to hear.

She shot out from behind the bar, grabbed the fisherman by the end of his scraggly beard, and pulled him toward the door. He stumbled and swayed and then took a swing at her.

Sue easily dodged the blow and then seized him in a headlock.

The fisherman waved his arms frantically as she choked him out.

There was fire in her eyes, a focused determination, as she squeezed harder until he was gagging and gasping for air.

Hayley watched in horror as the fisherman slowly began to pass out.

Fearing she might kill the drunk, Hayley finally blurted out. "Sue, stop!"

As if suddenly freed from a trance by the sound of Hayley's voice, Sue released the fisherman and he collapsed to the floor. She turned to Boyd.

"Get him out of here."

Boyd dropped his comic book on the table, and hustled over, bending down and grabbing the half-conscious fisherman in a bear hug and herding him out the door.

Liddy stepped forward and put a gentle hand on Sue's arm. "Thank you for coming to my defense."

Sue just grunted, shook Liddy's hand off, and went back behind the bar without saying another word.

Hayley couldn't believe it.

She had never seen a woman possess such powerful physical strength.

Sue had dispatched her unruly customer, who must have had at least twenty-five pounds on her, without batting an eye.

There was no doubt in her mind that Sue, despite her claim of having left him alive on that beach at the lobster bake, could easily have strangled the smaller, wiry Jackson Young.

Chapter 14

Boyd came back inside the bar after a few minutes, and told Sue that Lewis had promised to go home quietly. However, he had just sat back down and picked up his comic book when the Taylor Swift song playing on the jukebox ended and everyone in the Starfish Lounge heard a man outside yelling.

It was a drunken Lewis screaming at the top of his lungs about how he was going to ruin Sue by filing a lawsuit for assaulting him.

Sue was fed up. She picked up the phone and called the police.

By now the mounting drama of the situation was enough for Mona and Corey to call off their latest game of pool, and wander back over to the front of the bar where Hayley and Liddy were on the edge of their seats waiting for Sue's next move. No one wanted to plug a quarter in the jukebox and play another song because they didn't want to miss a moment of the show playing out at the Starfish Lounge.

Sue marched outside and started screaming at Lewis, telling him she had already called the cops so if he didn't get the hell out of there he would be arrested. Lewis hollered back that he was happy the police were on their way so they could arrest *her* for attempted murder. From the far end of the bar, a man Hayley hadn't even noticed before who was slumped over in the corner, his head cradled in his crossed arms, was roused from slumber, and in an annoyed, scratchy voice, yelled, "What the hell is all that racket?"

It was Rufus, the eighty-something barfly, and Ellie's grandfather.

He glanced around, momentarily unaware of where he was, but he quickly noted the familiar surroundings and settled into a sense of relief. He was safe and sound at his regular watering hole. Rufus winced, probably from a massive hangover, and then barked, "Where the hell is Sue? I need another whiskey!"

At that moment, a siren wailed in the distance, growing in volume as it got closer. All the remaining patrons in the bar, not many since last call was not that far off, excitedly filed outside to witness the dramatic scene unfolding. Everyone, that is, except for Rufus, who dropped his head back down on the bar and covered his head with his hands to pray the pounding away.

Hayley, Liddy, Mona, Corey, the chatty young tourists with the RV, Boyd, and a few others gathered outside to see Lewis, enraged, taking wild swings at Sue, who easily dodged them. As he charged at her again, she stuck out her arm and flattened the palm of her hand against his forehead, keeping him at bay as he repeatedly took swings at her with his spindly, rubbery arms, missing her by a mile.

A squad car rolled up in front of the bar and Sheriff Daphne, with a stern face and professional demeanor, climbed out of the car and slowly walked over to where Lewis was taking his pathetic potshots at Sue.

"All right, Lewis, I think you've made your point. Now it's time to settle down," Sheriff Daphne said.

"You need to arrest her! She viciously attacked me!" Lewis wailed.

"The only person who seems to be attacking anyone right now is you," Sheriff Daphne said, exchanging a quick smile with Sue.

"I ain't settling down until an arrest is made! You hear me, Sheriff?" Lewis yelled defiantly.

"Loud and clear," Sheriff Daphne said, unclipping a pair of handcuffs from her waist belt and snapping one on Lewis's right wrist. He struggled momentarily, but he was too inebriated to put up much of a fight and before he could break free, his left wrist was cuffed as well.

"You're under arrest, Lewis," Sheriff Daphne said coolly.

"On what charges?" he demanded to know.

"We can start with disturbing the peace and go from there. Sound good?"

"I'm going to sue you for every last dime you have," Lewis spit out at Sue before cranking his head around toward Daphne, who was pushing him in the direction of her squad car. "And I'm going to sue the police department for false arrest!"

"Well, maybe when you wake up tomorrow morning in the drunk tank, you'll have a change of heart," Sheriff Daphne said as she opened the back door of the car and shoved Lewis inside before slamming it shut on him, effectively locking him inside. He was still screaming, nose smashed against the glass of the window, smearing the glass with spittle and snot, but his voice was muted and most of his words unintelligible. The crowd could only make out a few and they were all four-letter ones.

Sue checked her watch and turned to her small crowd of customers who were bunched up by the entrance to the bar. "Folks, I'm sorry to say it is almost one o'clock so you missed last call. Time to call it a night, but please come again tomorrow."

Ellie strolled down the sidewalk toward the bar, her eyes widening as she took in the flashing blue lights on top of the squad car, the screaming drunk in the back, and the horde of people gathered outside.

Boyd lit up at the sight of her, and rushed over to her.

"Hi, Ellie," he said, pure joy in his voice.

"Hello, Boyd, nice to see you," she said shyly. "Who's been arrested?"

"Just Lewis. Again," Boyd said, rolling his eyes.

"Thank goodness. I thought it might be Granddad in the back of that squad car," she said with a relieved sigh.

"No, he's still inside. You here to pick him up?" Sue asked.

Ellie nodded.

"Boyd, why don't you go get him?"

Boyd bounded inside, a big, excited grin on his face.

Hayley turned to see Corey trying to give Mona a good night kiss, but once again, she expertly dodged it so his lips landed on her chin. It was awkward and weird but ridiculously cute. Mona was beside herself trying to keep her relationship with this handsome local strictly platonic.

Liddy, meanwhile, was busy dodging her new friends, the young couple touring the US in their RV, who were following her around, asking if she minded accepting their Facebook friend request. Liddy tried mightily to be polite but the strain on her face revealed she was at her wit's end.

Hayley yawned, ready to return to the cabin for a good night's sleep, but when she turned to Liddy's Mercedes, which was parked right out in front of the bar, she saw Sheriff Daphne printing out a ticket from her traffic violation handheld machine and slipping it underneath the windshield wiper after stuffing it in a small envelope. She headed back to her squad car, where Lewis had finally stopped screaming and was now out of view, presumably passed out on the backseat.

Hayley ran to catch up to her.

"Excuse me, Sheriff, why did you give us a ticket?"

Sheriff Daphne slowly turned around, and at the sight of Hayley, gave her a withering look, as if she was the last person she ever wanted to see.

"Your tires," Daphne sighed, eager to end this conversation and get back to the station and deposit Lewis in the drunk tank.

"What about them?"

"They're not turned in the right direction for hillside parking," Daphne said.

Her eyes locked into Hayley's and she stared at her, as if to say, *"You really want to fight me on this?"*

Hayley definitely wanted to fight her on this. "But the street is flat."

"No, it's not. There's a clear incline. Your tires should be turned toward the curb."

"This is ludicrous. What is your problem with me, lady?"

Sheriff Daphne's nostrils flared.

She didn't appreciate a visitor challenging her authority.

Hayley immediately regretted standing up to her.

She half expected the sheriff to pull out another pair of handcuffs and toss her in the back of the squad car with Lewis.

But Daphne just took a deep breath and said quietly, "I have no problem with you. I just have a problem with you violating the law. If you want to fight the ticket in court, be my guest."

She turned on her heel and marched over to her squad car, jumped in the driver's seat, and peeled away so fast Hayley imagined poor Lewis being tossed around from side to side in the back.

Liddy, having finally extricated herself from her new millennial friends, traipsed back over to her Mercedes, stopping in her tracks at the sight of the envelope tucked underneath her windshield wiper.

"What's that?" she asked, eyes wide.

"Traffic ticket," Hayley said. "Apparently, you didn't park the car properly on the hill."

"Hill? What hill?"

Liddy spun her head around looking for some kind of slope.

"According to the sheriff, Salmon Cove might as well be the streets of San Francisco," Hayley said, defeated.

"Oh, hell no! She is not going to get away with this!" Liddy roared, fishing her smartphone out of her purse. "I am going to fight this!"

She snapped photos of the tires, the car, the street, and all the surroundings from every angle, capturing the last of the patrons in front of the bar, including the young couple who waved excitedly, convinced Liddy wanted a memory of their time together.

"I'm going to bring so much photographic evidence to

court, that power-hungry policewoman's head will spin!"
Liddy said, determined.

Boyd led Rufus out of the bar and hustled him over to
Ellie, who smiled and gave her grandfather a quick peck
on the cheek. "Come on, Granddad. Time to go home,"
she said.

"You want me to escort you home, Ellie?" Boyd asked,
expectantly.

"No, not tonight, Boyd, we'll be fine. But thank you.
My car's parked just down the street."

The flash from Liddy's phone camera caused Rufus to
jolt and wave his arms in front of his face.

"Something's happening, Ellie! I think I may be having
some kind of stroke," he cried.

Ellie stared at Liddy's camera, a frown on her face.
"It's just a flash from a camera, Granddad. Nothing to
worry about."

And then she hustled him off, leaving Boyd behind
with a sad, disappointed look on his face. He turned and
shuffled back inside to help Sue clean up and cash out for
the night.

Having said good-bye to Corey, Mona joined Hayley,
who watched as Liddy continued snapping a slew of
pictures for her robust defense she planned to unveil
in traffic court. Assuming she would even bother returning to Salmon Cove once she got a date on the
docket.

"I think it is high time we finally head home to Bar
Harbor in the morning," Mona said. "If I stay here much
longer, I may crumble and do something I shouldn't with
Corey."

"I want to stay another day," Hayley said.

"But I thought—"

"That power-hungry sheriff clearly doesn't want us here, and she's doing everything in her power to get us to leave," Hayley said. "Well, when someone pushes me, I tend to push back. I am not going to be run out of town."

Chapter 15

"I'm so thrilled you chose to stay a bit longer so I could show you my appreciation for helping a friend in need," Polly said, biting into her lobster roll.

They were sitting at a picnic table with a stunning ocean view outside the Lobster Shack, a small takeout seafood joint located just outside of Salmon Cove.

"You didn't have to treat me to lunch," Hayley said. "I had a wonderful time selling your blueberry pies at the lobster bake."

She dipped a fried clam in some tartar sauce and popped it in her mouth, not expecting it to be so hot. It burned her tongue as she quickly chewed and swallowed and then chased it down with an iced tea, frantically waving her hands in the air.

Polly laughed. "I know, they just smell too good! It's impossible to wait until they've cooled down."

The potbellied owner of the Lobster Shack, wearing a stained white T-shirt, Bermuda shorts, and flip-flops, sweat pouring down his face from the grill, ambled over to the picnic table and set down a paper plate piled high with a feast of fried shrimp.

"Here, ladies, enjoy. On the house," he said, winking at Polly.

"Thank you, Buddy! They look delicious," Polly cooed, flirtatiously touching his thick, smooth forearm.

"Just don't forget to bring me another one of your peach cobblers one of these days," he said, wiping the sweat off his face with a dirty rag that was draped over his right shoulder.

"You can bet on it," Polly said, beaming.

"Better get back to the fryer," he said, nodding, a big smile on his face, and then he did an about-face and waddled back inside the small windowless shack with steam pouring out.

"You certainly have a lot of devoted fans of your baked goods," Hayley said, impressed.

"Well, yes, I've built up quite a loyal clientele. And everybody has their own personal favorite. Buddy here loves my cobbler. Sue at the Starfish Lounge always wants to buy all my banana muffins. Old man Rufus can't get enough of my blueberry pies, and his granddaughter Ellie is a huge fan of my lemon squares. And that boy who works for Sue, and is so smitten with Ellie . . ."

"Boyd."

"Yes, Boyd, he drools over my angel food cake with fresh strawberries. Then there is that handsome Corey Guildford who's been doting on your friend while she's been here, well, he's always coming around for my fudge brownies. I could go on and on . . ."

"Sounds like you're friends with everybody in town," Hayley said, blowing on a fried clam and making sure it was cool before taking a bite.

"Only the ones with a sweet tooth," Polly said, laughing. "I will say, we have our share of tourists, but once they clear out, there's not that many of us left and we tend to stick together. I love living in such a beautiful, quiet, idyllic place. You must understand, coming from Bar Harbor."

"Yes, small-town living certainly has its advantages, there's a certain comfort and safe feeling, except when something really disturbing and unexpected happens . . ."

"You mean that poor man they found murdered on the beach? It's such a ghastly thing to happen, especially on the day of the lobster bake, which everyone looks forward to every year. I've been having nightmares about it," Polly said, shaking her head. "I mean, who would do such a horrible thing?"

"Hopefully, the police will figure it out," Hayley said.

"It's just so shocking. Nothing like that has ever happened in Salmon Cove," Polly said, dipping a fried clam into a plastic cup of cocktail sauce.

Hayley nodded sympathetically, knowing her own hometown of Bar Harbor's crime rate, given her past experiences, was slightly higher.

They sat at the picnic table gorging on fried food, chatting and staring at the seagulls skipping over the water in the bay for another half hour before Hayley finally stood up and thanked Polly for lunch. They both headed to the parking lot where they air-kissed each other good-bye, and Hayley climbed into Liddy's Mercedes, which she borrowed to come here, and drove off, leaving Polly chatting with the gruff, greasy, adorable Lobster Shack owner, Buddy, who followed her out to personally see her off.

Hayley had barely driven half a mile when she noticed in the rearview mirror a squad car pull out behind her and follow her. Her grip on the wheel tightened as her heart leapt into her throat. The squad car pulled up close, tailgating her. Hayley kept her eyes fixed on the road and checked her speedometer. It read thirty-two miles per hour. The speed limit sign she had passed just a few hundred feet from the Lobster Shack was thirty-five miles per hour so at least she was confident she wasn't speeding.

The front windshield of the squad car was tinted so she couldn't see who was driving, but she sure as heck could hazard a guess.

Nervous, Hayley let up on the gas pedal, fearing she might go over thirty-five, which would give the officer driving so close behind her just cause to pull her over. The needle dropped all the way down to twenty-two miles per hour. She couldn't understand why she was so nervous. She wasn't doing anything wrong. But Sheriff Daphne was no fan of hers, if indeed that was her driving the squad car behind her, and she seemed to always be looking for an excuse to give her more trouble.

There was a traffic light up ahead.

She was just entering the downtown area.

The light turned yellow.

Hayley could have easily and safely sailed through the yellow light before it turned red, but she wasn't taking any chances. She slammed on the brakes and the Mercedes jerked to a stop. The squad car nearly plowed into her bumper it was so close.

She glanced through the rearview mirror again.

The squad car idled behind her ominously.

Hayley swallowed hard.

Waiting for the light to turn green was agonizing.

Finally, the traffic light mercifully flashed green, and Hayley carefully flipped on her right blinker and turned right to head down the street that led to the country road that would take her back to the cabin where Liddy and Mona were waiting. Hopefully, the squad car would keep going straight into town.

No such luck.

It stayed right behind her.

That's when she saw the flashing blue lights, and was forced to pull over. She turned the wheel sharply and scraped the front tire against the cement curb because she was so discombobulated.

Just as she suspected, the driver's-side door of the squad car swung open, and Sheriff Daphne got out in her uniform, wearing dark sunglasses. She swaggered up to Hayley's window. Hayley pressed the button to lower it and turned to Sheriff Daphne expectantly.

"Do you know why I pulled you over?"

"I have no idea. I was not speeding."

"No, you weren't."

"Broken taillight?"

"Nope."

"Expired registration?"

"Nope."

"Then what?"

"You were driving too slow."

"I beg your pardon?"

"Speed limit is thirty-five miles per hour. You were going under twenty at one point. Driving too slow can be just as dangerous as driving too fast."

"You have got to be kidding me," Hayley scoffed, throwing her arms in the air.

"Please keep your hands on the wheel where I can see them," Sheriff Daphne said, glancing in the backseat as if she half expected to find some sort of illegal contraband.

Hayley froze, fearing this woman might be looking for an excuse to pull out her gun and shoot her. She put her hands back on the wheel and squeezed so tight her knuckles were white.

"I'm going to let you off with a warning this time," Daphne said, adjusting her sunglasses.

Hayley sighed. "I appreciate that. Thank you."

"You know, I've been studying up on you," Daphne said, stone-faced.

"What do you mean?"

"I like to know who is in my town and what their intentions are so I did a little research, read a few issues of your local paper, and much to my surprise, I found out you fancy yourself some kind of crime fighter."

"I write a cooking column," Hayley said through gritted teeth.

"Oh, I think you're underselling yourself, Wonder Woman," Daphne said, casually fingering the gun in her holster just enough so Hayley would notice. "You've got quite the reputation for saving your town from a whole bunch of bad seeds. Well, let me tell you, this here isn't Bar Harbor. This is Salmon Cove, and this town belongs to me. And I won't stand for anyone engaging in that kind of nonsense here. This is my turf. Are we clear?"

Hayley nodded and stammered, "Y-Y-Yes, we're clear."

"I didn't hear you."

"We're clear!" Hayley shouted.

"Good, happy to hear it. You have a nice day. And stay closer to the speed limit," Daphne said, smirking as she returned to her squad car, jumped in, and sped off, leaving a cloud of dust blowing through Hayley's open window, causing her to cough.

Hayley sat in the Mercedes for five more minutes, trying to stop shaking, before she was calm enough to start the car and continue to the cabin.

Sheriff Daphne was trying her best to intimidate her enough so she would just leave Salmon Cove once and for all.

But why?

Why was her being here such a threat?

And was it related to the murder of Jackson Young?

Island Food & Spirits
by
Hayley Powell

Part One

Some of the most exciting and memorable times of my young life were when I packed up my duffel bag and headed to summer camp. And not just any summer camp! I absolutely cherished the two weeks I spent at Camp Pine Tree.

What's not to love about camp? Meeting new friends, swimming in cool scenic lakes, dressing up for skits on the outdoor stage, competing in sports competitions like archery and softball. But mostly I loved the festive nights by the campfire when all the campers and counselors would gather around and sing songs. To be honest, this particular activity stood out to me because the boys from the other side of the camp were invited too.

What made Pine Tree so special to me was the idea of arriving with a clean slate.

No one knew you! Unlike back at school where kids perceived you a certain way, there was no peer pressure. You weren't the target of any "mean girls" like Sabrina Merryweather, who was a constant thorn in my side. She would always pretend to like me, but then relish in any opportunity to sabotage me or make me look stupid!

The other huge upside was the presence of a fresh crop of boys from all over the state! It was a rite of passage to have a summer camp boyfriend! For a twelve-year-old girl, a summer romance was just about the coolest thing you could hope for because once you did go home, you could recount all the details to your friends, who loyally hung on your every word with rapt attention. Of course, the love story always got juicier in the retelling, but nobody seemed to mind. It was our responsibility to make it at least as exciting as the plot of *Dirty Dancing*!

This was my last summer as a camper because the following year I was scheduled to return as a counselor in training, so I knew I had to make these two weeks in July epic!

This was also the first summer my younger brother, Randy, was signed up to attend. He was not happy about it. Randy had never been to summer camp. He preferred spending his summers watching game shows on TV in the house, or if our mother forced him outside to get some fresh air, he made sure he had plenty of

his comic books to keep him entertained.
The idea of running around in the woods
behind our house held little appeal. So
the prospect of spending two weeks in
nature, sharing a cabin with boys he didn't
know, eating camp food, or as he called it
"prison slop," or participating in organized
sports was, well, in his words, "sanctioned
torture!"

Randy had been waging war with our
mother, Sheila, for weeks ever since she
announced she had enrolled him at Camp
Pine Tree. He threatened to run away, call
the child abuse hotline, hold his breath
until she relented, but no begging or pleading or tears streaming down his face caused
her to change her mind. She was going to
make sure he had this experience whether
he liked it or not!

On our last night at home before em-
barking on our summer camp adventure,
Mom served lobster tacos. This was not the
way to get on Randy's good side. He hated
lobster! We both knew what was happening. She was testing the recipe because
once we were safely spirited off to camp,
she could entertain a promising new beau.
Mom only bought lobsters when she was
trying to impress a new man in her life!

After a two-hour drive to Camp Pine
Tree, where Randy's last-ditch efforts to
wiggle out of going by pretending he
was suffering from food poisoning from
the one bite of lobster he was forced to try
the previous night failed, we arrived at the

registration tables just past the main entrance. I was already on cloud nine because across the parking lot was my last year's summer crush, Nate Hall. Our eyes met and he gave me a playful wink and nod. I smiled back shyly, which in camp language meant we were officially still a camp couple.

As excited as I was, Randy was twice as miserable. After only two minutes in his cabin, he ran back to the parking lot hoping to catch Mom before she left, only to see her driving away (he swears to this day she spotted him in the rearview mirror and sped up). When a sympathetic counselor led him back to the cabin, he walked right through a small patch of poison ivy, and so for the next few days, he suffered from a rash on his face and arms, causing his bunkmates to avoid him like the plague. To make matters worse, he quickly became the target of a couple of bullies, who rummaged through his duffel bag and found his Big Jim action figure (yes, action figure, not a doll as he would loudly point out!). The next morning Randy woke up to the sight of poor Jim swinging from the cabin rafters by a rope with a hangman's noose tied around his neck.

In the dining hall, he refused to eat the hot food and survived on cold cereal. One day, when it was his turn to be a table waiter for his cabin, he was carrying a large heavy tray with a full pitcher of bug juice (in the civilian world this is basically a very sugary Kool-Aid type of drink) and glasses to his table when he tripped over someone's outstretched leg and flew forward. The tray of bug juice launched into the air, as if in slow motion. Everyone watched as it finally came down and crashed to the ground, drenching everyone in the general vicinity.

Kids started screaming and shouting, others were laughing and pointing at poor Randy, who was so embarrassed he got up and started to run out of the dining hall, but slipped on the spilled juice and went right up in the air and landed on his butt to more guffaws and howling. He tried to pretend he had a broken leg in the hopes of going home early, but the nurse dismissed his claim and sent him back to his cabin, where he wrote a letter to Mom threatening suicide, but couldn't afford the cost of a stamp to mail it.

I wish I could say I was the ever-protective older sister keeping a close watch on my little brother, but I have to admit, I was too caught up in my Nate Hall summer romance of holding hands during our nature hikes, flirtatiously dunking each other while swimming in the lake, sharing s'mores and stealing kisses at the bonfire every night. I was completely oblivious to Randy's pain until one week in, when I found him sitting in the parking lot with his packed duffel bag on turnover day, when some kids left and new campers arrived. He was hoping Mom might have a change of heart and pick him up a week early. In fact, he had faked a stomachache and gone to the nurse's office, and while he was there, moaning on the examination table for effect, the nurse got distracted by a kid with a bloody knee. Randy crept over to her desk and called home. Mom wasn't there but he left a message on the answering machine, informing her he was dying, and only had a week to live! Well, the nurse caught him and called her back when she got home and told her everything was fine. He was going to be an inmate at Alcatraz for another week.

I really felt bad for him, and gave him my best pep talk, how we were at Camp Pine Tree together, how we were bonded by familial ties, and how I would be more sensitive to his predicament.

"This is going to be the best last week of camp ever!" I declared.

"How do you know?" he asked, sniffing.

"Because for the whole week you can tell yourself, 'This is the *last* camp week I'll ever have to live through because I'm never coming back!'"

That made him smile.

Suddenly I heard a familiar voice shouting from across the parking lot. "Hayley! Hayley Powell!"

I squeezed my eyes shut, slowly turning around, all the while praying to myself that what I was hearing wasn't true. But sadly, my luck had just run out. It *was* true. I knew that voice. And when I opened my eyes, there she was running straight toward me from across the parking lot, dragging a stylish L.L.Bean duffel bag on wheels in one hand and waving wildly with the other. It was Sabrina Merryweather! My arch rival and chief nemesis at school!

Of course, as she hugged me and with her fake smile told me how excited she was to be at camp with me, neither of us had any idea that the two of us would be trapped together in a life-or-death struggle for survival before the week was out!

To Be Continued

Hayley's Grown-Up Bug Juice Cocktail

Ingredients
1 ounce melon liquor
1 ounce coconut rum
1 ounce sweet & sour mix (prepared)
2 ounces pineapple juice

In a cocktail shaker filled with ice add all your ingredients.

Shake until mixed; then pour into a chilled cocktail glass.

Sit, sip, and relax out in the summer night.

Sheila's Man-Bait Lobster Tacos

Ingredients
2 tablespoons olive oil
½ cup thin-sliced red onion
2 cloves garlic, minced
1 teaspoon cumin
1 teaspoon chili powder
Pinch or more to your taste red pepper
    flakes
2 cups chopped lobster meat, cooked
1 cup salsa
4 8-inch flour tortillas

Optional ingredients: shredded lettuce, sliced avocado, chopped onion, sour cream, and your favorite jar of or homemade salsa.

In a large skillet over medium high heat your oil. Add the sliced onion and garlic and cook until they begin to soften. Add the cumin, chili powder, and red pepper flakes, and cook about a minute.

Add the cooked chopped lobster and salsa and heat until heated through.

Warm your tortillas on top of the stove or in a microwave for 30 seconds until pliable and divide the lobster mixture between the four tortillas.

Top with any of the optional ingredients and enjoy this scrumptious taco treat!

Chapter 16

"If this Sheriff Wilkes wants us to leave so bad, then I think we should just do what she says and get the hell out of here," Liddy said, zipping up her suitcase and rolling it over to the front door of the cabin.

"I won't be scared off," Hayley said defiantly.

"Hayley, as nice a time as I've had here, despite the dead body turning up on the beach, I want to go home. I have a lobster shop to run," Mona said. "Besides, if I see Corey one more time, I'm not going to be able to help myself. I'll jump his bones. And I'm a married woman!"

"Okay, fine, you win, we'll leave. But I just don't understand why Sheriff Wilkes is so determined to get rid of us," Hayley said, walking over and grabbing the handle of her own roll-away luggage.

"Who cares? We had our weekend getaway, one for the books I might add, and now I'm done," Liddy said, standing at the doorway. "Mona, could you be a dear and carry my luggage to the car?"

"Why can't you do it yourself?" Mona barked.

"Because you haul lobsters every day and are built sturdier. I just do Pilates once a week," Liddy said.

"More like once a year," Mona said under her breath.

"And I never once asked you for gas money so you owe me. You can pay me back with your brute strength."

Not in the mood to argue, Mona marched over to the door where Liddy was standing, snatched the handle of Liddy's suitcase, and dragged it outside to the car. "Fine, you just relax, Princess Kate."

Hayley rolled her luggage across the room and followed Mona out the door. Her mind was racing. It bothered her that she didn't know what Sheriff Daphne had against her, why she was so obsessed with them leaving town. Normally, she would just dive right in, asking questions, talking to the locals, digging for the truth. But they were in an unfamiliar town with people she didn't know, and it would just make the task harder.

This was one mystery Hayley Powell was not going to attempt to solve.

Mona was right.

It was time to go home.

Hopefully, another amateur sleuth, if not the police, would pick up the mantle and solve the crime of who murdered Boston travel writer Jackson Young.

After loading the trunk of the car with their luggage and piling into the Mercedes, the three friends, with Liddy behind the wheel, Mona riding shotgun, and Hayley in the back, drove off down the dirt path to the main road for the long trip back to Bar Harbor.

They had driven about two miles down the road, when Liddy slammed on the brakes and the car screeched to a halt at the side of the road. "I think I may have left my Chanel Sublimage La Crème back at the cabin!"

"Your what?" Mona asked, stretched out in the front passenger's seat.

"It's a beauty cream," Liddy said.

"It's an anti-wrinkle cream," Hayley corrected her from the backseat.

"Yes, so? It's why I look half my age," Liddy sniffed, waiting for them, even just one of them, to agree.

They didn't.

There was just a brief, uncomfortable silence.

"I don't want to go back. Just buy another one," Mona groaned.

"It costs four hundred dollars a bottle! I am not leaving without it!"

"Are you sure you left it back at the cabin?" Hayley asked.

"No, I'm not sure. If I did, it's on the kitchen counter since the cabin doesn't have a bathroom," Liddy said. "I remember applying some on this morning but I don't remember putting it back in my purse. Hayley, could you check for me?"

"We're never going to get home," Mona said, shaking her head, annoyed.

Hayley reached over and lifted Liddy's bag off the car seat next to her and rummaged through it, pulling out Breath Savers, lipstick, loose change, a compact, until she finally found a small white bottle of cream.

"It's right here, Liddy," she said, holding it up so Liddy could see it in the rearview mirror.

"Bless you, Hayley! I just had to be sure," Liddy said, pressing her foot on the gas and pulling the Mercedes back out on the road.

Mona closed her eyes to take a nap and within thirty seconds was snoring loudly.

Hayley picked up all the items she had spread out on the seat next to her and dropped them back inside Liddy's bag. She was just about to zip it closed when she noticed something stuck to the side. It looked like a loose credit card at first but then it dawned on her. It wasn't a credit card. It was a hotel room key card. She yanked it out and thrust it into the front seat so Liddy could see it.

"Is this what I think it is?" she asked.

Liddy glanced at it and gasped. "I forgot I even had that."

"It's the key to Jackson Young's hotel room. He gave it to you that night at the bar," Hayley said, excited.

"Hayley, I don't like that look in your eye, and I'm pretty sure I don't want to know what you're thinking."

Hayley thought about it for a moment.

"You know what, I'm sure the police have already swept the place for prints and clues, and housekeeping has scrubbed it clean, and there's probably a new guest in there already," Hayley said.

"No, I was talking to Bill and Vanessa, or Buck and Vera, I can't remember their names, you know, the irritating couple I met last night, well, their RV is getting serviced so they're staying at the hotel in town, and they told me the police will not allow the management to touch anything in that room during an active murder investigation."

"So the room is exactly how Jackson left it before he was killed?"

"I assume so," Liddy said, before catching herself. "What am I doing? I shouldn't be encouraging you!"

"Liddy, turn the car around," Hayley said.

"No, we're going home!"

Mona's snoring got louder, drowning out the sound of their voices.

"Mona, wake up! I can't hear myself think!" Liddy screeched.

Mona momentarily stopped snoring and snorting and repositioned herself so her face was smashed up against the window, her eyes shut, her tongue pressed to the glass like a suction cup. But less than ten seconds later she was snoring up a storm again.

"We can just slip in and then slip out. No one will even know we were there," Hayley pleaded. "Come on, I know you're curious."

If it had been anyone else staying in that room, Liddy would have held out and refused to go back. But it was Jackson Young. The man who had flirted with her, and made her feel so special, and then broke her heart by standing her up for the lobster bake. She was too emotionally invested not to want to know what might be in that hotel room.

Without saying another word, Liddy turned the car around and headed back to Salmon Cove while Hayley reached over the headrest of the passenger's seat and pinched Mona's nose shut to cut off her oxygen supply and stop her incessant snoring. Mona went quiet for a few seconds and then gasped and grunted and waved her arms in the air until Hayley let go. And then she shifted her body again, this time so she was facing Liddy and continued sleeping, and yes, snoring.

Liddy pulled the car into a parking space just down the street from the hotel, making sure the tires were less than an inch from the curb and turned out in case anyone might consider the flat street some kind of hill.

When she shut off the car engine, Mona was roused awake.

"Are we home already?" she said, sitting up.

"Not quite," Liddy said, eyeing Hayley, anticipating Mona's reaction when she heard the news.

"Where are we? This place looks exactly like Salmon Cove," Mona grumbled, rubbing her eyes.

"That's because we are in Salmon Cove," Liddy said.

"What the hell are we doing back here?" Mona yelled.

"Ask Hayley," Liddy said.

"Mona, I just want to check out Jackson Young's hotel room. It'll take five minutes," Hayley said, unfastening her seat belt.

"Why would you want to do that? We were told in no uncertain terms we are no longer welcome here! Why are we not getting the hint?"

"Have you *met* Hayley?" Liddy asked.

"I believe Sheriff Wilkes is acting mighty suspicious, and if her behavior has anything to do with Jackson Young's murder, I feel obligated to find out the truth, and our best chance of doing that is inside that hotel."

Mona knew she wasn't going to win this argument. "Okay, fine. But let's make it fast. I'm starving and that diner we liked on the way here is only open for breakfast and lunch."

"Ten minutes tops," Hayley assured her.

They got out of the car and casually strolled into the lobby of the hotel. The desk clerk was busy showing a guest points of interest on a map he had laid out and didn't even see them pass by. Instead of the elevator, they hurried up the staircase to the second level. When they reached Jackson Young's room there was a sign taped to the door: NO TRESPASSING PER ORDER OF THE SALMON COVE POLICE DEPARTMENT.

They all froze in place.

It was a clear, stern warning.

And it gave them pause.

"What should we do?" Liddy asked, holding the key card, hesitating.

"We've come this far. I say we go for it," Hayley said, eager to get inside the room and look around.

"I knew that would be your vote. What about you, Mona?"

"Just hurry up. I'll keep watch out here," Mona said, looking around to make sure no one was watching them.

Liddy sighed, inserted the key card, and a small green light lit up. They heard the door unlock. Hayley and Mona slipped inside and flipped a wall switch to turn on the light.

The room appeared perfectly normal. The bed was made. The room was very sparsely decorated. There was a TV remote on the nightstand and a notepad and pen but nothing else. No personal items in view.

"You take the bathroom. I'll look around here," Hayley said.

Liddy made a beeline for the bathroom, and Hayley started with a small suitcase propped up in the closet. She laid it out on the floor, unzipped it, and found nothing but some unironed shirts, dirty shorts, and smelly underwear. She then focused her attention on a black leather computer bag. There was a laptop inside, which she fired up, but didn't have the password to gain access. She searched the pockets of the bag but it was empty of any personal identification or papers. Jackson most likely had his wallet on him when he was killed so the police undoubtedly had already admitted it as evidence. Tucked deep inside a side pocket was a small photograph in a small, thin silver frame. It was a picture of Jackson with an attractive blond woman and three adorable children, two boys and a girl, standing on a peak with the Grand Canyon in the background. It looked like a family photo, and the silver frame suggested he carried it around when he traveled and kept it out to look at when he missed his wife and kids. She opened the back of the frame and took the photo out. On the back was scribbled *"Grand Canyon, summer of 2016."*

Liddy ambled out of the bathroom. "Nothing in there, just some men's toiletries and a lot of disgusting hair and shaving cream in the sink. It never would have worked with us, he's too much of a slob."

She noticed Hayley staring at the picture.

"What's that?"

Hayley handed the photo to Liddy.

She stared at it, grimacing, and then she thrust it back to her. "I should have known he was lying about being single. He probably does it all the time when he's on the road."

"I don't know, Liddy, something just doesn't make sense here."

"Everything makes perfect sense. He's a vile, lying cad who will say anything to get a poor, trusting, unsuspecting woman in the sack."

Suddenly Mona burst into the room, a harried look on her face. "We need to get out of here!"

"Why? What's going on?" Hayley asked.

"A housekeeper came out of a room down the hall and saw me guarding the door. She looked at me suspiciously and I think I saw her make a call on her cell phone as she pushed her cart around the corner."

"She could have been calling anyone," Liddy said, brushing her off.

"Sue told me Jackson hammered her with questions far beyond what a typical travel writer would want to know. What if he not only lied about being single, what if he lied about being a travel writer, too?"

"For what possible reason?" Liddy asked.

"Seriously, we can talk about this in the car, on the way

back to Bar Harbor, because I'm starting to get a real bad feeling about all of this!" Mona wailed.

"What if he's not here to write about Salmon Cove, but he's here looking into something else entirely?" Hayley wondered.

"Like what?" Liddy asked.

"I don't know, but Sheriff Wilkes told me she did some research on me, and found out my history of poking my nose into places it doesn't belong, and that seems to be making her extremely nervous, which would explain all the parking tickets and not-so-subtle warnings to leave town. I suspect she's hiding something and doesn't want anyone, especially us, to find out."

"Are you suggesting Sheriff Wilkes was the one who killed Jackson?" Liddy gasped.

"I'm not ruling anything out, but the dots do seem to be connecting," Hayley said.

"But what's her motive?" Liddy asked.

Hayley shrugged.

"You could always ask her yourself," Mona said softly.

"Sheriff Wilkes has no interest in talking to me," Hayley laughed.

"You could try. She's standing right there," Mona squeaked.

Hayley and Liddy whipped their heads around to see Sheriff Daphne Wilkes standing in the open door of the hotel room, her hand on the butt of her holstered gun, the hotel manager hovering behind her.

"Got a call someone might have ignored the warning on the door, and forced their way inside this room illegally," Sheriff Daphne said, a joyful lilt in her voice.

She was loving this moment.

Liddy bravely stepped forward and held up the room

key card. "No one forced their way inside. Jackson gave me his key. We are invited guests."

But even Liddy knew her argument was flimsy at best, and the sheriff was having none of it.

"I'm placing you all under arrest for breaking and entering," Sheriff Daphne said, with a big smile. "Thank you, ladies. You've just made my day."

Chapter 17

"Sonny . . . Sonny, it's me, Liddy, I know you're there so pick up! It's an emergency," Liddy sobbed, eyes brimming with tears, as she stood in front of Sheriff Daphne's desk speaking into the old-fashioned corded phone.

Daphne was seated upright behind her desk, typing keys on the keyboard of her desktop computer, busy with paperwork, but keeping one eye on Hayley and Liddy, whom she had escorted out of their cell to make their one allotted phone call.

Liddy, of course, insisted they call Sonny Rivers, her ex-boyfriend, and mercifully for them, a highly respected lawyer.

Liddy turned to Hayley, distraught. "He's not answering."

Hayley turned to Sheriff Daphne. "Can she hang up and try his office number?"

"One phone call means one phone call," Daphne said flatly, never taking her eyes off her computer screen.

"Stay on the line, Liddy. He'll have to come home eventually."

"There is a ten-minute time limit and then it is straight back to the cell with your friend," Daphne growled.

Liddy glanced at Hayley and mouthed the word *Bitch*.

They had left Mona in the cell, chatting with a teenager who got caught trying to steal OxyContin from behind the pharmacy counter at the local drugstore. The girl poured out her life story, and Mona always had a sympathetic ear. Hayley believed Mona would fit right in perfectly with the cast of characters in *Orange Is the New Black*, Hayley's favorite show on Netflix to binge-watch. She pictured Mona as the large, intimidating inmate whose physical appearance might scare you at first, but once you got to know her, she would turn out to be a protective Mama Bear and champion the underdog inmate who might get separated from the herd and vulnerable to an attack, and Big Mama Mona would make sure you were safe under her watch.

It was a comforting thought having Mona with them as they faced the prospect of serious jail time.

"Sonny! Sonny! Thank God!" Liddy screeched, cupping her hand over the mouthpiece of the phone. "Sonny just picked up."

"Yes, I gathered that," Hayley said, shaking her head. "Tell him to get in his car right now and drive to Salmon Cove!"

"Sonny, you are not going to guess where I am . . . Sonny . . . Stop it, Sonny . . . Stop . . . for heaven's sake, Sonny, shut up! I didn't mean for you to actually try to guess . . . I'll tell you! I'm in jail! Yes, we've been arrested! Hayley, Mona, and myself! You've got to get down here and get us out!"

Liddy bit her lip tightly as she listened to Sonny on

the other end of the phone, and her face started turning beet red.

"What's he saying?"

Liddy raised her hand and shushed Hayley.

She listened some more.

"Sonny, I don't care that you have to be in court in the morning . . . No, I don't care how important the case is, or how much money you're going to make . . . I am sitting in a jail cell, do you hear me, jail cell in Down East Hicksville, and I need to get out of here right now before I go absolutely insane!"

Hayley reached for the phone. "Let me talk to him."

Liddy pushed her away, keeping the phone clamped to her ear. "Sonny, where are you? It sounds echoey . . . your hot tub? I thought the doctor told you to steer clear of the hot tub until you got your blood pressure under control."

"He's barely thirty and he already has high blood pressure?" Hayley asked.

"Yes, and that's one of the pathetic excuses he used when we broke up. He said I was a big reason his numbers were so high. Can you imagine?"

Hayley kept her mouth shut, but yes, yes she could.

Suddenly Liddy gasped.

"Who was that?" Her eyes flared with fury. "Don't lie to me, Sonny. I heard someone giggling in the background. Is someone with you in the hot tub?"

"Liddy, for heaven's sake, it doesn't matter," Hayley wailed.

"It's a simple yes or no question, Sonny," Liddy snarled.

"Please don't tick him off, Liddy! He might hang up!" Hayley pleaded.

"Destiny? Isn't that your new paralegal? She's barely

out of high school!" Liddy cried. "You are the lowest of low, Sonny! It hasn't even been a week since our breakup and you're already playing around with some dim bulb floozy!"

Hayley pried the phone out of Liddy's fist and shoved her away, screaming into the phone, "Sonny, Sonny, please don't hang up!"

Liddy was still yelling even though she no longer had possession of the phone. "I don't care if she went to Stanford! You're a two-timing whore bag!"

Hayley, panicked, cried breathlessly into the phone, "Sonny, please tell me you're you still there!"

"I'm here, Hayley."

"Thank you, thank you. Now I'm begging you, please, you've got to come and get us out of here. We're going to be charged with breaking and entering."

"And tampering with an official police crime scene," Daphne added, almost smiling.

"Listen to me, there's no way I can drive all the way down to Salmon Cove tonight. I told Liddy I'm working on a very big case in Bangor and we're at a very critical juncture," Sonny said. "But don't sweat it. I have a friend near Salmon Cove. He's a good egg. We went to law school together."

"A lawyer?"

"Yes, his name is Oliver Hammersmith."

"Okay, how do we get in touch with him? We're only allowed one phone call and this is it," Hayley said, panic rising in her voice.

"No worries. I will call him and have him come down there before the hearing tomorrow, okay? He'll have you out by mid-morning, I promise."

"Thank you, Sonny," Hayley said with a sigh of relief.

"There's just one thing you need to know about Oliver before you meet him, Hayley."

"What's that?"

"How can I say this politely? There's a little too much yardage between the goal posts."

"I'm not sure I'm following you, Sonny."

"He's a couple of Froot Loops shy of a full bowl."

"What?"

"The wheel is still spinning but the hamster's dead."

"He's dumb! You're saying he's dumb!"

"No, I would never say he's dumb! Oliver is a friend. He's just a little slow on the uptake."

"What's the difference?"

"He wasn't the brightest in my class but he absorbed the basics. Trust me, he's a decent lawyer. He'll get you out."

"You are not reassuring me right now," Hayley said, gripping the phone tighter.

Hayley heard Sonny's paralegal Destiny cooing in the background. "How long are you going to be on the phone, baby? The champagne will go flat."

"I got to go, Hayley, I'll put in a call to Oliver right now. I promise."

And then the line went dead.

"What happened?" Liddy asked.

"He's calling a colleague he went to law school with, Oliver something, to come help us."

"Is he good?"

"Sonny says he's the best," Hayley lied.

She hated living with the truth alone, but Liddy was already having a meltdown over her ex-boyfriend's rapid-fire rebound fling with his paralegal.

Daphne stood up from her desk and waved for them to head back down the hall to the jail cell where Mona was waiting for them. She followed behind them, but halfway, she told them to stop.

They turned to face her.

"You know, ladies, there is the possibility I could have a change of heart and release you right now before any official charges are filed," Daphne said, folding her arms, relishing her power position.

"Really?" Liddy asked, wide-eyed and hopeful.

"All I would ask in return is that all three of you get in that Mercedes and drive out of Salmon Cove, and promise never to return."

"Yes, yes, you've got yourself a deal! We'll never come back! Ever! Ever! Ever!" Liddy screamed, jumping up and down and clapping her hands.

Daphne turned to Hayley for her response.

"We'll think about it," Hayley whispered.

Liddy's eyes nearly popped out of her head. "Think about it? What's to think about? We're taking the deal!"

"We need to talk to Mona first. She has family and history here. I'm not sure she'll want to agree to *never* come back," Hayley said.

"Of course she'll agree!" Liddy barked. "The alternative is sitting in jail and possibly living the rest of her life with a criminal record, even though I'm not entirely sure she doesn't have one already!"

Hayley turned and stared at Daphne, refusing to be intimidated. "Like I said, we'll think about it."

"Suit yourself. But don't take too long. My offer expires in the morning," Daphne said, reaching out and shoving them back toward the jail cell at the end of the hall.

Hayley did not want to make any kind of deal with this woman.

She clearly had some kind of ulterior motive for forcing them out of town.

And she just didn't trust her.

Not one bit.

Chapter 18

Judge Alvin King, a crusty, jowly cheeked, hefty man with big lips and bug eyes, sat behind his bench, wearing his black robe. He reached for a handful of jelly beans that filled a glass bowl next to his gavel and shoveled some into his mouth as he perused a set of papers in front of him.

"Okay, case number 16-CF-092, breaking and entering and tampering with evidence at a crime scene."

Judge King raised his eyes from the papers to look at Hayley, Liddy, and Mona, who stood nervously next to their lawyer, the rail-thin, bespectacled, balding Oliver Hammersmith, who appeared fidgety, unfocused, and somewhat confused.

"My, you ladies have been busy," the judge said with a smirk.

Hayley looked back to see Sheriff Daphne sitting in the back row, watching the proceedings. She was grinning from ear to ear and enjoying every minute of it.

"How do the defendants plead?"

Hayley cleared her throat, having been designated as spokesperson for the three of them.

"Your Honor, we admit we let ourselves into Mr. Young's room—"

"Ignoring the sign on the door that said, 'No Trespassing' by order of the Salmon Cove Police Department!" the young whippersnapper of a prosecutor, who was clearly out to make a name for himself in these parts, blurted out from the table across from them.

Judge King raised a hand for silence. "Let the defendants answer my question, Counselor."

"Yes, Your Honor," the prosecutor said, chastised.

"But we technically were not breaking and entering because Mr. Young had given my friend Liddy his hotel key card and told her to come by his room any time . . ."

There were a few knowing titters from a couple of onlookers in the courtroom gallery. Mr. Young's intent by giving Liddy his key was obvious.

"I appreciate your explanation, Miss . . ."

"Powell. Hayley Powell. We're from Bar Harbor and we've never had any trouble with the law. Well, okay, full disclosure, I was arrested one time but it turned out to be one big misunderstanding, and Mona here, well, she got into a physical brawl with a police officer a few years back, but to be fair, if his boss, the chief of police, had been around at the time of the altercation she never would have been arrested because the young officer was the one who technically started it—"

"I've never been arrested, Your Honor!" Liddy piped in proudly.

"Congratulations," the judge said, with a fake wide-eyed smile.

"Thank you, Your Honor," Liddy said, smiling, oblivious to his obvious sarcasm.

"Tell me, Miss Powell, are you a fan of courtroom dramas on TV?" he asked, smiling.

"Yes, I love them. Ever since I was a kid. *LA Law*, *The Practice*, you name it, I watched it."

"Very good," the judge said, nodding. "Then you probably learned a few basics about courtroom proceedings."

"Yes, Your Honor," Hayley said.

"Then it boggles my mind why someone who has seen so many courtroom dramas has no inkling that the correct response to my question is either 'Guilty' or 'Not Guilty'! I am not interested in hearing your life story and the life stories of your two friends!"

"Understood, Your Honor," Hayley said, bowing her head.

There was silence in the courtroom.

Judge King sighed. "Miss Powell?"

"It's Mrs. Powell, actually. Powell is my husband's name. Well, my ex-husband, we're divorced and he lives in Iowa but I kept his name to make things easier since my kids also have his name—"

"Mrs. Powell?"

"Yes, Your Honor, I'm sorry. I'm just really nervous and I tend to prattle on when I'm nervous."

"I can see that. How do you plead, Mrs. Powell?"

"Not guilty, Your Honor," Hayley said softly.

"Ms. Crawford?"

"Not guilty!" Liddy shouted dramatically.

"And Ms. Barnes?"

"What they said," Mona grunted.

"Work with me, Ms. Barnes, I need you to say it," Judge King groaned.

"Not guilty," Mona grumbled.

"Noted. Now, Mr. Cheatham, you've recommended bail be set at fifty thousand dollars per defendant . . ."

"What? That's outrageous!" Liddy yelped.

Hayley nudged Liddy's side with her elbow to give her the signal to keep quiet.

"Yes, Your Honor," the prosecutor said, standing up. "These ladies are not members of our community, they have no ties here, and you heard from their own mouths that two of them have a past criminal record—"

"Neither of us was ever charged, you little piss ant!" Mona yelled. "And I do have ties here! I came here every summer when I was a kid!"

Hayley glared at Mona to shut up.

The judge gave Mona a long, withering look and then returned his attention to the young prosecutor.

"It is my opinion they pose an extreme flight risk so I believe the bail amount should reflect that," the prosecutor said confidently.

"Mr. Hammersmith?"

Oliver Hammersmith said nothing.

"Mr. Hammersmith, are you still with us?" the judge asked.

Hayley glanced over to see their lawyer standing next to them, facing the judge, but his eyes were closed and his mouth was open. He was literally asleep standing up.

"Mrs. Powell, would you be so kind and wake up your counsel?"

"Yes, your Honor," Hayley said.

She gave Hammersmith a sharp jab in the ribs with the palm of her hand.

He jolted awake, snorting.

"Welcome back, Mr. Hammersmith," the judge said, starting to lose patience.

"Where am I?" he asked, disoriented.

"Salmon Cove Town Court," the judge said. "You're representing these three fine ladies who are charged with, well, we've already gone over all that."

"What the hell is the matter with you?" Hayley hissed.

"I'm sorry. I've been having insomnia lately. I didn't get much sleep last night so I watched a couple of movies on Netflix hoping they would make me fall asleep, but they were really good and so they kept me up instead—"

"I don't care! You need to focus! They're trying to set our bail at fifty grand apiece!" Hayley said with urgency.

"Fifty grand!" Hammersmith howled. "That's outrageous!"

"That's what I said!" Liddy wailed.

"Your Honor, it's totally unreasonable for the prosecution to request such an unfair bail amount when these three women are pillars of their community, and are only here in Salmon Cove to support our economy with their tourist dollars—"

"They're here because they allegedly broke the law and that's all I'm concerned about. But your point is well taken, Mr. Hammersmith. I'm setting bail at five thousand per defendant," the judge said, banging his gavel. "Next case."

Liddy turned to Oliver Hammersmith. "Do they accept credit cards? I can cover all three of us with my American Express Platinum card. I really want the Delta SkyMiles for my flight to Paris in the fall."

"Liddy, if they convict us, you will not be going to Paris or anywhere else except a jail cell!" Hayley squealed.

"We're not going to get convicted," Mona said calmly. "Sheriff Bitch-Face is trying to railroad us and we're going to stop her in her tracks."

"How are we going to do that? We actually did enter that hotel room illegally, we actually did tamper with evidence by searching Jackson Young's belongings, and to put the cherry on top, we have a lawyer who falls asleep standing up during our court hearing!" Hayley said, dissolving into full panic mode.

"I hate to be the bearer of bad news, ladies," Hammersmith said, zipping up his leather briefcase, which was scuffed and completely falling apart. "The court does not accept credit cards. Only a certified cashier's check from a licensed bond bailsman."

"Well, that's it, then. We're going back to jail. It'll be at least two days before we can arrange all of that," Hayley said, resigned.

"Hayley, honey, please tell me you are all right!" a woman's voice cried from behind them.

They all turned to see Polly Roper, in a flower-print blouse, navy skirt, and a straw floppy hat, rushing into the courtroom.

"I was having my morning coffee at the café this morning, and overheard someone say some tourists had been arrested. Well, when I called your cell phone three times and kept getting your voice mail, I got worried."

"It was confiscated when we were arrested," Hayley said, hugging Polly.

"I stopped by the police station and the officer on duty told me you were in court for your hearing so I ran right over," Polly said breathlessly. "How can I help?"

"You can find us a reputable bail bondsman," Hayley said, relieved.

"My bridge partner, Bessie! She's the local bail bondsman and notary public. I'll go over there immediately and post your bail."

"Polly, I can't ask you to do that," Hayley said.

"Nonsense, what are friends for? I trust you three not to blow town," Polly said, laughing.

"Don't bet on it," Mona announced.

"Mona!" Hayley snapped before turning back to Polly. "She's joking. I promise!"

"There's just one catch," Polly said, suddenly dead serious.

Oh no.

"What?"

"I've been devouring your columns at the *Island Times* website ever since we became buddies, and your recipes sound delicious. I'll post your bail *if* you promise to give me a lobster recipe you haven't shared with anyone else!"

"Deal! Deal! I'll give you every family recipe I have! Anything!"

"I'll have you all out by lunchtime," Polly said, racing out of the courtroom.

Polly was true to her word.

By the time the noon bell rang at the local fire department, Sheriff Daphne had released Hayley, Liddy, and Mona, and they gratefully hugged Polly, who was at the station to pick them up. And as if she hadn't been generous enough, she immediately escorted them across the street to the Sunshine Café and treated them to lunch. They slid into a booth, Hayley and Polly on one side and Liddy and Mona on the other.

"Polly, we can't thank you enough," Hayley said, exhausted but relieved.

"It was my pleasure," Polly said, perusing the menu. "I know how difficult and bullheaded Sheriff Daphne can be, and I suspect I know why she has it out for you."

"Why?" Liddy asked.

"Her," Polly said, pointing at Mona.

"Me? What the hell did I do?" Mona roared.

"Sheriff Daphne doesn't care that you three trespassed by letting yourself in Jackson Young's hotel room. She's actually upset that Mona here trespassed on her territory."

"What territory?" Hayley asked.

"Corey Guildford."

"I'm not following," Liddy said, confused.

"Daphne and Corey have been casually dating for the last nine or ten months!"

"That lying son of a—" Mona bellowed.

"Now calm down, Mona," Polly said, slapping her arm with her menu. "It's nothing serious, at least according to Corey. They've gone out a few times, and frankly at this point, I have no idea where they stand. But Daphne, from everything I've heard, fell hard, and is somewhat obsessed with him."

"So when she saw him around town with Mona, it sent her into a tailspin," Hayley declared, pounding her fist on the table. "Now it all makes sense. The traffic tickets, the stern warnings to leave town, they were all a means to get rid of us so Daphne could have Corey all to herself."

"What's she worried about? I'm a married woman!" Mona said.

"She doesn't know that. You never wear a wedding ring," Liddy said, pointing to Mona's bare ring finger.

"Well, that's only because I gained some weight over the years and the ring doesn't fit on my fat finger anymore!"

"You're not the first people to suffer from Daphne's abuse of power," Polly said, leaning forward. "She set her sights on Sue a while back too."

"What did she do?"

"Same as Mona, she got together with Corey. Just a couple of innocent dinners, nobody seriously thought they were dating, they were just friends, but Daphne went wild and started showing up at the Starfish Lounge, making sure they weren't serving minors, double-checking her liquor license, inspecting the place for health code violations, things that weren't even in her jurisdiction."

"Has anyone reported this behavior?"

"To the police? She *is* the police. And the Town Council has their heads buried in the sand. They don't want any trouble.

"Once Sue got the message, she dropped Corey like a hot potato, even as a friend. I'm surprised she still allows him to hang out at her bar. Daphne started leaving her alone when she saw Sue being wined and dined by another man these past few months."

"Who?" Liddy asked.

"You wouldn't believe me if I told you," Polly said, smirking.

"Try us," Hayley said, bursting with curiosity.

"Rufus."

"The town drunk?"

"That's the one," Polly said, glancing around to make sure none of the other diners were eavesdropping.

"Talk about strange bedfellows!" Liddy exclaimed. "He's got to be at least thirty years older than her!"

"It could just be a sweet friendship that Sue is playing up just to keep Daphne off her back, but one never knows!" Polly chirped, embracing her role as Salmon Cove's resident gossip.

Sue and Rufus?

This town just kept getting weirder and weirder.

Chapter 19

After leaving Polly, who had to rush off to judge a pie-baking contest at the senior center, Hayley, Liddy, and Mona walked back to Liddy's Mercedes, which was parked near the hotel where they had left it before they were arrested. Hayley immediately spotted the white envelope flapping up and down in the breeze underneath the windshield wiper. She glanced up at the sign directly in front of the car, which read NO OVERNIGHT PARKING.

"Well, all I can say is, this is the first legitimate ticket we've received since we set foot in this town," Hayley said, shaking her head.

"Can we just go back to the cabin so I can take a nap? I didn't get one moment's rest in that nasty jail cell," Mona whined.

Liddy fished out her car keys from her purse and pressed the remote, unlocking the doors. They all reached for their respective door handles, when suddenly they were stopped in their tracks by a high-pitched shrill.

"Well, look who's here!" a woman's voice screeched.

"Oh, Lord, it's them!" Liddy said, her whole body tensing up.

"Who?" Hayley asked.

"Bill and Vera from Ohio. They are the most annoying people I've ever had the displeasure of meeting. Quick! Pretend we didn't hear her and get in the car, and let's get the hell out of here!"

They all scrambled to get their doors open and to pile inside the Mercedes, but they were just not fast enough. The couple were on top of them in seconds. Hayley hadn't gotten a good look at them the other night at the bar. They were fresh-faced and young, probably in their late twenties or early thirties. He was tall, skinny, dark, with hairy arms and legs, and wore thick black glasses that just made his huge eyes more pronounced. She was a wispy blond flower child in a rucksack dress.

Liddy sighed, gathered her strength, and then swung around to greet them with a big fake smile. "Bill and Vera! How are you?"

"It is Buck and Vanessa," the young man corrected her, grinning from ear to ear, not offended at all.

"Right. Buck and Vanessa," Liddy said, turning and pointing at her friends. "These are my friends Hayley and Mona."

"Nice to meet you," Hayley said politely.

Mona just grunted. She was tired. And when Mona was tired, her manners evaporated and her whole demeanor got ugly.

"They're from Ohio," Liddy offered.

"Iowa," Vanessa corrected her.

"Right. I almost got it. They're right next door to each other," Liddy said through gritted teeth.

"Actually, they're not," Vanessa said with a giggle.

"Okay, so there's one state between them," Liddy whispered, desperate to change the subject.

"Not even close," Vanessa insisted. "There's Ohio, then

you move west and there is Indiana and Illinois and then you get to Iowa."

"Who cares? It's the Midwest! All those states are pretty much the same!" Liddy screamed, determined to end this impromptu geography lesson.

"People in the Midwest sure do care. We're very proud of where we come from," Vanessa said, remarkably still with a bright smile on her face.

"Liddy is right about one thing, honey. We are all the same. We are all Americans," Buck said.

Hayley half expected him to break out into a verse of "The Star-Spangled Banner."

"That's why we're on this RV tour of our great country, getting to know its people and the different traditions and history of each state. Iowa can be somewhat of a bubble," Buck said.

"So you quit your jobs and are just driving around in a camper? How long do you expect to keep this up?" Hayley asked.

"For as long as we're happy. We sold our home five years ago, our parents bought it for us as a wedding present, but we weren't interested in going the typical route of getting nine-to-five jobs, having babies, drowning in debt, so we chucked everything, sold the house and bought this camper and just pretty much go where the wind takes us," Buck said proudly.

"But with no jobs, how do you live? How do you pay for food?"

"It was a big house," Vanessa said with a wink.

In a way, Hayley admired them for living free and unencumbered, having no responsibilities except paying for gas and a hamburger at a truck stop.

"The best part is getting to know all the locals when we land in their towns," Buck said. "On the whole, everybody is real open and friendly, especially here in Salmon Cove."

"Yes, we've met some nice people here too," Hayley said.

"And some *not* so nice," Liddy quickly added. "Well, it's been a pleasure but we really need to—"

"People tend to open up to strangers and talk about things they might not normally discuss with someone they know. Like what happened to that poor travel writer Mr. Young, who was so brutally killed down on the beach a few days ago," Vanessa said, ignoring Liddy's cue that she wanted to leave.

"Yes, it was horrible," Hayley said, commiserating. "Just such an unimaginable thing to happen in such a quaint town."

"We heard before he was murdered, he was seen hanging around you, Liddy," Buck said, eyeing her intensely.

This surprised Liddy, and took her off guard. She fumbled and stuttered a quick response. "Well, yes, I met him. But I hardly knew him."

"Well, according to the clerk at the hotel when you tried to check in but there were no rooms, Mr. Young appeared to be quite taken with you. What word did he use, Vanessa?" Buck said, turning to his wife.

"Smitten," Vanessa said.

"Right. That's the word," Buck said, smiling, as he returned his gaze to Liddy, his eyes boring into her. "He was smitten with you."

"I suppose so, yes, but apparently it didn't last long. We made a date to attend the lobster bake, and he stood me up," Liddy said, supremely uncomfortable discussing this topic with two strangers.

"That must have made you very angry," Vanessa said.

"It did. I do not have a history of being stood up by

men," Liddy said with a defensive tone as she spun around to garner support from her friends. "Isn't that right?"

"No, she has men lining up to impress her," Hayley said, toeing the party line.

"What are you talking about? Sonny just dumped her!" Mona piped in, bored and grouchy.

"How many times do I have to tell you we are just taking a break . . . and apparently seeing other people!" Liddy wailed.

Buck deftly tried to turn the conversation back to Jackson Young. "Do you think there could have been another reason . . . besides your obvious charm and beauty . . . why Jackson was interested in you?"

"What? What do you mean? Of course it was my charm and beauty! What are you getting at? And why are you asking me all these personal questions!"

"You will have to forgive Buck, Liddy," Vanessa interjected. "Driving around in an RV all the time can be quite boring so he tends to find unusual ways to entertain himself, like getting involved in other people's dramas."

"Then take some of that house money and get a Netflix subscription! You can spend every night watching dramas!" Liddy yelled.

"I'm sorry. I didn't mean for you to take offense . . ." Buck said, reaching out and touching Liddy's arm.

She recoiled. She was done with these two. "If you'll excuse us, we need to go now! It's been a long, restless night and we didn't sleep a wink in jail—"

"*Jail?* You've been in jail?" Vanessa asked, eyes widening. "Why?"

"It is none of your business!" Liddy shouted. "Girls, please, let's just get the hell out of here!"

Liddy went to open the driver's-side door, but Hayley

gently moved her aside and steered her toward the backseat. There was no way she was going to allow Liddy to drive a car in her current frazzled condition.

They all piled inside, and Hayley drove off, watching Buck and Vanessa in the rearview mirror. They just stood there, watching them, stone-cold sober looks on their faces, hardly the bubbly, bouncy couple they had first appeared to be.

Who were they?

And why were they so interested in Liddy's connection to Jackson Young?

Chapter 20

When Hayley pulled the Mercedes onto the dirt road that led to the cabin, she immediately felt a sense of unease. When she could see the cabin she noticed the front door was wide open, and her fears were confirmed.

"Mona, did you remember to lock the door when we left?"

"Of course I did!" Mona barked defensively.

They all jumped out of the car, leaving their luggage they had packed in the trunk, and trudged over to the door to inspect it.

The wood on the frame was severed and the lock on the door was mangled.

"Somebody must have used an ax or a sledgehammer to bust their way in," Mona said, shocked.

They slowly poked their heads inside to look around.

The place was ransacked. Chairs were tipped over on the floor. The lumpy old couch in the center of the room had been torn apart and stuffing spread everywhere. Even the ratty old curtains on the windows had been ripped off the rods and cast aside.

Mona cautiously stepped inside first to survey the damage, followed closely behind by Hayley and then

Liddy, who kept herself close to the door for a quick escape if necessary.

"What were they looking for?" Liddy asked, visibly shaken.

"Beats me," Mona said, shuffling around the room, kicking into a corner some broken glass that had smashed on the floor when the intruder, or intruders, had cleared off the kitchen counter of some beer mugs and dishware. "But they sure as hell did do a number on this place!"

"Do you think this has anything to do with Jackson Young's murder?" Liddy asked.

"I haven't a clue," Hayley said, shrugging.

"Should we call the police?" Liddy asked, searching her bag for her phone.

Hayley scoffed. "What for? Sheriff Daphne won't care. She probably won't even bother to show up here let alone investigate."

"To be honest, I wouldn't be surprised if this was her doing to scare us into leaving town," Mona said, walking around the room, carefully picking up a couple shards of glass before anyone stepped on them.

"Oh, Mona, I don't know if she would go to those lengths . . ." Liddy said.

"She's made no bones about keeping me from Corey. And she's proven she'll do anything to make that happen by falsely arresting us!"

"Well, it's only fair to point out again that we did enter that hotel room knowing it was illegal," Hayley reminded her.

"Whose side are you on?" Mona growled.

"Just keeping it real, as the kids say," Hayley said.

"They don't say that anymore, Hayley. You're about five years behind the times," Liddy said.

"Thank you for reminding me just how out of touch I am, Liddy," Hayley said, annoyed.

Suddenly a scream flew out of Liddy's mouth, startling Hayley and Mona.

"Liddy, what's wrong?"

"That's my makeup bag on the floor. I must have been in such a rush to leave this place I forgot to pack it! I knew I left something behind!" she cried, still clutching the doorframe and refusing to come all the way inside the cabin. "Mona, would you mind picking up my lipstick over there and putting it back in my makeup bag, oh, and I see my mascara in the corner, it's very expensive, I bought it in Spain, and I don't want some rat running off with it!"

"I am not your housemaid, Liddy! Why don't you come in here and pick up your own junk?" Mona bellowed.

"I can't," Liddy said quietly.

"Why not?" Mona asked, throwing her arms up in the air.

"I . . . I'm . . . s-scared," Liddy stammered.

Hayley walked over to Liddy and took her gently by the arm. "It's okay, honey. I know it's a shock to come back here and find the cabin looted."

"Looted? It doesn't look like they actually took anything, I mean, seriously, what kind of thief wouldn't bother to take imported mascara from Spain?" Liddy scoffed.

"A thief who doesn't give a whit about your stupid expensive makeup!" Mona yelled.

"It's not like *you* have to worry about someone stealing anything of yours, Mona," Liddy sniffed. "You own nothing of real value, least of all that ridiculous sweatshirt you insist on wearing to bed that belongs to your husband, the one with the picture of a lobster and the phrase, 'Just looking for a good piece of tail!'"

Mona chuckled. "He loves that sweatshirt. He'd kill me if he found out I took it from his drawer and brought it with me. But it's just so comfy."

"Well, when you wear it, it sends an entirely different message," Liddy reminded her.

Mona's eyes went wide. "Damn! You're right. I never thought about that!"

"Liddy, whoever broke in here is clearly gone, so there is no reason for you to be afraid anymore. It is perfectly safe now," Hayley said.

"You really think so?" Liddy said, eyes darting around the cabin.

"Look around. It is just the three of us, and if it makes you feel any better, Mona and I will take turns staying up tonight to keep watch just to make sure no one tries to come back," Hayley assured her.

"Okay," Liddy said, before slowly, hesitantly, with Hayley's help, stepping inside the cabin.

Mona marched past her and outside to the car to carry their bags back inside since it looked like they were going to be stuck in Salmon Cove at least one more night, if not more. She came in struggling with Liddy's luxurious four-wheeled Louis Vuitton suitcase with cowhide leather trim.

"Thanks, Mona, you can just put them over by the closet," Liddy said.

"You do it! I got at least two more loads in the trunk I've got to get in here," Mona growled, walking back outside.

Liddy sighed, and pulled the suitcase by the handle over to the closet before setting it down on the floor and unzipping it. "I want to hang a few of my tops so they don't get more wrinkled than they already are from being packed in here all night!"

She removed one red silk number from the suitcase,

stood up, and opened the closet door while Hayley grabbed a broom and began sweeping up the broken glass on the floor.

As Liddy absentmindedly reached for a hanger, her eyes suddenly went wide and she let out a bloodcurdling scream, which caused Hayley to jump.

A large man, over six feet, in a black T-shirt and jeans and wearing a nylon stocking mask over his face, lunged out of the closet and wrapped his hands around Liddy's throat. He shoved her forward as Hayley watched in shock before coming to her senses and rushing over to help her friend by pummeling him on the back with the edge of the broom handle.

Hearing the screams from outside, Mona rushed back from the car, appearing in the doorway, shocked to see Hayley frantically buffeting a man over the head with a broom as Liddy's eyes nearly popped out of her head as he squeezed his giant hands around her throat!

Mona sprang into action, and raced over to them, leaping onto the man's back and getting him into a chokehold.

He was big and strong, but quickly got spooked by the all-out assault. He released his grip on Liddy's neck and tossed her aside, catapulting her halfway across the room. She smacked face-first into the battered and dusty icebox, before slumping to the floor, dazed.

Mona kept her arm fastened tightly around the robber's neck, and he stumbled, as she squeezed tighter, cutting off his oxygen supply. This just made him madder and more determined to shake her off before he got too light-headed and passed out. Meanwhile, Hayley kept up the blows with the broom handle, whacking his arms and legs.

The assailant jerked his body back toward the wall, slamming Mona against it, one, two, three times, hoping to dislodge her. But Mona was in the zone, hooting and screaming like a mother gorilla protecting her young.

But on the fourth try, he gave it his all, and the impact knocked the air out of Mona, and she stopped hollering, and let go. She fell to the floor, but managed to reach out and grab the man by the foot as he tried to run.

Hayley aimed for his groin, but he anticipated the move and threw his hands out in front of it and grabbed the broom handle, wrenching it from Hayley's grasp. He then wielded it like a baseball bat and bashed the side of Hayley's head. She saw stars and stumbled back, maintaining her balance but disoriented.

The man, in one final violent act, used his free foot to swing it around and kick Mona in the face. Blood spurted from her nose and she instinctively let go of him and covered her face to avoid any further blows.

The masked man bolted out the door and disappeared into the woods.

Hayley raced over to Mona, who waved her away. "I'm fine. It's just a nosebleed."

"Liddy? Liddy?" Hayley shouted, jumping over the debris on the floor to get to her friend, who had crawled to her knees, a hand pressed over her forehead.

She glared at Hayley.

"It is okay to come in, Liddy! It is perfectly safe, Liddy! Don't be afraid, Liddy!" Liddy yelled, mocking Hayley's reassuring tone.

Hayley had an overwhelming sense of relief. As long as Liddy was giving her a hard time, that meant she was not seriously hurt.

But Liddy had been right about one thing.

There was no reason to feel safe in Salmon Cove anymore.

Island Food & Spirits
by
Hayley Powell

Part Two

The best summer camp week of my life turned into one giant epic fail after the sudden and surprise arrival of Sabrina Merryweather on the scene at Camp Pine Tree. It started on a rainy Monday when we were stuck in our cabin during a downpour, and I decided to cheer up my fellow cabinmates by sharing my weekly care package from my mother including her delicious, gooey, can't-miss homemade brownies. I was a hero to the girls for approximately two minutes until Sabrina presented us with her own care package from her parents—a large cooler stocked with chilled containers of fresh lobster dip and boxes of expensive gourmet crackers! She began handing them out to her fellow campers to dramatic "ooohs" and "ahhhs."

Seriously? Fresh lobster dip?

How could my mother's brownies compete with that?

One point, Sabrina! And me? A big fat zero!

It was all downhill from there.

Any activity I signed up for like archery, or swimming, arts and crafts, whatever it was, Sabrina signed up too and made it her personal mission to outscore me or, out-swim me, or simply make me look bad. The adorable finger puppet I made from chenille stems and feathers paled in comparison to her detailed diorama of the JFK assassination made from a cardboard box, crepe paper, and Legos.

The final straw was on Wednesday when I showed up late at the dining hall because I had to talk my brother, Randy, out of mailing our mother yet another note threatening suicide if she didn't come pick up him up ASAP. I strolled into the hall and stopped in my tracks, my face contorting into a mask of horror when I saw Sabrina sitting in my usual spot at the dining table right next to my camp crush, Nate Hall, who stared at her like a lovesick puppy, hanging on to every word that was pouring out of her big, fat mouth! In fact, the whole table of diners were enthralled with whatever story she was spinning at that moment. She glanced over at me in mid-sentence, smiled and winked at me, and then turned her attention back to Nate, who as of that moment, was Sabrina's new summer camp crush!

I was hurt and humiliated and I ran back to the cabin, threw myself on my bunk, cried into my pillow, and then pretended to be fast asleep when everyone came back to the cabin at curfew.

Sabrina was giggling as she entered the cabin with the other girls and as she climbed up on the bunk above me and slipped under the covers related some flirtatious remark Nate had said to her. It took every ounce of willpower not to shove my feet so hard up against the bottom of her bunk she would fly up and fall right to the floor in a big splat! Maybe she would break a leg and be forced to go home! I could never do it, but just the thought of me doing it made me feel a little better.

I tossed and turned, unable to fall asleep, and that's when I saw Sabrina quietly make her way down the ladder next to the bunk. She tossed on a hoodie, grabbed her small flashlight, and went out the door. She was obviously heading to the "outhouse" as we lovingly called it, which was actually a basic bathroom situated behind the cabin outfitted with a few showers and commodes.

A few minutes later, the camp bell that summoned us to all activities and meal times began ringing loudly, startling my other cabinmates awake. Outside there was lots of shouting and screaming, and then we heard one of our camp counselors ordering everyone through a bullhorn to get out of the woods!

We all scrambled out of bed and grabbed the first thing we could find for our feet as our own counselor, Sarah Jane, rushed us out the cabin door. Once we were outside, we could see the entire sky lit up like the Fourth of July! My heart leapt into my throat as I quickly realized the air was thick with smoke and flames engulfed the trees, quickly spreading toward the cabins!

Dozens of firemen raced onto the scene yelling at us to evacuate the woods immediately! We all turned and ran in the opposite direction as fast as our legs could carry us past the cabins as the fire raged behind us. Our counselor found an old trail that led to the main road and we headed in that direction.

A sick feeling soon settled in my stomach as I glanced around and realized Sabrina wasn't with us. She must still be in the outhouse. I shouted for our counselor, who was ahead of me herding everyone to safety, but she was too far away to hear me. I was scared, not sure if I should go back, but my instincts kicked in, and I turned and raced back toward the fire.

I passed a group of boys who were running down the trail in a panic, and even caught sight of my brother, Randy, who had a big grin on his face, thrilled that this disaster probably meant we would have to go home early! I just prayed he didn't have anything to do with how the fire started!

I reached the outhouse, screaming for

Sabrina as loud as I could over the roaring of the fire and the husky voices of the firemen yelling to one another as they fought the blaze. I raced inside and checked every stall and the shower area but there was no sign of her! I hurried back to our cabin, calling for Sabrina, but didn't see her there at first. I hoped she had found a means of escape and was with another group or had caught up with ours. Then, suddenly, I noticed a light coming from underneath my bunk. I dropped to my knees and peered under it, and sure enough, there was Sabrina curled up in a tight ball, crying, scared to death, the flashlight lying beside her.

I reached under the bed and pulled her out, and she grabbed me, sobbing, and hugged me tight as I led her back down the path. Behind us we heard a loud explosion and I looked back to see our cabin shaking violently as a large tree landed on the roof and sparks flew everywhere.

Sabrina screamed hysterically, unable to move, and the air was now so thick with smoke neither of us could see anything! So I gripped Sabrina's hand even tighter and just ran blindly into the night, dragging her along behind me, until we ran smack into the arms of a fireman, who finally led us both to safety.

Our parents were notified, and by the next morning, our mother arrived to take us home. She was happy to see us alive and well, but mortified at the sight of Randy, who had refused to shower for the whole two weeks and was caked in dirt. He ran past her and jumped in the backseat of the car and refused to come out until we were home. He promised me he had nothing to do with the fire, and luckily, a few weeks later, we heard a couple of hikers had camped out nearby and not properly put out their camp-fire, so Randy was officially in the clear.

Sabrina spent the rest of the summer showering me with gifts of lobster dip to show her appreciation, and even presented me with a lovely friendship bracelet and matching necklaces where each of us had half of a heart on a chain and mine said "Best" and hers said "Friends."

Sabrina and I met every day at a popu-lar café in town and she introduced me to mint iced teas that were so refreshing and delicious, we would sip them for hours re-hashing the dramatic events of the summer to anyone who was willing to listen, embel-lishing the details to make ourselves seem like true movie heroines!

On the first day of school that fall, I rushed into the cafeteria at lunchtime. I had been looking forward to this all morning when finally I would be seated at Sabrina's table with her posse, feeling the warmth from all the attention I would surely re-ceive from her clique as she told them how the two of us had almost perished in a roar-ing forest fire, and how I had heroically and selflessly saved her life.

With a big smile on my face I made a beeline for her table, but as I approached, she turned her head toward me, and just looked at me with a blank stare. In the blink of an eye, I knew that our summer friendship was over, and things were back to normal. And so, I quietly turned around and walked over to a corner table and sat by myself, that is, until my real BFFs, Liddy and Mona, joined me and we laughed and gossiped, and I realized I was the lucky one, not Sabrina, to have such real and true friends by my side.

I've changed up one of my favorite childhood summertime drinks, mint iced tea, and made a more adult version to satisfy my craving for a yummy cocktail!

Minty Iced Tea Cocktail

Ingredients
4 or 5 mint leaves
2 ounces bourbon
Your favorite brand of iced tea
Lemon slices for garnish (optional)

In a small bowl crush up four or five mint leaves then put them in a cocktail glass, add ice, the 2 ounces bourbon and top off with your iced tea. Garnish with lemon if you would like.

Here is a yummy lobster dip to add to your favorite crackers while you enjoy your cocktails!

Sabrina Merryweather's Favorite Lobster Dip

Ingredients
Meat from two cooked 1¼ lobsters,
    chopped up in small pieces
1 tablespoon diced onion
1 tablespoon lemon juice
1 8-ounce package softened cream cheese
1 tablespoon prepared horseradish

Mix all your ingredients in a blender until fully incorporated and fairly smooth. Transfer to a bowl. Cover and chill in the refrigerator for at least two hours, the longer the better for the flavor. Remove and share with your family and friends, who will be eternally grateful!

Chapter 21

As they cleaned up the ransacked cabin, Corey happened to call Mona's cell phone to inquire about spending the afternoon with her. Upon hearing the news of the break-in and their violent encounter with a masked intruder, Corey insisted on jumping in his truck and racing right over with Sadie in tow to check on them despite Mona's loud protestations that everything was fine and there was absolutely no good reason for him to come over.

Hayley and Liddy instinctively knew that Corey was using the surprise attack as an excuse to see Mona again, but Mona instantly dismissed their theory and scolded them for acting like dippy, nitwitted high school girls trying to fix up their bestie.

"He's not coming over just to see me," Mona declared. "He wants to make sure all of us are okay!"

Within minutes, they heard a truck pull up outside and the door slam, and then they saw Corey Guildford burst into the cabin with Sadie hot on his heels, tail wagging. He blew right past Hayley and Liddy and headed straight to Mona, whom he grabbed in a tight hug, and whispered in her ear as he patted the back of her head, "Honey, are you okay?"

Mona grimaced at the sight of Hayley and Liddy exchanging knowing looks, and pushed him away. "I told you on the phone, I'm fine, now get off me."

Corey stared at Mona, his soft, caring eyes taking in her face, transfixed.

"We're fine too, Corey, thanks for asking," Liddy hollered from across the room.

Corey snapped out of his reverie and turned to them. "I'm glad to hear it. So he was hiding in the closet?"

"Yes," Hayley said, pointing, "Over there."

Corey walked over to the closet and poked his head inside. "He must have heard you arriving, and didn't have time to escape, so he hid in here."

"Yeah, thanks for figuring that out for us, Captain Obvious," Mona said, snorting.

It was clear what Mona was doing. She was completely overcompensating for the fact that she really liked this guy by making fun of him and treating him like dirt.

Hayley and Liddy were not buying it for a minute.

And neither was Corey.

He ambled back over to Mona, and squeezed her cheek with his thumb and forefinger. "I love it when you try to act bitchy. It's downright adorable."

"The whole thing nearly gave me a heart attack," Liddy said.

Sadie perched next to Hayley, and she knelt to pet her. "Well, we're safe now that we have our very own guard dog, right, Sadie?"

Sadie panted and closed her eyes, intoxicated by Hayley's gently and lovingly stroking her fur.

"Did you get a good look at him?" Corey asked.

"No! I told you on the phone, he was wearing a mask," Mona sighed impatiently.

"I mean physically, was he tall, short, lean, fat, could you make out any identifying characteristics at all?" Corey asked.

"He was definitely big," Hayley offered. "And I'd say he was on the heavy side, he had some bulk to him, but he was wearing a long-sleeve shirt and jeans so it's not like we saw a distinctive tattoo or birthmark, or anything like that."

"It all happened so fast! After he hurled me into the refrigerator, I don't remember anything at all!" Liddy cried.

"Did you already call the police? I'm surprised I beat them here," Corey said, perplexed.

"We . . . uh . . . we didn't call them," Hayley said.

"What? Why not?"

"Because we're afraid Sheriff Daphne will show up herself, and find a way to blame the whole thing on us!" Liddy said.

"Blame *you*? That's crazy," Corey said. "Why?"

"Because she hates us!" Mona shouted.

"What?" Corey asked, still confused.

"She's been targeting us ever since we arrived in Salmon Cove, Corey," Hayley calmly explained. "Ticketing our car every chance she gets, arresting us for tampering with evidence, but then offering not to charge us if we just quietly leave town."

"Why would she do that?"

There was a long, pregnant pause.

"Because of you," Hayley said quietly.

Corey looked at all three of them, flummoxed and upset.

"I don't . . . I don't understand . . ."

"I think you do, Corey," Hayley said softly. "She is in love with you, and ever since Mona came to town, she's seen her as a major threat."

"But Daphne and I are not in a relationship!" Corey roared, striking a defensive posture. "I mean, yes, we went out to dinner a few times over the last year or so, but it was all very casual and friendly, nothing serious."

"Well, apparently, Sheriff Crazy Pants doesn't see it that way!" Mona barked. "She believes she's your girlfriend!"

Corey made a beeline for Mona and took her hands in his, squeezing them tightly. "Mona, I swear, I consider Daphne a friend. Sure, at first when I asked her out, I thought maybe we might forge some kind of relationship, but after a couple of dates I knew in my heart she wasn't the one so I backed off and tried to keep things simple and friendly. I thought she got the message and was okay with that. Mona, read my lips. Daphne is *not* my girlfriend!"

"Makes no difference to me," Mona said, wrenching her hands free from his grip. "I'm a married woman."

"I'm very well aware of that. You've reminded me of that fact about a dozen times since you got here."

Hayley noticed a hurt look cross his face for an instant, but he quickly covered and stepped closer to her.

"Mona, there's something I've been wanting to get off my chest ever since you arrived in Salmon Cove," Corey said solemnly.

Hayley and Liddy exchanged looks, wondering if they should step outside, but neither willing to move a muscle and miss a moment of the scene that was about to unfold.

"No!" Mona yelled.

"No, what? I haven't said anything yet!"

"No, I don't want to hear it! Whatever it is you have to

say, keep it on your chest . . . your muscled, hairy, hot, sexy chest! Just keep it there, do you hear me?"

"I can't, Mona."

"Yes, you can! I'm warning you, Corey, don't say anything!"

"I love you," Corey said, eyes welling up with tears. "I've loved you for years, ever since we were kids, but I was never man enough to say anything, and then I heard you got married back in Bar Harbor after you graduated from high school and had a boatload of kids, and I was happy for you! I figured we were never meant to be, so I moved on. But there is a reason I never married, Mona, I've always kept you in my heart, and I didn't think it was fair to marry someone else, knowing deep down she would never be my number one."

Liddy gasped, grabbing Hayley's shirtsleeve for support. The drama of this moment was almost too over-whelming for her. "This is the most romantic moment that's ever happened to me, and it's not even happening to *me*!"

Mona didn't say a word.

She just started at Corey, a blank expression on her face.

"When you came back here, I tried my damnedest to keep my feelings in check, and not let on how I felt. But you hadn't changed a bit. You were still the plain-spoken spitfire you always were, the one I fell in love with, and well, I had to admit to myself I was still in love with you. I'll always love you," Corey said softly.

Hayley noticed Liddy's entire weight leaning on Hayley's arm as she swooned. She feared Liddy might faint.

Mona stood frozen in place a few moments before slowly nodding her head as she signaled Corey that she had heard him and understood what he was saying. And then, she reared back and slapped him hard across the face with the palm of her hand.

"Well, snap out of it!"

Mona was a big fan of Cher's Oscar-winning performance in *Moonstruck*. Actually, it was Hayley who was the fan when they first went to see it as kids. Mona thought it was a syrupy, boring, ridiculous movie. But she clearly remembered the seminal scene of Cher's reaction when Nicolas Cage professed his love because she had literally just re-created it.

But Mona didn't stop there.

She slapped him again.

"Stop saying you love me! What the hell am I supposed to do with that information? I'm married, you hear me, married!"

"I know," Corey said, eyes downcast. "I just couldn't let you leave again without me at least putting it out there. I never would have forgiven myself."

Corey turned and walked back over to Sadie, who sensed he was hurting. He leaned down to rub her head and the dog soothingly licked his cheek, the exact spot where Mona slapped him, which was now turning a faint red. "Ready to go, girl?"

Sadie wagged her tail and started to follow him out.

Corey stopped at the door, and turned around, a sad smile on his face.

"Good-bye, ladies, safe travels home."

And then he was gone.

Chapter 22

"Well, I'm certainly glad that nonsense is over," Mona announced after Corey left.

"Did you see the look on his face, Mona? The poor man was devastated," Liddy said, shaking her head, clutching a hand to her heart.

"That's not my problem! He knew all along I was married and that nothing could happen between us! He should've just been more careful and not gone all soft on me," Mona said, averting eye contact with them, turning away as if she was trying her best not to release a sudden flood of tears.

"I think it was very brave of him to open up like that and take a chance," Hayley said.

"Brave? That wasn't brave! That was stupid! Look where it got him! Now he's all sad and depressed, which makes me feel bad. The big lug should've kept his mouth shut! We were having a nice time together and he had to go and ruin it! I've had it with Salmon Cove! I want to go home now!" Mona cried.

"We can't go home yet! We need to stay and face these ridiculous charges," Hayley said.

"No, we don't!" Mona declared. "We can just leave! Right now! Just get in the car and drive home!"

"Mona, we can't sneak out of town. Polly will lose the bail money she posted on our behalf! Leaving her high and dry wouldn't be right," Hayley said firmly.

"Hayley is right, Mona," Liddy said. "Polly was very sweet to bail our butts out of jail. If it wasn't for her, we'd still be there."

"She won't lose her money if we accept Sheriff Wilkes's deal" Mona said, folding her arms.

"You mean promise to leave and never come back *ever*?" Hayley asked.

"That's what I'm saying!" Mona said.

"But Mona, Salmon Cove holds such warm childhood memories for you. This cabin has been in your family for generations, and . . . well, what about Corey?" Hayley asked gently.

"What about him? I'm sick of that man fawning all over me! I'm sick of getting harassed by the local sheriff everywhere we go! I'm sick of always being front and center wherever there's a crime! I'll be happy if I never have to come back to this place ever again!"

"You're just worried if you stay here much longer, you'll do something you will regret," Liddy said.

"Yeah, and I guess there's that, too!" Mona barked as she furiously zipped up her suitcase. "So are we going to call the sheriff and take the deal?"

"No," Hayley said.

"No?" Liddy asked, surprised.

"You two can take the deal and go, but I refuse to allow that woman to try to dictate where we can go, who we can see, and what we can do. That's abuse of power and yes, we may be at risk for a heavy fine or even some jail time, but it's a risk worth taking to show her that she will not get away with intimidating us!"

Hayley noticed their halfhearted looks of support.

". . . Or intimidate just *me* if you two decide to get out of Dodge," Hayley said quietly. "So go on, you two can go. I won't hold it against you."

Liddy looked at Mona, who was stone-faced, and then back at Hayley. "Of course we're going to stay! We would never in a million years desert our best friend, right, Mona?"

"I really just want to go home and see my kids," Mona said, tapping her foot nervously. "And I normally can't stand my kids!"

Liddy stared at Mona, narrowing her eyes. "All for one and one for all, Mona . . ."

"Okay, yes, I'll stay, damn it! But I will never forgive you if we wind up serving six months in jail and I lose my lobster business!"

"Good, we're all in agreement," Liddy said, and then turned to Hayley. "So what's the plan?"

"Plan?"

"You're the one so determined to stay. You must have a plan," Liddy said, stepping closer to Hayley.

"I hadn't really thought that far ahead before I gave that rousing speech. I don't actually have a plan," Hayley said, shrugging, somewhat embarrassed.

"Why does it always depend on me to come up with a plan?" Liddy said. "Okay, the first thing I am going to do is call Sonny, and if he's not busy cavorting with his new paralegal, I'm going to get some honest-to-goodness legal advice so we're not just relying on that ignoramus Opie what's his name?"

"Oliver, Oliver Hammersmith," Hayley offered.

"Yeah, that dunce," Liddy said, grabbing her cell phone off the rickety, dusty kitchen table and tapping numbers with her finger on the screen to unlock her phone.

She clamped the phone to her ear and waited as it rang.

"Sonny, it's me, Liddy! Are you alone?" she asked pointedly. "Well, yes, I feel I need to ask because I have no idea who you might be with now that you're free to pursue anything in panty hose!"

Liddy sighed, rolling her eyes at Hayley and Mona as she listened to Sonny talk, using her right hand like a puppet to make a gesture of someone chattering on and on incessantly.

"Don't take that tone with me, Sonny! You lost that right the day you decided you wanted to take a break! No, no, Sonny, if you don't calm down I'm going to hang up!"

"Don't hang up, Liddy! Please, get on topic!" Hayley begged.

Liddy nodded. "Sonny, I don't know what you were thinking hooking us up with that nitwit Orville Thunder-head!"

"Oliver Hammersmith," Hayley corrected her again.

"Whatever! He is a moron, Sonny! He took a nap during our hearing and he was standing up! This is who you sent to save our hides? What on earth were you thinking? No, no, you listen . . ."

"For the love of god, Liddy, let the poor man speak!" Mona screamed.

Liddy raised her index finger to signal Mona to be quiet.

"Okay, Sonny, I'm listening . . ."

Hayley wished the phone conversation was on speaker because she was uneasy about solely relying on high-strung Liddy to absorb and process all the information she was getting from Sonny.

Liddy noticed Hayley's and Mona's nervous, angst-ridden faces, and gave them an encouraging smile and thumbs-up.

"Yes, I understand, but what about Hayley and Mona?" Liddy asked, listening to Sonny intently.

Hayley and Mona exchanged concerned looks.

"Okay, fine. Talk to you later, Sonny," Liddy said, ending the call.

"Well, what did he say?" Hayley blurted out, unable to handle the suspense.

"He wants me to drive over to Oscar Hammerhead's office . . ."

"Close enough," Hayley sighed.

"And we're going to get Sonny on the phone so he can talk to Oscar, or is it Owen?"

"It doesn't matter, Liddy! Just tell us what Sonny said!" Hayley wailed.

"They're going to have a conference call and Sonny is going to talk Ollie through a very detailed courtroom strategy, and he wants me there to take notes so if he drifts off point in the courtroom I will have Sonny's written instructions in front of me to help him get back on track."

"That actually sounds like a good plan," Hayley said, surprised and relieved.

"Well, let's go over to his office right now then," Mona said. "We're wasting time here."

"There's just one thing," Liddy said. "Sonny wants me to go to Hammerhead's office alone."

"But why? If we are going to discuss strategy, Mona

and I should be there too because our futures depend on it!" Hayley insisted.

"Sonny understands that, but apparently Sledgehammer has a thing about crowds . . ." Liddy said.

"What do you mean crowds?"

"Being in close quarters, like a small office, with more than two people. The courtroom is different because it's wide and open, but he's extremely claustrophobic, and can't focus on the task at hand, and Sonny says it is imperative he stay focused."

"What kind of loony tunes character are we dealing with here?" Mona bellowed.

"Okay, fine. Two people. But you are one person, Liddy, so that means either Mona or I can come along too, right?"

"No, Sonny will be there."

"But he won't even be in the room! He will be on the phone!" Hayley yelled, exasperated.

"I guess just a voice still counts as another person in the room," Liddy said. "Do you really want to argue about this? We need to nail down our defense!"

Hayley threw her arms up in the air, giving up.

They ran out to the car, and with Liddy driving, drove back to the Salmon Cove business district, taking great caution to stay well under the speed limit, but not too slow, to avoid getting stopped by Sheriff Daphne or one of her minions. Liddy dropped Hayley and Mona off near some shops, and told them to meet her at six PM at the Mews, a nice waterfront restaurant she had researched online, that served a pricey but well-reviewed dinner menu. They agreed, and spent the next two hours walking up and down the street in the business district, poking their heads into various boutique stores, but their minds were on what was happening at Oliver Hammersmith's office.

They ended up at the Starfish Lounge and had one drink to kill time, and then just before six, they strolled down Main Street and on to the outskirts of town where the Mews was situated with a stunning view of the bay.

They sat at the bar and had a cocktail and waited for Liddy, but she was apparently running late, so when their reservation time came and went, they decided to be seated by the hostess and split a fried calamari appetizer. By seven Liddy was still a no-show. Hayley texted her and received no response. She tried again at seven thirty and then again at eight. Still nothing. She then called Oliver Hammersmith's office and got his voice mail. Office hours were from ten to six and she was told by the secretary's polite voice to call back tomorrow.

By nine PM Hayley and Mona were more than just a bit concerned. It was so unlike Liddy to be completely incommunicado. Perhaps she somehow inexplicably spaced on their dinner plans and had just driven back to the cabin after her meeting with Hammersmith. They paid the bill and called a taxi to take them back to the cabin. But when Hayley and Mona were dropped off by the cabdriver, they found the cabin dark and deserted. Inside, there was no sign of Liddy. The place was just as they had left it. Hayley tried calling Liddy's cell phone one more time and she was sent directly to voice mail.

Something was seriously wrong.

Chapter 23

When the first rays of sunlight peeked through the trees in the woods surrounding the cabin the following morning, and Liddy still had not returned, even stalwart Mona was trying desperately not to join Hayley in full-fledged panic mode.

"This is so unlike her. I mean, Liddy thrives on keeping everyone abreast of her schedule every waking moment," Hayley said. "She wouldn't just go somewhere and not text or call us."

Mona rubbed her eyes and yawned as she shook her head, completely at a loss. Neither of them had slept a wink all night. They just sat up waiting and worrying and speculating on her whereabouts.

"So what should we do?" Mona asked.

"We have to go out there and look for her," Hayley said, pouring herself a strong cup of coffee to shake off her bone-weary exhaustion.

"How? We have no car. We're stuck out here in the middle of nowhere."

"We're going to have to call someone to help us,

someone who can drive us around, and I think we both
know who that person is," Hayley said calmly and deliberately.

"Hell no! We are *not* calling Corey!"

"Mona, this is no time to be stubborn! Liddy could be
hurt! What if her car somehow skidded off the road into
a ditch, and she's trapped and crying for help, but nobody
can hear her? Did you think about that? Time could be
of the essence!" Hayley yelled.

Mona flinched. She couldn't argue with that. She
sighed, and grabbed her phone off the kitchen counter
and called Corey.

He arrived at the cabin in less than fifteen minutes to
pick them up. They squeezed into the cab of his pickup
truck, Mona forcing Hayley to climb in first so she would
be stuck in the middle, separating her from Corey. Sadie
wagged her tail in the bed of the truck.

Corey peeled away, but once he hit the main road, he
slowed down to a crawl, scanning both sides of the road to
check for skid marks and any other signs of an accident.

By the time they reached the business district, it was
close to eight thirty, which, according to the voice mail
message they had received, was the time the law office of
Oliver Hammersmith was open for business.

Corey dropped Hayley and Mona off, and told them he
was going to go pick up some breakfast sandwiches and
coffee for them while they spoke to the lawyer. If it was
going to be a long, grueling day searching the area, they
were going to need their strength. He drove away, and
Hayley and Mona entered the small office in the center of
town, basically an add-on to the main building, which
housed a far busier and more prestigious real estate
business.

They walked into the cramped space, where there was

a tiny desk so close to the entrance they banged the edge
of it when they opened the door. Behind the desk was a
rotund elderly woman with more than a passing resemblance to Mrs. Claus with her white hair tied in a bun and
tiny reading glasses teetering on the bridge of her nose.
She even wore a red sweater to keep warm from the blast-
ing air conditioner. She turned her attention away from her
desktop computer and greeted them with a tight smile.

"May I help you?"

"Yes, we're here to see Mr. Hammersmith," Hayley
said, returning her smile.

"Do you have an appointment?"

"No, we don't, but it's an emergency," Hayley said.

Oliver Hammersmith's office door was open halfway,
and he was clearly visible sitting behind his desk, feet up,
paper cup of steaming coffee in front of him, reading the
print edition of the local paper.

"I'm sorry. He's booked this morning," Mrs. Claus said
as she gazed back at her computer screen and tapped a
few keys on the keyboard, perusing his schedule. "How
about next Friday?"

"You don't understand," Hayley said patiently. "We are
clients of Mr. Hammersmith. He is currently representing
us in a court case and—"

"I understand, but I'm afraid he just can't see you
right now."

"Excuse me," Mona interjected. "But can I just point
out that we have a clear view of the guy at this very
moment. We can see him in his office reading the paper!
He doesn't look that busy!"

"Mr. Hammersmith never meets with anyone before
noon. He needs his mornings to prepare himself, reflect
on what is expected of him for the day, it's all part of his

process," the secretary said, a little discomforted by Mona's aggressive demeanor.

"Screw that! We need to talk to him right now! It could be a matter of life and death!" Mona screamed, pounding the door wide open and marching inside.

Hayley threw an apologetic smile at the secretary and then followed Mona.

Oliver Hammersmith, startled, threw his paper in the air and kicked his cup of coffee with his shoe so it spilled all over his desk. He jumped to his feet.

"What? What is this?"

The secretary pushed her way into the office behind Liddy and Mona. "Mr. Hammersmith, I'm so sorry! I told them you were unavailable but they refused to listen and barged right in!"

Hammersmith began hyperventilating with short, quick gasps, as if he was asthmatic. He clutched his chest. "There are too many people in here! One of you has to go! This is making me very uncomfortable!"

"Well, we're not going anywhere! Not until you talk to us!" Mona said, folding her arms and glaring at him.

Hammersmith, unnerved, turned his wide, alarmed eyes to his secretary and between gasps, said, "Alice, go next door and find a rag to clean this mess up! But wait until these ladies leave before you come back in here, okay?"

"Yes, Mr. Hammersmith," his secretary, Alice, huffed, glaring at Hayley and Mona, galled by their rudeness, before quickly retreating out of the office.

Agitated by the mess on his desk in front of him, Oliver picked the newspaper up off the floor and dropped it on the desktop to soak up some of the spilled coffee before it cascaded over the side and onto the carpet.

"Now, ladies, about your case—" he said, discombobulated, trying in vain to focus.

"We're not here about our case," Hayley said. "We're here about our friend Liddy."

"What about her?" he asked, still staring at the desk to make sure the coffee didn't start dripping off the side.

"She's gone," Mona said.

"Gone where?"

"We don't know," Hayley said, sighing. "We were hoping you could help shed some light on the situation. Do you remember what time she left your office yesterday?"

"She wasn't in my office yesterday," Hammersmith said, tapping his foot nervously, still staring at the newspaper and coffee. "Do you think the paper has absorbed enough to keep the coffee from spilling on the floor?"

Hayley couldn't take it anymore. She grabbed some tissues she had in her bag and lined wads of them up along the edge of the desk as a barrier like tiny sandbags to stop the flow of coffee.

"There! Is that better? Can you focus on our conversation now, Mr. Hammersmith?"

Incredibly, it worked. He was satisfied his office carpet was safe. He finally looked at them for the first time.

"We had an appointment, but she never showed," he said. "I had my colleague Sonny Rivers waiting on the line. I tried calling the cell phone number she gave me, but she never answered. I must have left three or four messages. Sonny is a very busy man, so after a half hour, he hung up and I went on to my next meeting."

"But she dropped us off yesterday only a couple blocks from your office. She was on her way to see you," Hayley said, her heart beating faster, a sickening feeling growing in the pit of her stomach.

"What can I say? She never made it," he said, shrugging, totally unconcerned. "Are we done here? I can see Alice is back with that rag, and I'd like her to come in here and wipe up my desk, and unfortunately that can't happen if there are too many people here—"

Mona looked as if she was about to lose it, but quite surprisingly, she held her tongue.

"Well, if you hear from her, please call us," Hayley said, scribbling her cell phone number on a writing pad with a pencil. "Will you please do us that favor?"

"Of course. We still need to discuss your case and how we plan on proceeding. Sonny has a few ideas on our defense and I concur—"

"That's not our priority presently," Hayley said through gritted teeth. "But thank you."

Hayley and Mona left the office. Alice waited until they were clear and then she rushed in with the rag to sop up the coffee that had soaked through the tissues and was now seconds away from pouring over the side of the desk like Niagara Falls.

Outside, they spotted Corey waiting for them at the intersection. He was parked in a loading zone so they hurried toward him before Sheriff Daphne spotted him and he got a citation.

At the sight of them approaching, Sadie's tail wagged faster and faster.

Mona stopped in her tracks and whispered, "Uh-oh."

"What is it?"

Mona pointed across the street. "Look."

Hayley followed her gaze to the other side of the street where Liddy's black Mercedes was parked next to another NO OVERNIGHT PARKING sign. It sat there, abandoned, with yet another printed traffic ticket stuffed underneath the windshield wiper.

Chapter 24

"Hayley, where is she? What are we going to do?" Mona said, her face tightened, worry lines forming on her forehead, in a rare display of distress.

"We have to stay calm," Hayley said, failing to reassure her. "Now the car is parked directly across the street from the Starfish Lounge. Maybe someone saw her yesterday."

She took Mona's hand and they crossed the street and went into the Starfish Lounge, which had just opened its doors for the day a few minutes earlier. There were a smattering of early-day drinkers, including reliable barfly Rufus sipping a whiskey on the rocks in the corner, a couple of local fishermen drinking beer at a small table in the back, and part-time employee Boyd, who sat in a booth near the door, taking a break, reading a new issue of his alien invasion comic book series.

Behind the bar, Sue replenished her clean glassware, which had been left to dry on some towels behind the bar overnight.

"Mona, you go question those guys in the back while

I talk to Sue," Hayley suggested as Mona nodded and ambled over to strike up a conversation with the fishermen.

"Morning, Sue," Hayley said, sliding up on a barstool.

"Well, good morning," Sue said, looking up with a smile. "Must have been a rough night if you're starting this early."

"Yes, it was a pretty rough night, in fact," Hayley said, solemnly. "We seem to have lost our friend."

Sue noticed Mona chatting with the fishermen. "You mean the short, mouthy one with the expensive jewelry?"

"Liddy, yes, that's the one," Hayley said.

"You sure she didn't just hightail it back to Bar Harbor? She didn't appear to be a big fan of Salmon Cove as I recall," Sue said, lining the clean glasses along a low shelf just above the ice cooler.

"I'm positive," Hayley said. "Her Mercedes is still parked across the street. It looks like it's been there all night, with a traffic ticket to prove it. Did you happen to notice it when you locked up the bar and left last night?"

"Can't say that I did, but I've got to admit, I was pretty wiped out when we closed last night. I had a tough time herding out the customers after last call, and the floor was so sticky it took Boyd an hour to mop the place, and someone threw up in the men's room, so I wasn't too aware of my surroundings when I finally got out of here and slogged home."

"Who was here for last call yesterday?"

"The usual suspects. Rufus, Boyd was here working, of course, that couple visiting from out of town, the real friendly, gabby ones, I forget their names, Bob and Vera . . . ?"

"Buck and Vanessa," Hayley offered.

"Yeah, them, they've been here every night. We had a big crowd of college kids here for the summer who are working as singing waiters at that restaurant where the kids perform show tunes between dinner courses. They were big drinkers, pretty rowdy, in fact, but relatively harmless . . ."

"Anybody else you can think of?"

"It was awfully crowded, like I said, it was a challenge pushing everybody out the door when I tried to close."

"And you personally never saw Liddy at any point yesterday?"

"No, I haven't seen her since you were all in here the other night."

Hayley took a deep breath, not looking forward to approaching the next subject, but she decided to just go for it anyway. "Sue, I heard a rumor . . ."

Sue leaned in, excited. "I hope it's a juicy one."

"It's about you and . . ." Hayley nodded in the direction of the old man nursing his whiskey at the other end of the bar. ". . . Rufus."

Sue laughed heartily. "I see you've been talking to Polly Roper."

"Yes, I have," Hayley said.

"She's been peddling that story for weeks now. You have to understand something about Polly. She thrives on drama and scandal, even when there is none. She's a total gossip fiend," Sue said, shaking her head.

"So there is no truth to the rumor that you and Rufus are dating . . ."

"Dating? That's rich!" Sue guffawed. "No, ma'am, that story has been blown way out of proportion. I suppose the whole damn thing got started because I do have a taste for older men, I've dated a few in the past, one in particular after I got out of the military. He was loaded and nice enough to loan me the cash to open this bar, but it didn't last very long, and I paid him back . . . with interest . . .

and there were a couple of married ones I may have gotten friendly with over the years, which I tried to keep on the down low for obvious reasons, but let's leave it at that . . ."

"So definitely not Rufus?"

"Look, I like Rufus, and we have gotten close . . . but not in the biblical sense! I just find the old coot fun and interesting to talk to, he's had quite a life, and yes, I have treated him to a few meals just to hear some of his stories, but give me a break. When I say I like older men, I mean men under eighty years old!"

"Got it!" Hayley said. "You're just friends."

"Why are you so interested in my love life? How does this help you find your friend?"

"I just have this feeling that there's something larger going on here with that travel writer Jackson Young getting murdered on the beach and our friend Liddy simply vanishing into thin air. I don't know, I'm trying to get to know as much as I can about this town and the people in it to figure out how all the pieces of this very strange puzzle fit together . . ."

"Well, I'm sorry to tell you, you're wasting your time pumping *me* with questions. I don't have anything to do with all that nasty business," Sue said, turning away.

She was done talking.

And Hayley wasn't anxious to get her ire up like the late Jackson Young did at the beach on the day he was murdered.

Hayley slid off the barstool and approached Boyd, who was in a booth, immersed in his comic book.

Before she even had a chance to open her mouth, Boyd looked up at her with a blank stare and said, "They're here."

"Who?"

Boyd glanced at the cover of his comic book, which

portrayed some slimy lizard-like creatures stomping their way through Washington, DC, and overrunning the White House.

"Oh, you mean, the aliens, yes, you told me," Hayley said, resisting the urge to roll her eyes. She sat down across from him. "Boyd, did you by any chance see my friend Liddy at any point yesterday around town? You remember her, right? Attractive, brown curly hair, kind of a loud, spitfire personality?"

Boyd buried his face back inside his comic, reading it, studying the pages like an impressionable Baptist boy at his first Bible study class.

"Boyd?"

He refused to lift his eyes from the pages.

"I know you can hear me. Did you see her?"

"No," he grumbled before jumping to his feet, rolling the comic book up, and stuffing it in the back pocket of his jeans. "I got to get back to work."

Hayley watched him hurry off, not sure if he was telling the truth or not. He was such a peculiar young man, very tough to read.

Mona soon arrived at Hayley's side as she stood up from the booth. "So those two fishermen in the back said they were here last night, but left early because they had to head out at five this morning to haul their traps. They both remember leaving here around seven thirty and seeing Liddy's Mercedes parked across the street."

"So whatever happened to her must have happened right after she parked her car to go to the meeting with Oliver Hammersmith and before she arrived at his office, because she never made the meeting nor did she ever return to her car at any point after that."

"Hayley, I'm scared. What could have happened to her?"

"I don't know, but I'm beginning to suspect maybe

there's something to this alien invasion Boyd's been going on about. Maybe they've beamed her up to the mother ship. It's the only thing that makes sense at this point," Hayley said, at a loss.

They started to head out of the bar, but Hayley, spotting Rufus, who was now starting in on a fresh whiskey, hunched over the bar, stopped to talk to him.

"Good morning, Rufus," she said brightly.

Rufus squinted at her with bloodshot, weary eyes and managed to grunt, "Morning."

"Do you recall seeing our friend, Rufus? Her name is Liddy . . ."

"The jailbird, yeah, you're all jailbirds. I heard about you ladies getting thrown in the clink," he slurred as his chuckle erupted into a coughing fit.

Hayley waited for him to down his whiskey and kill his cough before she continued.

"You heard right . . ." Hayley sighed. "But our friend, Liddy, she's disappeared and we're very worried . . ."

Rufus banged his glass on the bar for Sue to refill it. She glanced over, sighed, grabbed the bottle of Jack Daniels, and poured some in his glass.

"I'll never let them put me in jail," he said, leaning forward, teetering on the edge of his barstool to the point where Mona took a step forward to catch him if he fell off. "I got some sleeping pills hidden in a false bottom drawer back at my place, real strong ones, I swear if the cops show up at my door, I'll swallow the lot of them. I'm never going to jail, you hear me? Never!"

He was in his own little world, lost in his own strange, fuzzy thoughts.

"Why would they throw you in jail, Rufus?" Mona asked, suspicious. "Have you done something that would give them cause to arrest you?"

"No, I'm innocent! Clean as a whistle! But you never know how they might try to railroad you," he slurred, spit flying out of his mouth so high Mona tilted her head to dodge it.

"Rufus, about our friend . . ." Hayley tried again.

"She's gone," Rufus said, gulping down his whiskey.

Hayley and Mona exchanged worried looks.

"What do you mean gone?"

"She left."

"Left where?" Mona barked, quickly losing patience.

"Town, she left town!"

"You saw her?"

"Yesterday when I was walking down the street to come here. She got in her fancy-ass car and drove that way!" Rufus said confidently, pointing in the direction of the road that led out of town.

"And what time was that?" Hayley asked.

"About three thirty, four at the latest. I guess it was the same time I got here. You can ask Sue, she was here, she knew what time I came in," he said, pounding his empty glass on the bar, demanding yet another round.

Sue gave him an irked look and then decided to ignore him while she talked to another customer.

"Thanks, Rufus," Hayley said, before taking Mona by the arm and pushing her out the door and into the street. "That makes zero sense. According to everybody else we've talked to, Liddy's Mercedes has been parked in that spot since yesterday, which means he's either confused . . ."

"Or deliberately lying to us," Mona said ominously.

"Why would the old town drunk lie to us? He obviously wasn't the one who snatched Liddy because he was right here at the Starfish Lounge in plain view of everyone until his granddaughter Ellie probably came to pick him up at closing."

"Maybe the old stewed prune has something to hide!" Mona said.

Hayley stood in front of the Starfish Lounge, mystified. Something downright sinister was going on in this otherwise picture-perfect Maine coastal town.

The fear inside her was growing rapidly. But she was determined to get to the bottom of this because Liddy's life could very well depend on it.

Chapter 25

Hayley knew they had to wait at least twenty-four hours since they last saw Liddy before they could legally file a missing persons report at the police station. Liddy had dropped them off in town at four PM the previous day before heading off to her appointment with Oliver Hammersmith. It was now ten minutes to four. So Hayley and Mona raced over to the local police station and burst through the front door, stopping at the small reception desk manned by a fresh-faced young recruit with big, kind eyes and an eager smile. He was bursting out of his nicely pressed cream-colored uniform, probably because he kept stuffing handfuls of jelly beans into his mouth from the glass bowl on top of the desk that was clearly intended for visitors. The judge, the police, they all seemed to love jelly beans.

"How may I help you, ladies?" he asked, smiling so hard there were veins popping out of his neck.

"We're here to report a missing person," Hayley said, ravenously eyeing the jelly beans since they hadn't eaten since breakfast.

"Oh, no! That's terrible!" he gasped, but more like a

friendly neighbor rather than a helpful police officer on duty to protect and serve.

Hayley and Mona stood there waiting for him to take action, but he didn't make a move. He just stared at them, smiling, before realizing that he probably shouldn't be grinning from ear to ear after such a serious claim. So he very awkwardly contorted the smile into a concerned pout.

"Who's missing?"

"Our friend Liddy Crawford, we haven't seen or heard from her since yesterday and we are very worried," Hayley said.

"Oh, my, I am so sorry," the pudgy young man said as he noticed Hayley glancing at the jelly beans.

He pushed the bowl closer to her. "Jelly bean?"

"Thank you," Hayley said, snatching a handful and gratefully popping them into her mouth.

There was a lingering silence as the chubby-cheeked police officer full of compassion gazed at them with the same sad pout.

Mona turned to see Hayley chewing a mouthful of jelly beans so she decided to take charge and stepped forward, slamming her hands down on the reception desk. "So is there some kind of report we can fill out so you guys can start looking for her, or do you want to, you know, put out an APB?"

"What's that?" he asked with a curious look on his face.

"What's what?" Mona asked, confused.

"That last part you said. AB—what?"

"APB! An All Points Bulletin! It alerts all the squad cars in the area about our missing friend with a complete description so they can keep an eye out for her!" Mona yelled.

"There's no need to do all that. We just have one squad car! I can just radio Sheriff Wilkes and tell her myself," he said, smiling.

Hayley swallowed the jelly beans and leaned forward. "Please, Officer . . ."

"Richter, Billy Richter," he said, offering his hand.

Mona was about to slap it away, but Hayley beat her to him and politely shook his hand.

"Officer Richter, we're wasting valuable time . . ."

"Call me Billy," he said brightly.

"Billy! Right. Okay, Billy, can we at least get started with some paperwork, because there's *always* paperwork to fill out!"

"Sure, why don't you sit over there and I'll get the process started," he said.

"Thank you," Hayley said, grabbing Mona, who stared glumly at the obnoxiously chipper young man, by the shirtsleeve and pulling her over to a couple of uncomfortable folding chairs.

They sat down and waited for him to get up from his desk, but he just sat there, smiling at them.

Hayley sighed. "Are you going to bring us the paperwork or do we have to go somewhere to get it?"

"I'm not authorized to hand out any forms. I'm just a part-time receptionist for Sheriff Wilkes. I'm not really an officer, but I'm studying to be. I guess I should have mentioned that when you called me Officer Richter, but I just loved the sound of it! Officer Richter! I'm hoping maybe I will be someday, but I flunked the first test and I have to wait three months before I can take it again!"

Hayley reached out and grabbed Mona's shirtsleeve

again because she instinctively knew Mona was about to leap out of the chair and beat the crap out of the kid, but Hayley held firm and kept Mona fastened in her seat.

Mercifully, Hayley spotted the squad car pull up out front and Sheriff Daphne get out and stroll into the station. She instantly spotted Hayley and Mona and grimaced.

"What are you two doing here?"

Hayley jumped up and raced over to her. "Our friend Liddy has vanished into thin air and we're afraid something bad has happened to her so we came here to file a missing person report!"

"When did you last see her?"

"Yesterday," Hayley said. "She had a meeting and dropped us off in town around four and we never heard from her after that! She was supposed to meet us for dinner—"

"It hasn't been twenty-four hours," Sheriff Daphne said, glimpsing at the clock hanging on the wall.

"Yes, we waited until four o'clock. You can see right there, it's four o'clock," Hayley said, desperation rising in her voice. "That's twenty-four hours!"

"It's three fifty-seven," Sheriff Daphne said flatly.

Mona threw her head back and howled, "You've got to be kidding me!"

Sheriff Daphne turned to Billy behind the desk. "Send them into my office when it's four o'clock."

She stared at Hayley, waiting for her to dare challenge her, and then ambled off down the hall to her office.

Mona lunged forward after her, but Hayley held her back, and whispered urgently into her ear, "We *need* her."

They sat back down and stared at the clock until it was exactly four, and then they both sprang from their seats and bounded over to Billy behind the desk.

He looked up at them again with his big, eager smile.

"It's four o'clock, we'd like to see Sheriff Wilkes," Hayley said calmly.

Billy glanced at the clock. "That one's a little fast. My computer still says three fifty-nine."

Hayley squeezed Mona's hand tightly, silently warning her not to overreact.

To her surprise, Mona remained steady and calm, but she did notice her biting her lip to keep herself from saying something she would regret.

After about fifteen seconds, Billy's adorably chubby face lit up. His computer clock obviously had finally flashed four o'clock.

He stood up and came around his desk.

"This way, ladies," he said. "Can I get you some coffee?"

"I think we're both wired enough, thank you," Hayley said, shaking her head.

He ushered them into Sheriff Wilkes's office. She was just sitting there, not doing anything, making a point of showing them that she had no intention of helping them until she was legally required.

"Sit down," she said, gently rubbing her neck with her hand and wincing.

"Pain in the neck?" Hayley asked.

"Yeah," she said, staring at them. "A couple of big ones."

There were so many things Hayley wanted to say to her, but she couldn't risk ticking her off. Liddy was missing and the situation was dire.

"I have a theory," Sheriff Daphne said, sitting back in her chair and folding her arms across her chest.

"What's that?" Mona asked.

"I don't think your friend just up and disappeared. I don't think this is foul play at all. What I think is your friend got nervous about your upcoming trial, maybe she wasn't the instigator, maybe she was dragged along by her two friends, and she panicked because the two of you were refusing to take my very generous offer, so she just blew town to leave you two to deal with the whole big mess. Yup, that's what I think."

"Liddy wouldn't do that," Hayley said, anger rising in her voice.

"Maybe you don't know her as well as you thought," Sheriff Daphne said. "Maybe she's the only reasonable, clearheaded one of the three of you."

"We've known each other since we were kids," Hayley said.

"Yeah, she's never been reasonable or clearheaded!" Mona wailed.

Sheriff Daphne watched them, saying nothing, doing her best to intimidate them and make them feel uncomfortable.

Hayley couldn't take it anymore. "My brother-in-law is the police chief of Bar Harbor so I know a few things about the law, and I know that once someone has been missing for twenty-four hours, it is your responsibility as an officer of the law to accept a missing person report, so we are not leaving here until you allow us to file one."

"Fine," Sheriff Daphne said through clenched teeth. She sat forward in her chair and unfolded her arms. She clicked a few keys on her keyboard and then turned to them, stone-faced. "What's her name again?"

"Liddy Crawford," Hayley said, relieved.

"How do you spell it?"

"Which one? Liddy or Crawford?"

Sheriff Daphne looked at her with disdain, and said, "Both."

She was not going to make this easy by a long shot.

Suddenly the phone on the desk rang.

"Excuse me," Sheriff Daphne said dismissively before picking it up. "Yes, Billy, what is it?"

She listened for a few moments and then hung up and jumped to her feet. "I'm sorry, ladies, something more pressing has come up and I need to go."

"What's more pressing than a missing person?"

"Another body has been found," she said, charging out from behind her desk.

"A body? Who?" Hayley cried.

Sheriff Daphne ignored the question and bolted out of the office. Hayley and Mona chased after her back into the reception area where they found Billy, pale and shaken.

Sheriff Daphne stopped briefly to address Billy. "Call the coroner's office and have them meet me there."

Billy nodded as he reached for the phone, his hands quivering as he punched in some numbers.

Hayley raced to catch up to Sheriff Daphne, desperate. "Please, Sheriff Wilkes, we have to know, is it our friend?"

But Sheriff Daphne just shook her off and said as she flew out the door, "Hang tight, I'll be back in a few hours."

And she was gone.

Mona was already hovering over Billy.

"Come on, kid, what do you know? Whose body did they find? At least let us know if it was a man or a woman!"

Billy looked around to make sure no one was within earshot, and then quietly whispered, "It's a man. He's a local."

Hayley sighed, tears of relief streaming down her cheeks.

"Who?" Mona insisted.

Billy was clearly scared of his boss, but in the presence of Mona, a very aggressive and frightening force, he was utterly out of his mind petrified. "The sheriff will *kill* me if she finds out I told you anything."

"We won't tell her, I promise," Mona said, surprisingly calm, which made Billy even more nervous. "Come on, Billy, you know you want to tell us."

"Old man Rufus, she found him dead as a doornail."

"She? Who is she?"

"Sue, the owner of the Starfish Lounge."

Island Food & Spirits
by
Hayley Powell

My ex-husband, Danny, and I didn't have a whole lot of money for fancy vacations in our early years as a married couple, or as I refer to them, "BK"—"Before Kids." But we made it a point to scrape just enough cash together to at least get away for a nice long weekend once every summer! Both of us adored Old Orchard Beach, about three hours south of Bar Harbor near Portland. Every time we went there, we would treat ourselves to a nice hotel, some special meals out, lots of soothing cocktails, and if we were lucky with the weather, a few sunny days lounging at the beach.

We always spent the winter and spring months squirreling away our spare change and extra cash in an old cookie tin that belonged to my grandmother, which I kept in a high cupboard over the top of the stove.

Well, the day had finally come to make our hotel reservation, and so I needed to deposit our vacation savings at the bank. I carried up a step stool from the basement, climbed up on it, and retrieved the cookie tin. It seemed lighter than the last time I had dropped a few coins in it, but I didn't think much of it until I lifted the lid and peered inside. Instead of jangling coins and lots of green paper money, all I found were about a dozen slips of white paper with a note scribbled on each one. I snatched one out of the tin and unfolded it, and sure enough, scrawled in Danny's familiar handwriting were the words, *"I owe you $ Love, Danny."*

My blood started to boil. I glanced at the clock on the kitchen wall. I still had a few hours before Danny would come marching through the back door, asking for his dinner. I needed to calm myself. And my foolproof way of doing that was to feed myself. So I went to the fridge and grabbed last night's leftover Lobster Seafood Casserole with its wonderful chunks of lobster, fresh-picked crabmeat, and small peeled Maine shrimp and popped the casserole dish right into the microwave. Within five minutes, I was gobbling it up, and I could feel my blood pressure slowly going down.

After scraping the last bits out of the casserole dish with a spoon, I was feeling much better until my eyes fell on that cookie tin sitting on the counter and I got mad all over again. So I went to my reliable Plan B. A nice cocktail. I pulled out my homemade blueberry simple syrup to make my favorite summertime refresher, a Blueberry Gin Fizz Cocktail. Well, that did the trick. After two of those, I was relaxed and feeling pretty happy.

That is, until Danny breezed through the door. He took one quick look at the empty pitcher of Blueberry Gin Fizzes, the empty, scraped-clean seafood casserole dish and the opened cookie tin sitting on the kitchen counter, and he knew he was in big trouble.

Danny's mouth opened and a litany of excuses began pouring out, but I stopped him by raising my hand in the air and staring at him coldly. He got the message. He stopped talking.

I didn't scream, or yell, or cry, I simply informed him in a low, controlled voice that I didn't care how he did it, or what he needed to do to replace the missing money, but he was going to do it because I desperately needed a vacation, and if he didn't want me filing for divorce before Labor Day, he would find a way to make it happen. Danny nodded vigorously, promising me we would leave on schedule in one month's time.

Well, exactly one month later, to my surprise and delight, we were in Danny's car driving to Old Orchard Beach! I didn't know how he did it, and I didn't ask because frankly I didn't care. All I cared about was we were on our way.

Three hours later my hopes and dreams of a magical weekend faded fast when we pulled up to a large, dilapidated, old dark and dingy home with its paint peeling, some of the shutters on the windows hanging sideways and some completely gone, an overgrown front yard, and one crooked old sign above the front door that said VACANSY. That's not a typo. The proprietors didn't know how to spell.

All of a sudden I had visions of those creepy old homes in Stephen King's novels. Danny quickly explained that he hadn't been able to raise enough money for our fancy beach vacation, but he knew I desperately wanted to get off the island for a weekend, so he booked the only place he could find online that he could afford. He also proudly told me that even at the low price he paid, all our meals were included. So much for my dining out at quaint restaurants with ocean views fantasy. We were roughly twenty miles from the ocean.

I opened my mouth to tell him how disappointed I was, but Danny quickly jumped out of the car and hurried up the steps and into the house to check in. I reluctantly began hauling our luggage out of the trunk. Suddenly I had a feeling I was being watched so I stopped and looked around, but didn't see anything. I grabbed Danny's duffel bag, pulled it out, and dropped it on the ground next to me, and then I heard a loud rustling sound coming from the bushes on the side of the house. I paused to listen, and heard a low, steady growling. And then I locked eyes with the biggest and dirtiest dog I had ever seen in my life, and

he happened to be foaming at the mouth.
After a few tense moments of a standoff,
he sprang toward me.

All I could think as I stared at this
mangy beast running at me was *Cujo*, that
scary Stephen King novel with the devil
dog from hell who tore people apart with
his sharp teeth! I screamed at the top of my
lungs, hauled butt up the rickety old steps,
and burst right through the screen door of
the old house, screaming bloody murder,
with the dog nipping at my heels.

As I crashed into the foyer, Danny, who
was talking to a short, stout old woman,
whipped around in surprise and stared at
me as I stammered hysterically about being
chased by a wild rabid dog.

The old woman chuckled and told me,
"That's just sweet ole Charlie. He loves
people, and is just excited to say hello to
you."

I turned to look at sweet ole Charlie,
who was panting and growling on the other
side of the screen door. He didn't strike me
as sweet at all. He was staring at me with
hungry eyes.

The old woman introduced herself as
Edna, and suggested I might like to go out
back and get some fresh air on the porch
while Danny finished checking in. She
pointed to a door down the hall.

Slightly shaken, I decided it might be a
good idea, and I walked down the hall and
out into the backyard that was laden with

thick weeds and dead-looking trees, and I sat down in an old wicker chair on the back porch.

As I glanced around, I noticed just beyond the trees past a sagging fence was a large cemetery filled with old headstones. Wilted flowers in vases had been scattered around the graves.

I contemplated getting up to read some of the old headstones, but I stayed fastened to the wicker chair because I knew if I started seeing the names of family pets, I would probably drop dead from a heart attack given how much *Pet Sematary*, another Stephen King novel, kept me up at night for weeks after reading it.

I relaxed in the old wicker chair, and was close to nodding off, when all of a sudden I saw a skeletal-looking old man with sunken cheeks and long white hair slowly sit up from one of the graves, like he was rising from the dead!

I let out a bloodcurdling long shriek and then all went black.

When I woke up I found myself in a dark room. I was disoriented at first, not sure where I was, but then it all came back to me. After I screamed and fainted dead away on the porch, I was awakened by Danny a few seconds later, gently shaking me. I could hear Edna yelling out in the yard, "Darrell, I told you to stop taking your cat naps out here in the family plot while you are weeding, you damn near scared the poor girl to death!"

Danny suggested I take a nap before dinner, which was the first good idea he had come up with all year. Edna led me to a room, and I was so tired, I didn't even bother switching on the lights, I just crashed on top of the bed, pulled a blanket over me, and fell fast asleep.

Now fully awake, I was feeling foolish for passing out on the porch earlier, and so I made the decision to just make the best of our new accommodations. I was going to enjoy this weekend come hell or high water!

I felt around the side of the bed until I came in contact with an old lamp sitting on the nightstand, and flipped the switch on, bathing the room in a soft light.

I gasped, almost choking, as my eyes darted around the room at the horror! Everywhere I looked there were clowns. I hate clowns! They terrify me! Ever since I was a little girl! And now I was trapped in this room, surrounded by them, all laughing at me, with their big red noses and wide lips and painted white faces and wild, unruly hair and colorful party hats! It was awful! Just like, yes, here it comes, another Stephen King novel I had devoured in grade school, *It*! There were clowns on the wallpaper! Toy clowns on the bookshelf! I glanced down at the squares on the handmade quilt that was draped over me, and yes, it was embroidered with, you guessed it, clowns!

I let out a deafening scream, and high-tailed it out of there as fast as I could, flew down the stairs, and almost collided with Edna, who had darted out into the hallway from the kitchen when she heard the commotion.

Choking back sobs and trying not to blubber in front of a stranger, I attempted to compose myself all the while muttering about my fear of clowns attacking me. She didn't flinch. She just took my hand and guided me to the dining room and set me down in a chair next to Danny. At the head of the table was Darrell, the grave napper, who stared at me dumbfounded. I let out a sigh. Mercifully it was time for dinner.

Danny reached over and patted my knee and I tried to relax as Edna smiled and said, "Your husband called ahead and told me about your favorite dish so I prepared it special for your first night here."

She lifted the lid off the casserole, and announced, "Voila! Seafood casserole!"

Both Danny and I gasped out loud and clapped our hands to our mouths as we stared at the live, wiggling and jiggling baby squids crawling on top of a huge pile of spaghetti. It was the grossest thing I had ever seen!

We both pushed back so hard from the table that Enda dropped the lid, which hit the casserole dish, and turned it over. The slimy squids rolled all over the table. Darrell reached out and picked one up, popping it in his mouth.

Enough was enough! We bolted out the front door, past the barking, growling, snapping dog from hell luckily tied to his leash (friendly my foot), jumped in the car, and drove out of there as fast as we could, never stopping once until we crossed the Trenton Bridge and were safely home.

I can confidently claim that Edna's seafood casserole doesn't come close to my own special recipe. So trust me on this and try the recipe below! But first, relax with a Blueberry Gin Fizz Cocktail. I had a few after we got home from our ill-fated Old Orchard weekend and they sure did the trick!

Blueberry Gin Fizz Cocktail

<u>Ingredients</u>
3 cups frozen or fresh blueberries
½ cup sugar

2 cups gin
½ fresh-squeezed lime juice
Club soda

In a medium saucepan combine your blueberries, sugar, and water and bring to a boil. Once boiling, turn down heat and simmer for six minutes. While simmering, mash the berries as much as you can. When done, strain the syrup into a cup and let cool.

In a pitcher add the gin, lime juice, and cooled blueberry syrup and mix well together.

Fill a glass with some ice and blueberry mixture about halfway and top with some club soda. Enjoy this refreshing beverage by yourself or with friends.

Hayley's
Lobster Seafood Casserole

<u>Ingredients</u>
½ pound cooked lobster meat, rough chopped
½ pound crabmeat
¼ pound shrimp, peeled and deveined
¾ cup chopped onion
1½ cups mayonnaise
1 cup shredded cheese (your choice)
8 ounces evaporated milk
1 teaspoon kosher salt
1½ teaspoons ground black pepper
1 sleeve Ritz crackers
4 tablespoons butter

Mix together the first 9 ingredients in a greased casserole dish.

Finely crush the Ritz crackers in a bowl. In a small sauce pan melt the butter and pour over the crushed crackers, stirring to mix well. Pour crackers evenly over the top of the casserole.

Preheat your oven to 375 degrees and cook the Lobster Seafood Casserole for 20 to 25 minutes until hot and bubbly and crackers are nicely browned.

Let sit for ten minutes, serve, and enjoy.

Chapter 26

Old man Rufus lived in a modest, single-level clapboard house located on a quiet residential street just a few blocks from the police station. After Mona strong-armed Billy into scribbling the address down on a Post-it note and handing it over to her, she and Hayley hoofed it over there on foot, arriving to find Sheriff Daphne's squad car parked out front and a small crowd of gawkers hanging out on the sidewalk and in the street in front of the house.

Sitting on the stoop just outside the front door was Rufus's granddaughter Ellie, in a pretty pink sundress, slumped over, her face buried in her hands, sobbing. Hayley made sure Sheriff Daphne was nowhere in sight before she worked her way through the gaggle of onlookers and hurried up the walk to reach Ellie.

"Ellie, I'm so sorry . . ."

She looked up at Hayley, her eyes red from crying, and wiped her runny nose with the back of her hand.

"I just got here . . . the sheriff wouldn't let me go inside . . . somebody in the crowd had to tell me what happened . . ." she said, choking.

Hayley sat down next to her and gently put an arm around her shoulders but didn't say anything. She sensed

Ellie just needed someone there with her, and none of her nosy neighbors was offering any kind of emotional support at the moment. They were too busy whispering and gossiping with one another.

"I know my grandfather could be challenging, and when he drank too much he was a downright pain in the butt, but he was a good man . . . and . . . well, I just can't believe he's gone!" Ellie sobbed.

Hayley held her tighter, and Ellie covered her face again with her hands and leaned in to rest her head on Hayley's chest as she cried. Hayley stroked the back of her hair with her hand to comfort her.

Suddenly Boyd raced around the corner, walking fast, in a full sweat, his face full of worry. He stopped at the sight of Ellie inconsolable and weeping, and he melted on the spot, pushing past a few onlookers who stood in his way, in order to rush to his beloved's side. He looked as if he wanted to shove Hayley aside and take her place as Ellie's savior of the moment, but he resisted the urge. Instead, he reached out with a big, fleshy hand and softly touched her bare forearm.

"I got here as soon as I heard," he said, out of breath.

Ellie looked up at him, and there was relief in her eyes. Hayley let go of her as she jumped to her feet and fell into his embrace, blubbering.

Boyd gave Hayley a look that said, *"You can go away. I'm here now!"*

"Ellie, did the sheriff tell you how your grandfather died?" Hayley asked in a soft, soothing voice.

Ellie shook her head. "She refused to tell me anything!"

"It was the aliens!" Boyd said, anxious and upset. "I'm telling you they are here and among us."

Good Lord, not this again, Hayley thought, rolling her

eyes. Ellie did not deserve to hear the paranoid delusional rantings of a comic book obsessive. And fortunately, she didn't have to because at that moment Sheriff Daphne marched out of the house.

Ellie broke free from Boyd's bear hug and rushed over to Daphne, who was leaning into her squad car to grab her radio.

"Sheriff Wilkes, please, I have to know how my grandfather died!"

Sheriff Daphne held up her hand for silence and then spoke into her radio. "Billy, I want you to call the coroner and let him know I have assessed the situation and I believe we're dealing with a death from natural causes, but he's welcome to draw his own conclusions if he still wants to come all the way out here."

"Roger that," Billy's disembodied voice said followed by static.

"So you believe his old body just gave out?" Ellie asked, sniffling.

Sheriff Daphne looked at her for the first time, took in her fragile face and broken spirit, and finally mustered up some sympathy.

She nodded solemnly. "He was well into his eighties, Ellie. It happens."

"Can I see him?"

Sheriff Daphne instinctively began shaking her head no, but she couldn't help but feel sorry for the pathetic, needy, wispy, distraught girl in front of her, so she sighed, relenting, and said, "You can come with me inside but just for a minute, and don't touch anything."

"I won't, I promise!" Ellie said, her voice cracking.

"Do you want me to come with you, Ellie?" Boyd asked, worried for her.

"No, Boyd, you better stay out here," she said quietly

with a half smile. "But I appreciate you rushing over here to be with me."

Boyd beamed, thrilled over the validation.

She liked him, she really liked him.

Sheriff Daphne took Ellie by the arm to lead her inside to see her grandfather when she noticed Hayley standing next to the front stoop.

She stopped abruptly.

"If I see your head poking around inside this house at any time, I swear I'll knock it off!" Sheriff Daphne warned, scowling.

And then she continued on inside with Ellie.

Mona walked over to Hayley. "I say we get the hell out of here before Sheriff Cruella De Vil finds another excuse to arrest us!"

Hayley nodded in agreement and they turned to go when Sue suddenly stumbled out of the house, her face wet with tears.

Hayley approached her. "Sue, I'm so sorry, I heard you were the one who discovered the body."

Sue choked back more tears as she nodded. "Rufus was at my bar every morning when I opened the doors and left every night when I closed them. Every single day, like clockwork, but not today. Shortly after you left earlier today, he said he wasn't feeling well and he went home. Later, I called to check up on him and got no answer. I didn't think much about it at first, I thought maybe he was taking a nap or something, but I must have tried three more times and he never picked up. I started to get worried so I just came over to check on him. He told me where he hides the spare key in case of an emergency. The TV was on in the living room and I found him in his kitchen, on the floor. At first I thought maybe he had just fainted, but then I kneeled down to touch him, and he was so cold, and that's when I knew . . ."

"The sheriff believes he died of natural causes," Hayley said.

Sue sniffed. "Of course she does! That will save her a boatload of paperwork."

"You think she's wrong?"

"No, I didn't say that, I mean, I'm realistic, I know Rufus was in his eighties. But I drove him around town all the time to his appointments and just last week he had a complete physical and the doctor told him he was in excellent health for a man his age."

"Just goes to show you never know," Mona said. "My older brother was a marathon runner, in tip-top shape, didn't drink or smoke, and he had a heart attack in the shower! It really hit close to home, and made me think I need to live my life differently."

"You mean take better care of yourself?"

"Hell no!" Mona yelled. "If my goody-two-shoes brother can follow all the rules and still have a heart attack, then I'm going to eat and drink as much as I want because all our days are numbered!"

"That's not necessarily the lesson I would take from your story, Mona," Hayley said. "But okay."

"I know Rufus drank like a fish, and that's never good, especially for someone as advanced in age as he was," Sue said.

"He was at your bar drinking every day of the week," Hayley said.

"The logical thing for me to do is accept what the sheriff says and be done with it, start planning the memorial service, but I can't. I want a thorough autopsy," Sue said.

"Do you have reason to believe he might have died from something else?" Hayley asked.

"I honestly don't know. The sheriff makes perfect sense. All the signs point to natural causes, but my gut is telling me there's something else going on here."

"What?" Mona asked.

"I can't quite put my finger on it. But Salmon Cove has had two deaths in the span of a week, and that doesn't necessarily raise a red flag, I mean, people die all the time, right? But unlike the sheriff, I'm not willing to let go of another possibility just yet."

Murder.

She was talking about murder.

"Sue, Jackson Young was strangled at the beach. When you found Rufus's body, did you happen to see if there were any marks on his neck?"

"No."

"What about signs of a break-in or struggle?"

"No, not that I could tell."

"So there were no obvious signs that Rufus could have been a victim of the same killer," Hayley said.

"No, like I said, it's just a feeling I have."

Hayley had the same feeling.

Two deaths in a small, quiet town that normally had an infinitesimal crime rate.

And then there was the matter of a mysterious disappearance.

They still couldn't find Liddy.

And they were not going to leave Salmon Cove without her.

Chapter 27

"What? Are you two out of your friggin' minds? No, no way, absolutely not! Count me out!" Mona roared as she slammed down her mug of beer on the bar at the Starfish Lounge, where she and Hayley had gone to re-group and figure out what to do next in their search for Liddy.

"But Mona, if Sue's hunch is right, and Rufus's death was not from natural causes, and if it is related to Jackson Young's murder and Liddy's disappearance, then the only way for us to find some possible answers is to search Rufus's house for clues that might help us determine if there was any foul play involved," Hayley implored.

"Hayley, have you forgotten that we are already facing serious breaking and entering charges not to mention tampering with a crime scene?" Mona asked, red-faced, in total disbelief that she would even suggest such a plan.

"But you heard Sheriff Wilkes say herself that she believes Rufus died from natural causes so there is no crime scene!" Hayley said.

"She's right," Sue said, refilling Mona's beer mug from the tap and setting it back down in front of her. "And Rufus has made me the executor of his estate so I have every right to let myself in with the key I know he keeps hidden and go through all his paperwork, and there is no law that says I can't bring a couple of friends along with me."

"This is crazy!" Mona cried.

"She can't arrest us again!"

"Come on, have you met the woman? She'll do whatever she has to in order to take me down and keep me away from Corey!" Mona said, shaking her head. "No, I'm sorry, I'm done playing Marg Hell-of-a-burger."

"Who?" Sue asked, a puzzled look on her face.

"You know, the crime scene investigator from that TV show, you're always watching the reruns, Hayley!"

"Marg Helgenberger!" Hayley said.

"Yeah, her!" Mona said, sipping the foam off the top of her beer mug. "I'm done doing that."

"Fine," Sue said. "You can stay here and watch the place while the two of us go!"

"If I stay, can I drink for free?"

"Yes, on the condition you serve any customers who happen to come in. Can you make a decent cocktail?"

"Does a bear—?"

"Thank you, Mona!" Hayley shouted, cutting her off. "We won't be long."

It was a short drive back to Rufus's house from the Starfish Lounge. When Hayley and Sue got there, the street was empty of people who had been hanging around earlier and the squad car that was parked in front of the house was long gone. The body had already been picked up and shipped off to the morgue and the house was locked up tight. Sue made a beeline for a flowerpot that sat on the right of the front stoop. She lifted it up and picked up a shiny silver key, which she used to unlock the front door. Hayley followed her inside.

There was a dank, musty smell throughout the whole house. Tiny dust balls blew across the floor like tumbleweeds and the whole place seemed to cry out for a thorough cleaning.

"Sue, I'm curious, why didn't Rufus make his granddaughter Ellie the executor of his estate?"

Sue shrugged. "Beats me. He did mention to me once he didn't want to expose her to all of his secrets. He wanted her to remember him as just her sweet loving granddaddy."

"What secrets was he talking about?"

"I asked him the same question, but he changed the subject. I figured I'd find out eventually once he died and so . . ."

"I guess we're about to find out."

In the living room, Hayley stopped to look at a wall full of hanging pictures. There was one of Ellie when she was just a girl, maybe ten years old, cute as a bug. She posed like a teen model. There was one of Rufus's son and Ellie's dad, who had died tragically in a plane crash. At the end she found a portrait of Rufus, maybe thirty years younger, with a beautiful, olive-skinned, dark-haired beauty.

"That's Rufus's late wife, Annabelle. A real looker, wasn't she?" Sue said, coming up behind Hayley.

"I'll say, she's gorgeous. Did you know her?"

"No, she died before Rufus moved up here to Maine. From what Ellie told me, her death nearly destroyed him. A part of him wished he would've died shortly thereafter so he wouldn't feel so lonely, but he hung on for another ten or so years . . . until today," she said, sniffing, fighting back her emotions.

"You should make sure Ellie gets that. It's a nice thing to have to remember her grandparents."

Sue reached up and lifted the framed picture off the nail that it was hung on, and was surprised to see a small, gaping hole in the wall.

Hayley stuck her hand through it, felt around, and then pulled it out. She knocked several times on the wall. "It's hollow. Might be some kind of storage space. What do you think is in there?"

Sue gave Hayley a conspiratorial look, and then marched into the kitchen, rummaged through some drawers, and returned with a hammer in her hand.

"What are you going to do with that?"

Without answering, Sue reared back with the hammer and pounded it hard against the wall near the hole, creating a wider space.

"Sue! You can't just tear the whole wall down!"

"I'm not! I'm just creating a wide enough space to see what's in there!"

"Letting ourselves in the house is one thing, but legally speaking, this might be a stretch!"

"As the executor of Rufus's estate, it is my responsibility to obtain all available information inside the house, wherever it may be, in order to properly execute his last will and testament."

"If the whole bar thing doesn't work out, you can always become a lawyer."

Sue kept pounding. It was a very thin wall and plaster and wallpaper fell away to the floor, creating a mess, until Sue managed to stick her entire head through the hole to see what was there. She then quickly pulled it out.

"It's too dark. I can't see anything. Hand me your phone," she said.

Hayley grabbed her phone from the pocket of her shorts, opened the flashlight app, and handed it over to Sue, who hacked off more of the wall with her hammer until she was able to wedge both her head and her hand with the phone through the opening.

"Oh my God!" Sue yelped.

"What? What do you see?" Hayley screamed, fearing it might be yet another dead body.

Sue extracted herself and then began madly smashing the wall with her hammer until almost half of it came crashing down, enough space for a whole person to actually fit through. She climbed inside. Hayley waited for a moment, but couldn't stand the suspense anymore, and followed her. She was immediately swatting away cobwebs and sneezing from the dust and plaster, but once she was able to open her eyes and look around, she gasped in surprise.

Sue was standing next to four garbage bags stuffed with money.

"Come on, let's count it!" Sue said, excited, as she picked up one of the bags and tore it open.

After ripping open all four bags as well as a stack of manila envelopes full of papers and legal documents, Sue spent the next twenty minutes greedily counting the cash while Hayley perused the mountain of papers they had found.

After dumping the last bag of bills onto the floor and sorting and counting them, Sue let out a whistle.

Hayley looked up from a binder full of past tax returns she was painstakingly inspecting. "How much?"

Sue swallowed hard and said, "Almost eight hundred thousand dollars."

"Eight hundred thousand?"

"That's a lot of whiskeys at my bar!"

"How did Rufus get his hands on so much money and what was it doing hidden behind this wall?"

"I don't know, but I sure as hell hope I'm not just the executor, but I'm actually listed in his will!"

"But from everything you told me, Rufus lived a very simple life. It wasn't like he was walking through town throwing money around all the time! Why not spend some of it?"

"Maybe he wanted to keep a really low profile."

"Because the money wasn't from his life savings but from ill-gotten gains?"

Sue laughed. "It's ridiculous! I mean, I knew the man well and never once did I ever get the impression he was some kind of criminal mastermind."

"That's because criminal masterminds work very hard to *not* give you that impression."

"I just don't believe it, Hayley," Sue said.

"Look, I've been going over his past tax returns, ones dating back to when his wife was still alive. Something stood out to me. Look at this one from 2005," she said, handing the return to Sue.

She gave it the once-over and looked up at Hayley. "So? Looks like a typical tax return to me."

"Look at the Social Security numbers."

Sue studied the numbers listed. "They're sequential."

"Exactly! Social Security numbers are assigned at birth and by region, which would mean Rufus and Annabelle would've had to have been born right next to each other in the same town, but if you look at the photo that was on the wall, Annabelle was at least ten years younger than him."

"So you're saying . . . ?"

"Rufus and Annabelle might not be their real names. They could have established fake identities with fake Social Security numbers," Hayley said.

"Then who are they?"

"Let's keep looking."

Sue grabbed a stack of manila folders off the pile and tore into them as Hayley continued examining the tax returns. Sue emptied out one folder on the floor. She picked up a piece of paper and studied it.

"What is that?"

"Looks like a prison visitation application Rufus filled out to see someone named Miles O'Shannon," Sue said, flipping the page.

"Prison? Let me see that," Hayley said, snatching the form from Sue. She read it over and then looked up. "Do you still have my phone?"

"Oh, yes, sorry," Sue said, picking it up off the floor and handing it to her.

Hayley did a quick Google search on Miles O'Shannon and when the results loaded the first face she saw was a strikingly handsome man with Cary Grant looks.

"I've seen that face before. It's Ellie's father. She showed me a photograph just the other day," Hayley said.

"Her name is not O'Shannon," Sue said. "And I thought she said her father died in a plane crash."

"That's what she told me, too. But according to this article in the *Boston Globe* he's still very much alive and serving a life sentence in prison for first-degree murder," Hayley said, skimming through the article on her phone.

"Do you think she just made up that story about her

father dying in a plane crash because she was embarrassed he had been put away for murdering someone?"

"Did you ever ask Rufus about his son?"

"I did once. He was drunk, and just said, 'Whatever Ellie told you is the truth, and that's all I have to say on the matter.' So I dropped it."

"The article says it was a mob hit, a restaurant owner who blew the whistle on a protection racket, and that Miles O'Shannon . . ." Hayley said, and then gasped.

"What?"

"Miles O'Shannon is the son of notorious Boston crime boss Enos O'Shannon, who has been on the FBI's Most Wanted List for over ten years."

Hayley hastily tapped the name Enos O'Shannon into the search engine, and several images popped up of a man bearing a disconcerting resemblance to Rufus.

"When did you say Rufus moved to Salmon Cove?"

"About ten years ago," Sue said, shocked. "After his wife died."

"The same time the Boston prosecutor brought racketeering charges against Enos O'Shannon. He was lucky enough to avoid a number of convictions over the years, mostly because key witnesses ended up disappearing or got rubbed out, but this particular case was stronger than anything they had on him before, and it looked like he was finally going to be put away for good. They issued a warrant for his arrest, but he blew town before they had a chance to arrest him," Hayley said, scrolling down farther.

"I just can't get my head around the fact that Rufus is a big-deal mob guy," Sue said. "I mean, it sounds so preposterous!"

"He's dyed his hair and put on some weight and may have even had a nose job, but it's definitely him!"

Hayley intensely kept loading article after article on her phone, stopping at one, and holding the phone closer to her face, squinting at a picture.

"What is it?" Sue asked, looking over her shoulder.

"The byline for this article has a picture of the reporter who wrote it, and it looks just like . . ."

She pressed a finger to the picture to enlarge the image and stared at a good-looking young man in a jacket and tie with glasses that made him look intellectual. He appeared slightly different, more professional, but there was no mistaking who it was. She turned the phone so Sue could see the picture.

"Hey, isn't that—?"

"Jackson Young! But that's not his real name. He's actually Conner Higgins, and according to this mini-bio next to his name he is a freelance investigative journalist. It's all starting to make sense!"

"Jackson, I mean Conner, came here because he got a tip where Enos O'Shannon might be hiding out?"

"Yes, posing as a travel writer, but when he got here, Rufus, or Enos, may have been tipped off about him, and killed him before he could expose him!"

"But Hayley, Rufus was an old codger, healthy, yes, but still really old. Do you honestly believe he could be strong enough to strangle a fit, able-bodied, thirty-seven-year-old man?"

"Not likely, but the evidence is overwhelming that Jackson Young or Conner Higgins was killed due to his investigation of Enos O'Shannon's whereabouts, and I'm afraid—"

Hayley's hands began to shake and she put down her phone.

Sue stepped forward and took her hands into her own, trying to get them to stop trembling.

"What is it?"

"I just have this awful feeling that Liddy's disappearance is also tied up in all of this, and since we now know that we're dealing with a murderous crime family that has wiped out witnesses in the past, then that could mean—"

It was too frightening to think about.

Chapter 28

"As much as it pains me to have to do this," Hayley said, "we have to take what we've found and call the police."

"Sheriff Wilkes?" Sue asked, incredulous.

"What other choice do we have? We have to alert some kind of authority figure, and she's the only one this town has at the moment."

Sue shrugged. "Okay, I'll call her and have her meet us over here."

Sue pulled her phone out of the back pocket of her pants and was about to punch in her security code when a thump startled them both.

Hayley and Sue looked at each other, and then a rattling sound caused both of them to jump.

Someone was trying to enter through the front door.

"Did you lock the door after we came in?" Hayley whispered.

Sue nodded.

The rattling became more violent.

Someone desperately wanted to get inside the house.

Hayley and Sue froze in place.

And then the rattling stopped.

They waited a few moments, standing still, staring at each other, both distressed.

There was a long silence.

"Do you think whoever it was is gone?" Hayley said in a hushed tone.

"Probably just a couple of kids fooling around . . ."

A window in the kitchen was smashed and glass spilled to the floor.

They heard the lock on the sill inside unlatch with a click and the sounds of a man huffing and puffing as he climbed through and inside the house.

"Ow! I just cut my finger on some broken glass!" a man's voice wailed.

Hayley had heard the voice before.

But she couldn't quite place it.

And who was he talking to?

Hayley and Sue flattened themselves on either side of the gaping hole, knowing it wouldn't take long for the intruders to notice it once they entered the living room.

Hayley poked her head around to peer through the hole, and in the hallway, she saw the back of a man crossing to the front door, unlocking it, and opening the door to let another person into the house.

He sucked on his finger and whined, "It really hurts!"

"Don't be such a baby!" a woman said as she swept inside.

It was Vanessa, the chatty, annoying tourist who had come to Salmon Cove with her husband and tried so desperately to make friends with Liddy.

"Did anybody see you waiting on the porch?" the man asked as he looked to make sure no one had seen them come inside the house, and then he shut and locked the door. When he turned around, it was unmistakably Vanessa's loyal and equally grating husband, Buck.

Except now they were not acting like the cheery, enthusiastic, happy couple enjoying their five-year road trip in an RV. They were serious, focused, methodical as they fanned out and searched the house. Hayley knew it was only a matter of seconds before one of them would come into the living room and see the bashed-out wall.

"Vanessa! Come look at this!"

They heard the shuffling of Vanessa's boat shoes as she hurried in from the kitchen.

"Someone obviously beat us here," Vanessa said.

"Unless the old man did it himself before he kicked it," Buck said.

"Go take a look and see what's in there!"

Hayley and Sue braced themselves.

They were about to be discovered.

"Why do *I* have to do it?"

"Because you know from our training exercises at Langley that I have a serious case of claustrophobia."

Buck sighed, but before he had a chance to walk over and climb through the hole and find them, a gross, hairy rat ran across Hayley's shoe and she yelped in surprise. It squeaked as she shook her foot, kicking at it, and then it disappeared into the blackness.

It was deathly quiet for a moment.

Hayley heard a clicking sound, like a gun cocking, which was followed by another.

"Who's there?" Vanessa demanded to know.

"Come out with your hands up!" Buck ordered.

Hayley and Sue eyeballed each other, waiting to see what the other one was going to do first.

"I'm not fooling around! Come out of there, nice and slow!"

Hayley sighed. She wasn't going to do anything stupid especially since Buck and Vanessa had come to Rufus's house armed, so with her hands in the air, she stepped back through the hole and into the living room, followed on her heels by Sue.

Buck and Vanessa gaped at them, both surprised.

"You're Hayley, right? Liddy's friend," Vanessa said, confused.

"Hayley Powell," Hayley said nervously, staring at the barrels of their guns that were pointing at her and Sue. "Nice to see you both again."

"What the hell are you doing here?"

"I'm here with Sue," Hayley said weakly.

Buck turned to Vanessa. "She's the owner of the Starfish Lounge."

"I know who she is, Buck! I want to know what these ladies are doing in his house!"

Sue stepped out from behind Hayley, making a snap decision to take the reins. "Hayley generously offered to help me go through Rufus's personal effects. I am the executor of his estate, and so I have the grave responsibility of producing all the necessary paperwork in order for the lawyer to effectively execute his will!"

"Is that your mess?" Vanessa asked, nodding to the large hole in the wall.

Sue nodded. "Yes, it is. We found some important personal items that Rufus stored back there."

"What kind of personal items?" Vanessa asked.

"None of your damn business!" Sue said. "We have every right to be here, but you two are guilty of breaking and entering!"

"She's right, we didn't exactly go by the book here," Buck said softly, cringing.

Vanessa reached into the side pocket of her baby blue

windbreaker jacket that she wore over a pink halter top
and pulled out an official-looking silver badge, which she
flashed at them. "We're FBI."

Hayley blurted out a nervous giggle. "You're what—?"

"How do we know for sure? You can buy a badge like
that at Toys 'R' Us!" Sue yelled.

Vanessa lowered her gun and marched up to Sue, and
held the badge close to her face. "Take a good look. Trust
me, it is real."

Hayley eyed the pistol Buck still had trained on them.
"Could you please stop pointing that gun at me? We
won't try to run, I promise."

Buck had almost forgotten he was holding it, and then
flipped the safety lock and stuffed it in the back of his
khaki shorts.

"We told you what we're doing here. So why don't you
tell us what *you* are doing here?" Sue said, eyes fixed on
Vanessa.

"I'm Agent Stiles, this is my partner Agent Goodman,"
she said.

"Husband," Hayley said.

"No, partner, as in work colleague, we're not married,"
Vanessa corrected her.

"You sure bicker like a married couple," Hayley said.

"Hell, we're even in couples therapy twice a week,"
Buck added.

Vanessa shot him an irritated look and then continued.

"We were sent here to look into the death of an investigative journalist—"

"Jackson Young . . . ?" Hayley offered.

"Yes," Vanessa reacted, taken aback. "But his real
name is—"

"Conner Higgins," Hayley said.

Vanessa nodded, impressed. "When Higgins was found

murdered here, the agency began to suspect it might be related to a story he had been working on, one we were well aware of."

"Enos O'Shannon," Hayley said.

"Yes, that's right," Vanessa said. "Are you sure *you* are not working for the FBI?"

"Oh, no, that's silly!" Hayley laughed. "I'm just a newspaper columnist, but not the kind you think, I don't write the sort of pieces Jackson, I mean Conner, did, you know, about criminals and corruption, mine are about food because I love to cook, and I love to eat, but I'd be lying, however, if I said I didn't have a somewhat morbid interest in crime, you see my brother-in-law is the chief of police in Bar Harbor, and sometimes I find myself getting involved in one of his investigations, which by the way annoys him to no end—"

"Excuse me, is this going to last much longer? I feel like I'm listening to the audio version of your autobiography," Vanessa said, exasperated.

"I'm sorry, it's just that you two are carrying guns, and I hate guns, they make me very nervous, and when I'm nervous I can't stop talking—"

"Sorry, I'll put it away," Vanessa said, following Buck's example and flipping the safety lock and stuffing it in the back of her white shorts. "Anyway, we were sent here to find out why Higgins was killed, and if it was related to Enos O'Shannon, who the FBI has been trying to catch for decades."

"I think you may have finally found him," Sue said.

"We do too. Once we saw Rufus at your bar, he was on our radar, and we were surveilling him until we could confirm his identity, but then he up and died on us so we came here to his house hoping to finally find the proof that O'Shannon and Rufus were one and the same."

"Did Rufus know the FBI was onto him?" Hayley asked.

"I don't think so, why?"

"Because if he thought the feds were closing in, he might have taken his own life. He told me at the bar that he would never serve a day behind bars for anything because he was too old, too set in his ways, and he was never going to allow that to happen. I thought it was kind of odd at the time, but now it all makes sense."

"We have no reason to suspect he did commit suicide. O'Shannon is as slippery as an eel, if he had an inkling we were on this trail, he would have disappeared from Salmon Cove never to be seen or heard from again."

"What about his granddaughter Ellie?" Hayley asked.

"We don't believe at this time that she is even aware of her grandfather's real identity. She was just a young girl when he brought her here after her father was convicted and sentenced to life in prison," Buck said.

"So tell me, Agent Powell," Vanessa said with a healthy dose of sarcasm. "Is the proof we are looking for behind that wall?"

"Yes," Hayley said.

"Is anything else back there that we should know about?" Vanessa asked, a hint of suspicion in her voice.

Hayley and Sue flashed knowing glances at each other, not sure they were ready to give up all that money. Sue tried to signal Hayley to keep her mouth shut, but Hayley knew it was a lost cause. The government would reclaim it eventually.

"There's some money . . ." Hayley said.

"How much money?" Vanessa asked.

"About eight hundred thousand dollars," Sue said, regretful that she didn't have a chance to remove the money and hide it somewhere safe out of the FBI's reach before they got caught.

"Give or take," Hayley added.

Buck and Vanessa gawked at them, their jaws nearly dropping to the floor.

Chapter 29

Vanessa and Buck, or Agents Stiles and Goodman, and the higher-ups at the FBI insisted on keeping the Enos O'Shannon story under wraps at least until they had a chance to complete their investigation. If the press got wind of the story of one of the FBI's Most Wanted hiding for years in plain sight in a small Maine coastal town, Salmon Cove would be inundated with trucks and reporters from all the major news outlets and become the focus of intense worldwide attention.

Although Vanessa played her cards close to the vest, Buck was the more inexperienced agent, and thus a little more free-wheeling and chatty, and before Vanessa could shut him down, he revealed to Hayley and Sue that the working theory they were going to present to their bosses was plain and simple. Rufus aka Enos O'Shannon strangled Jackson Young aka Conner Higgins when the investigative journalist came too close to ferreting him out and exposing his secret life in Salmon Cove in an article.

This didn't make sense to Sue and she let them know it.

"I'm happy to hear your opinion, but you ladies can stand down now, we're on it," Vanessa said through clenched teeth, annoyed at having to deal with a pair of know-it-all amateur sleuths.

"But Rufus was never at the clambake. He spent the entire day drinking at my bar," Sue insisted.

"You were with him the whole time?" Vanessa asked.

"Well, no, I spent a little time down at the clambake . . ."

Arguing with the murder victim, but Hayley knew Sue wouldn't admit to that in order to save herself heaps of grief.

"But he was there when I left and he was there when I came back," Sue said.

"How do you know he didn't slip out after you were gone, kill Conner Higgins at the beach, and then hurry back to the bar before you returned?"

"Because it's impossible," Sue said, eyeing Hayley, knowing she was going to have to tell the entire truth.

"Why?"

Sue sighed. She knew the jig was up. "Because I went to see Jackson Young, I mean Conner whatever, myself. I was angry because he kept asking me a ton of personal questions, now I know why. He was really a reporter, and we had it out on the beach, but I swear on my life, when I left him he was still alive. And that's why I know it couldn't have been Rufus who killed him. When I got back to the bar Rufus was sitting on his same stool, drinking his same whiskey, telling his same stories. There was no way he could have strangled that reporter and beat me back to the bar. It's humanly impossible!"

Vanessa sized up Sue. "We'll take your story under advisement."

"It's not a story! It's the truth!" Sue said.

Vanessa turned and signaled Buck.

It was time to go.

"Wait!" Hayley yelled, rushing forward. "My friend Liddy, she's missing and I'm extremely worried!"

"What do you mean missing?"

"She was on her way to a lawyer's office in town yesterday, and she told us to meet her for dinner a couple hours later, but she never came and when we contacted the lawyer, he said she never showed up to their scheduled meeting."

"Did you contact the sheriff?"

"Yes, but she's not taking me seriously, and I believe her disappearance may be somehow related to the Enos O'Shannon case."

"In what way?" Vanessa asked, skeptical.

"I—I—well, I'm not really sure," Hayley stammered. "But Liddy got quite friendly with Jackson Young before he was killed, and it just seems like too much of a coincidence that all of this would be happening and then she just disappears without a trace—"

"Look, I'm sorry to cut you off, but this unfortunately is not our jurisdiction. I suggest you go back to the sheriff if she doesn't turn up soon. She can bring us in if it turns out to be a kidnapping or anything like that. Now, if you will excuse us, ladies, we have a lot of work to do."

Buck walked over and opened the door for them.

Sue glanced at the hole in the wall and looked at Hayley. She obviously didn't like the idea of leaving these two FBI agents alone in the house with all that money.

As Sue followed Hayley past Buck and out the door, she stopped and whispered in his ear, "If I read that there was less than eight hundred gees found at this house, then I'll know you skimmed some for yourself, and you can be sure I'll make the biggest stink the FBI has ever seen!"

Buck shook his head and slammed the door behind them.

Outside, Hayley's mind raced.

She couldn't just wait and do nothing.

She had to somehow find Liddy.

Sue, reading Hayley's worried face, put a comforting hand on her shoulder. "Don't worry. We'll find her. I'm going to head back to my bar now and relieve your friend Mona. She's been covering for me almost two hours. Can I drop you somewhere?"

"The sheriff's office," Hayley said, determined. "She can't ignore me forever."

They jumped into Sue's car and drove the few blocks to the police station. Hayley told Sue to give Mona the message to call Corey and have him drive her back to the cabin just in case Liddy had somehow magically returned and was looking for them. She would grab a cab and meet Mona back there when she was finished with the sheriff.

When Hayley walked into the station, receptionist Billy was preoccupied pounding his fist against the glass of a snack vending machine that had just eaten his coins. He didn't notice her so she seized the opportunity to slip past him and down the hall to Sheriff Daphne's office.

She found the sheriff talking on the phone.

"Yes, sir, I understand. This is a very delicate situation. There will not be any leaks coming from the local police, you can be sure of that!"

She noticed Hayley standing in the doorway, and she grimaced.

"Yes, sir, good-bye, sir," she said into the phone before hanging up. She stared at Hayley, trying to stay calm. "That was the mayor. He was bringing me up to speed on everything. Apparently, he was just contacted by the director of the FBI. Can you believe that? Our little small-town mayor on the phone with the head cheese of the FBI!"

"Sounds like a very big deal," Hayley said.

"It is! Nothing this exciting has ever happened in Salmon Cove. It seems we have a big-city mobster right out of *Goodfellas* hiding out in our midst!"

"You don't say," Hayley said, stone-faced.

"Yes, it turns out Rufus, the town drunk, is really Enos O'Shannon, who has been on the run from the feds for ten years to escape racketeering and murder charges. Who would have guessed little old soused Rufus would be on the FBI's Most Wanted List?"

"Sounds crazy," Hayley said, playing along.

"But you already know all this, don't you?"

Hayley's whole body tensed.

"According to the mayor, who was told directly by the director of the FBI, you were found by two of his field agents at Rufus's house with all the evidence not to mention four bags stuffed with cash."

Hayley knew she had to defend herself. "I didn't break in because I was with Sue, who is the executor of Rufus's estate and—"

"I don't care!" Daphne blurted out, interrupting her. "Do you hear me? I don't care! If I wanted to, I could arrest you all over again! You are a menace to this town, and you just won't leave anything alone, and I am damn sick of it! I am sick of you disrupting things! This is my town and I will not put up with this anymore!"

"This isn't your town! You don't own it or its people! You are here to protect and serve not bully and intimidate! Go ahead! Arrest me again! Show everybody how strong you are, how in control you are, how you rule this town with an iron fist! Who are you trying to impress? If it's Corey Guildford, trust me, this isn't the way to go about it!"

Daphne sat back in her chair, stunned.

She hadn't expected Hayley to come back at her so aggressively.

And she certainly didn't expect her to utter the name Corey Guildford.

"I know all about your unrequited love for Corey, and I honestly might think it was cute if you weren't so consumed with jealousy! How dare you abuse your power as the sworn-in sheriff of Salmon Cove to scare us out of town just so the object of your affection would be out of reach for my friend Mona! Well, for your information, Mona is married and totally loyal to her family, and so even if she did harbor feelings for Corey, and we both know he certainly harbors feelings for her, she poses no threat to you!"

Daphne stood up, eyes blazing with anger, staring Hayley down.

"You can flash your badge all you want, write as many tickets as you can, or toss me and my friends back in jail, but that's never going to make Corey love you!"

Hayley braced herself.

Daphne stood stoic for a few moments, but then her lip began to quiver.

No one had probably confronted her head-on like this ever before.

And Hayley half expected her to lunge across her desk and wrap her big strong hands around her throat and squeeze the life out of her.

But she didn't.

She just stood there, fighting back her emotions.

"Please, Sheriff Wilkes, I'm desperate. I know something bad has happened to my friend and I need your help!"

Daphne sat back down, plucked a tissue out of a box, and wiped her eyes before balling it up and tossing it in the trash can next to the desk. And then, finally, she looked up at Hayley and said, mustering as much professionalism as possible, "Tell me again when you last saw her."

Island Food & Spirits
by
Hayley Powell

The first summer after my divorce I decided it might be a good idea to take the kids on a weekend getaway. It had been a particularly rough and busy couple of months for all of us dealing with life without a husband and father in the house, and I wanted to make sure the kids were adjusting well with all the big, monumental changes so I planned a mini vacation of hiking and swimming in Southern Maine near the coastal town of Kennebunkport. I found a quaint little hotel with a swimming pool on the outskirts of town. The kids were ecstatic. We had barely walked into our room before they were changed into their bathing suits and racing for a dip in the pool. I was happy to be left on my own to stretch out on the bed and dive into the new Lisa Jackson novel I was dying to read before dinner.

Later that evening, as we walked the short distance to a local favorite seafood restaurant the desk clerk had told us about, Gemma was still chattering on and on about the impossibly cute boy her age she had met at the pool that afternoon. Dustin hung back, rolling his eyes, speaking volumes with his facial expressions. He was not as impressed.

After the hostess seated us and Gemma was still talking about "Hot Sean," I knew I was going to need a stiff cocktail. One stood out on the menu, a delectable-sounding chilled rum and orange juice cocktail called Mountain Sunset. It was a done deal. We ordered a round of Lobster-Stuffed Mushrooms for our appetizer, and Dustin and I devoured the whole plate because Gemma was too busy talking to put anything in her mouth. When she noticed the empty plate, she insisted we order another round, which we did in addition to another Mountain Sunset Cocktail for Mother, because I knew in my gut we were in for a long, chatty night.

By the time our entrees arrived, Gemma dropped the bomb that "Hot Sean" had invited us all to go boating with him and his father the following day.

I noticed Dustin shaking his head vigorously from side to side, making clear his wishes, and counting on me to put a stop to this crazy idea right now. He knew I had been making a concerted effort to keep him happy during this difficult time of upheaval, and was not above using that to get what he wanted.

"Gemma, I'm sure your new friend meant well, but his father probably won't appreciate him inviting total strangers on a boating trip," I said.

She was ready for that one.

"No, his father was there when he invited us! He encouraged the whole thing! And FYI, mother, Sean's dad is a total hunk! Plus, he's recently divorced, just like you!"

The last thing I needed in my life at that point was a fix-up. But Gemma was so excited, and Dustin needed to learn a lesson about not always getting his own way, so after one more sip of my Mountain Sunset Cocktail, I sighed and said, "Okay, let's do it."

Dustin was apoplectic. He had visions of hanging by the pool the whole weekend and playing video games on his phone. This was not part of the plan! But I had visions too. Baking in the sun with lots of wine and cheese on board a beautiful yacht sailing around the harbor off Kennebunkport. You certainly couldn't beat that!

Gemma gave me the cell number of Sean's father, Dave, after we returned to the room, and I called him to confirm the details. He sounded very pleasant, with a deep, masculine voice, which I hate to admit, sent shivers up my spine. Dave gave me an address for our GPS and told us to be there at eight in the morning. After I hung up, I kept picturing my TV crush Mark Harmon on the other end of the phone and I melted.

No! Stop it, Hayley! I said to myself. The last thing I needed or wanted in my life was a relationship with a man because now was the time to focus on the kids and myself.

The following day, as I punched the address into our car's GPS, I was a little surprised to see we would be heading north away from the coast. But I didn't question it. We ended up driving forty-five minutes until we pulled up to the side of the Kennebec River. Suddenly my stomach started to churn as I realized what was happening. We weren't going sailing along the coast in a yacht. We were going white-water rafting!

Dustin glanced out the window, and as it hit him what we were about to do, he yelled, "Mom! Put the car in reverse! Let's get the H out of here!"

Gemma whipped her head around in the passenger seat and hissed, "You better behave today!"

And then she jumped out of the car, all smiles, and waved as Sean bounded up to greet us. A short distance behind him was Dave, who was a far cry from Mark Harmon. He was actually *more* handsome! In fact, he took my breath away, like that old '80s song from the cute shaggy-haired crooner Rex Smith!

Both father and son were tanned, had toothy white smiles, and were dressed exactly alike in crewneck T-shirts, cargo shorts, and boat shoes.

After the introductions, Dave led us down to the river where our raft awaited. I led Dustin by the arm, squeezing it tight to make sure he didn't make a run for it. Dave helped us on with our life vests, and as he smiled at me, and strapped me into my vest, my heart was racing and I thought to myself, *How bad could this be?*

Well, as it turns out, bad. Really bad.

In fact, it was a horror show! We had barely set off from the river's edge before we found ourselves being knocked around, tossed up in the air, drenched in water as the raft crested over the raging white-water rapids. Gemma, who had been holding hands with "Hot Sean," bolted away from him and scrambled over to hug me tightly. We were both terrified as we screamed at the top of our lungs, praying to make it out of this whole ordeal alive!

Dave, who looked exhilarated, sat in the back of the raft with a paddle in one hand and fist-pumping the air with the other, loving every minute of it.

He shouted to us, "This trip is well known for its eleven rapids that are classified as IV and V rapids! Isn't it awesome? What a rush!"

I hated him.

He was no Mark Harmon.

Mark Harmon would have known I was not enjoying this, and found some way to get me and my kids off this hair-raising hell ride!

Gemma felt the same about "Hot Sean" as he was a carbon copy of his dad, waving the paddle and fist-pumping, laughing and whooping as we careened down the rapids.

Then I had a horrible thought.

Dustin.

What happened to Dustin?

Had he fallen overboard?

I looked around and saw him holding on to the ropes on the side of the boat completely soaked, screaming and shouting with joy, having the time of his life as the waves completely washed over him, the video games awaiting him on his phone the furthest thing from his mind!

After thirty more of the scariest minutes of my life, the rafting nightmare came to a merciful end. As did Gemma's budding romance with "Hot Sean." We were both sore, soaked, and shivering and threw ourselves on the ground, thankful to finally be on dry land.

Dustin, on the other hand, was jumping up and down, begging Dave to let us do it again. I politely declined with a tight smile on my face. Gemma waved good-bye to "Hot Sean" without even a quick peck on the cheek, and I could tell from the disappointed look on his face that he knew his short-lived weekend romance was definitely over.

We hightailed it out of there and back to the hotel while Gemma lamented that she should probably give her eighth-grade suitor

Stewie another chance because he had brains, and was captain of the Chess Club, and wanted to do whatever *she* wanted to do. Gemma was officially over her jock phase.

Dustin was disappointed we wouldn't be going back out on the rapids that weekend, so we tried to make up for it with some more Lobster Stuffed Mushrooms at our favorite nearby eatery, which I have to admit I chased down with a couple of Mountain Sunset Cocktails in order to recover from my recent near-death experience.

Mountain Sunset Cocktail

Ingredients
12 ounces orange juice
3 ounces light rum
2 tablespoons grenadine
Lime slice for garnishing (optional)

Combine your orange juice and rum. Set aside 1/3 of the mixture and pour the rest into two glasses.

Add the grenadine to the saved orange juice and rum mixture, then slowly pour into your glasses, letting it settle to the bottom.

Hopefully, it will look like a sunset, but not to worry if it doesn't because it tastes delicious either way!

Lobster Stuffed Mushrooms

<u>Ingredients</u>
2 shallots, thinly sliced
2 lobster tails, cooked and chopped into
    small pieces
3 ounces cream cheese, room temperature
8 ounces mushrooms, stems removed
    (chop up the stems and set aside)
⅓ cup gouda cheese, shredded
2 tablespoons chives, diced

In a skillet heat the two tablespoons olive oil over medium heat. Add your shallots and sauté until caramelized.

Add the chopped lobster meat, cream cheese, chopped mushroom stems, and Old Bay seasoning, and turn the heat to medium low. Stir until all the cheese is melted and everything is combined.

Place your mushrooms on a baking sheet open side up and spoon your cheese mixture into the mushroom.

Sprinkle your gouda over the tops of the mushrooms.

Heat your oven broiler to high heat, then put your mushrooms in the oven and broil until cheese is melted hot and bubbly. Remove from oven and garnish with the chives and serve and get ready for a lobster inspired treat!

Chapter 30

After leaving the police station, Hayley called Mona, who was back at the cabin waiting for her. Mona confirmed that Liddy still had not returned, which just fueled Hayley's growing sense of dread.

She quickly filled in Mona on what she and Sue had found at Rufus's house.

There was silence on the other end of the phone when she finished.

"Mona? Are you still there?"

"I'm here," she said, exhaling. "Man, oh man! That is one whopper of a story! And I always thought growing up that Salmon Cove was the most boring place on earth!"

"I know, I'm still trying to process it all! But the good news is, Sheriff Wilkes is finally taking Liddy's disappearance seriously, and she is calling in some state troopers to help find her. We also have a couple of FBI agents in town who might also lend a hand."

"I'm scared, Hayley," Mona said, her voice cracking.

It was rare for Mona to show much emotion other than anger or annoyance. And it was unheard of for her to show fear. But despite her protestations to the contrary, she cared deeply for Liddy. They had been bickering and insulting each other ever since they became friends in the second grade, and that's quite a long history.

"I know, Mona, me too," Hayley said solemnly.

"Where are you now?"

"I'm in town. Liddy's Mercedes is still parked where she left it, and wherever she is, she has the keys with her. I'm going to call a cab to take me back to the cabin."

"Okay, but hurry back. I'm climbing the walls here all alone!"

"I'll be there as fast as I can. In the meantime, why don't you call Corey and see if he'll come over with his truck? We're not going to want to sit around the rest of the day just waiting. I think we should go out again and keep looking."

"I'll call him right now," Mona said, hanging up.

Hayley knew there was just one cab driver in town because he was usually hanging outside the Starfish Lounge around closing time to drive any inebriated patrons who might stagger out of the bar safely to their homes. She looked up his number on her phone, and then called him.

"Ryan's Taxi, this is Ryan," a man said, distracted.

"Yes, I need a pickup in downtown Salmon Cove."

"Sorry, I've got an airport run to Bangor. I won't be back until late this afternoon," he said.

"Okay, thank you."

She ended the call, sighed, and then pressed Mona's number again.

"Hi, what's up?" Mona said.

"I can't get a taxi. Do you think Corey would mind swinging into town and picking me up on his way out to the cabin?"

"I haven't been able to reach him. I got his voice mail and just left a message," Mona said.

"Well, I guess I'm going to just have to walk," Hayley groaned.

"But it's something like three miles! It'll take you over an hour!"

"Well, I'm always saying how I need to exercise more. Here is my chance," Hayley said, shuffling off down the road that led out of town. "See you when I get there."

It was midday, the sun was blazing, and Hayley wasn't wearing a hat. She felt the intense heat against her cheeks, and worried she would suffer from a case of sunburn, but she trudged along, picking up her pace. Drops of sweat formed above her brow and she wiped them away with her hand. She forgot to pick up a bottle of water at the general store to keep hydrated, which was dumb. But she was determined to get back to the cabin. There was no way she was going to turn back now. She could replenish her fluids when she got there.

A couple of cars sped by, and Hayley thought about sticking her thumb out and hitching a ride, but she decided against it. If she kept pushing and making good time, she just might power walk her way back to the cabin in an hour flat.

She heard another vehicle approaching from behind. She glanced back to see a pickup truck speeding along the road toward her. At first she thought it might be Corey, and felt relief that Mona had finally gotten through to him, but as the truck got closer, she noticed it was red. Corey's truck was white. It slowed down as it pulled up next to Hayley.

Boyd sat behind the wheel. He was in a white tank top scuffed with dirt marks and wore a Boston Red Sox baseball cap on his head. He lowered his cheap sunglasses to the bridge of his nose. "What are you doing all the way out here?"

"Just walking back to the cabin where we're staying," Hayley said.

"Walking? But it's so dang hot! I mean, it's so hot out, the chickens at my daddy's farm are laying hard-boiled eggs!"

He laughed heartily at his own joke.

Hayley forced a smile, and said, "Good one."

"Why don't you hop in and I'll give you a ride the rest of the way?"

Hayley thought about it for a moment. Her feet were tired and she was sweaty and uncomfortable, but her gut told her to say no.

She should just stick to her original plan.

"That's awfully kind of you, Boyd, but I'll be fine."

"Are you crazy? I'm offering you a free ride! My truck has air conditioning!"

"I know, but I'm almost there and the walk will do me good," she said politely.

"You're not almost there. I know where the cabin is. You're still about two miles out."

"Thank you, Boyd, but I'm good."

She started walking.

At this point, she just wanted to get away from him.

He pulled his truck forward and drove alongside her.

"You're not fooling me, you know," he said.

He was no longer smiling. He looked grim, suspicious, and wary.

"I'm not sure what you mean, Boyd," Hayley said, still walking.

"Yes, you do. You're one of them, aren't you?"

"One of what?"

"*Them!*"

He was talking about the aliens he was reading about in his comic books, the ones he was so immersed in during his breaks at the Starfish Lounge. At first she thought it was harmless, but then when he kept suspecting actual real people like Liddy of being among their ranks, she was slightly disturbed. But now, on the side of the road, all alone with him and his wild machinations, suddenly she felt a sharp sense of danger.

"Boyd, you're not making any sense!"

"It makes perfect sense! You and your friends show up here in town, strangers I've never seen before, scouting the area, taking notes on our habits and behavior, reporting back to the mother ship!"

Hayley had heard enough. "Get real, Boyd! If we were aliens planning an invasion, why would we bother coming here of all places? Why wouldn't we go to Washington, DC, and take over the White House?"

"Because you want to start with the small communities and spread out from there so by the time you do reach the power centers, you're too big to stop!"

Damn, the kid had it all figured out.

But she wasn't going to indulge him any longer.

"Leave me alone, Boyd."

She started walking again, eyes straight ahead, hoping another car might come along at any moment that she could flag down to get her the hell out of here.

Boyd pulled his truck up next to her again.

"I won't let you do it! I'm going to do whatever it takes to stop you!"

She refused to look at him.

She just kept walking.

And he kept driving alongside her.

"Please, don't make me do this," Boyd said, in a grave tone.

That's when she heard a click, like a gun cocking.

Hayley whipped her head around to see Boyd leveling a shotgun at her out of the driver's-side window.

She instinctively threw her hands up. "Boyd, no! Please, don't shoot!"

"Then get in the truck."

Hayley did as she was told.

At this point, she just wanted to stay alive.

Chapter 31

Boyd kept his shotgun resting in his lap, the barrel pointing right at Hayley, as he drove his truck several miles out of town, pulling off the main road onto a dirt path that led through the woods. It was a bumpy ride, and the shotgun kept rattling up and down, and Hayley feared it might accidentally discharge and blow her head off!

Boyd gripped the steering wheel with one hand, his fingers wrapped around it so tight his knuckles were white. His other hand was around the shotgun, his finger gently resting on the trigger.

They pulled up in front of a dilapidated, rickety old farm house. The paint on the walls was peeling, a couple of windows were cracked, part of the roof was missing and covered with a blue tarp, there was some rusty farm equipment in the yard that was overgrown with weeds.

Boyd jammed the truck into park and then lifted the gun, edging it closer to Hayley, who leaned back as far away as she could from the end of the barrel that lightly touched her nose.

"Don't you dare try anything! I don't want to have to

shoot you, and get your slimy green alien blood all over my upholstery!"

"Boyd, how many times do I have to tell you, I am not an alien—!"

"You're lying! I know the truth! I know everything! Now get out!"

Hayley hesitated, not wanting to find out what he was going to do with her, but left with no choice, she carefully reached over and opened the passenger's-side door. She slowly slid out and stepped down to the ground, clasping her hands behind the back of her head.

Boyd hustled out the driver's side, keeping his eyes fixed on her, and his gun raised. He motioned for her to turn and walk toward the house. Hayley did what she was told. He ordered her to stay right and walk over to some metal sloping outside cellar doors. A crowbar had been wedged between the handles to keep anything, or anyone, from getting out.

Hayley turned back to face Boyd.

"What's down there?"

"The other one," Boyd said.

"The other what?"

"Alien! Like you! I captured it! I'm going to do whatever it takes to keep you monsters from destroying us! I'm going to save the world!"

Hayley gasped.

Was he talking about Liddy?

Boyd raised his gun, jabbing it toward Hayley, who flinched. "Now get down there! Now!"

Hayley knelt down and removed the crowbar, and then opened one of the cellar doors. She walked down the wobbly wooden steps. She shivered as she reached the bottom of the dark, damp, and moldy basement. She stopped for a moment to try to adjust her eyes to the dimness, but Boyd poked her in the back with the barrel of his gun, prodding her to keep going. Once they reached the other end of the cellar, Hayley could see something balled up in the corner. She squinted to get a closer look. Somebody was sitting on the ground, back against the cement wall, knees up with arms hugging them, head down.

"Liddy, is that you?"

The head suddenly popped up, and Liddy, her face smudged with dirt, her curly black hair sticking out in all directions, eyes wide with hopeful relief, choked back tears.

"Hayley?"

She sprang to her feet, arms out, and ran to hug Hayley.

"Stay where you are, alien queen!"

Liddy stopped short and sighed. "He's a crazy loon, Hayley! He thinks he's living the sequel to *Independence Day*, and we all know what a sucky movie that was!"

"Just stay calm, Liddy, we'll be all right," Hayley said softly.

"You two lizards will remain my prisoners until I can gather an army of rebels to fight back and foil your diabolical plot to colonize Earth!" Boyd spit out.

"Lizards? Do we look like lizards?" Hayley asked, insulted.

"He thinks we're wearing human suits," Liddy said, shaking her head. "Oh, he's a real character, let me tell you."

Boyd walked over to Hayley, a menacing look on his face, and he held out his free hand, while holding his shotgun in the other, pressing the barrel against Hayley's rib cage. "Give me your phone. I don't want you down here sending a signal to the mother ship with your location!"

Hayley sighed, reached into her back pocket, and pulled out her phone. She held it out, but dropped it before Boyd could grab it. He instantly had his finger back on the trigger of his gun.

"You did that on purpose! Pick it up!"

Hayley slowly, deliberately bent down to get her phone. She felt around in the dark for it briefly and then found it. When she touched the screen, the light came on, momentarily blinding Boyd, who covered his eyes, giving her the chance to speed-dial Mona. She quickly pressed a button on the side to make the light go out.

"Hurry up!" Boyd yelled.

Hayley handed him the phone, which he stuck in his shirt pocket, and then he backed away, shotgun still trained on them, until he reached the wooden steps.

He turned around and headed back up and outside where he shut the cellar door and slid the crowbar back between the handles to lock them inside.

Liddy hugged Hayley, sobbing. "I can't believe all of this is happening! What are we going to do? That boy is clearly out of his mind!"

"We need to remain calm, okay? Tell me how you got here!"

"It all happened so fast! One minute I had parked my car and was walking down the street toward Oliver Hammersmith's office for our meeting, and then the next thing I knew, someone was throwing a potato sack over my head and dragging me away. I tried to fight back, but he was too big and too strong and he must have punched me in the head or something because everything suddenly went dark, and when I came to, I was down here!"

Hayley looked around for some means of escape like a small window or another set of stairs that led up to the main house.

"I've already searched everywhere for a way out, Hayley, there is none," Liddy said, resigned.

"I just hope I was able to get a call through to Mona before he took my phone."

"He took mine, too! When I woke up down here, I was on the floor and he was on his knees next to me, his hands in my pants! I expected the worst, if you know what I mean, but he just wanted my phone! He said he wanted to make sure I didn't take any more pictures!"

"Why would he care about that?"

"He thought I was photographing locals here in Salmon Cove and sending the images up to the mother ship so they could identify them and then abduct them to use for our probing and harvesting experiments! I'm telling you, that guy could win a gold medal for being a grade-A screwball!"

"When did he see you taking pictures?"

"At the bar, the night that drunken fisherman got too rowdy and Sue called the police, and we were all herded out on the street, and there was a ticket on my car, remember?"

"Yes, you wanted to record photographic evidence that your tires were close enough to the curb to prove the ticket had no merit!"

"Boyd was definitely at the scene, saw me snapping pictures, and let his imagination run wild. I definitely got a lot of the patrons who were milling around outside the bar in the background of some of my shots."

"Rufus was also there that night," Hayley said, her mind racing.

"The town drunk? Yes, I think he was. So?"

"So we've discovered a lot more about him since I last saw you," Hayley said. "His name isn't even Rufus, it's Enos O'Shannon, a crime boss from Boston who has been on the run for ten years, wanted for racketeering and murder."

"Murder?" Liddy gasped. "Wait, do you think he may have had something to do with Jackson's violent death on the beach?"

"Possibly, because Jackson was lying about his true identity, too. His real name was Conner Higgins, and he was an investigative journalist trying to locate O'Shannon."

"Investigative journalist? So he was actually here on a top-secret, high-stakes reporting assignment and that's why he had to break our date? Oh, I can't tell you how relieved I am!"

"Liddy, your love life is not really an urgent priority at this moment, if you don't mind."

"Fine, okay, I get it. It all makes sense now. This O'Shannon guy strangled Jackson, or whatever his name is, because he was onto him."

"But O'Shannon is eighty-something years old and Higgins was a robust young man fully capable of taking care of himself. So maybe he talked someone else into doing it for him."

"Somebody like Nutcase McCrazy up there!" Liddy gasped. "Of course! The old man saw him reading his comic books in the bar every night! He must have known he was a simpleton who could be easily manipulated, so not only did he convince him Jackson was part of the alien plot, but us as well."

"Rufus was clearly seen in the photos you took that night, and he couldn't let those get out, especially in a courtroom where you were defending a traffic ticket! He couldn't risk anyone recognizing him!"

"So he had Boyd break into our cabin and try to find my phone, and when that failed, he snatched me off the street because he knew I must have had it on me!"

"Someone's done a real number on Boyd's head convincing him that you are an alien queen, but now his paranoid mind has run amok and he thinks we're all aliens! Including me, which is why he drove me here at gunpoint!"

"O'Shannon probably didn't plan that part! That's what you get when you collude with an insane person!"

"There's just one problem!"

"What?"

"O'Shannon is dead."

"Dead? He *died*? Just how long have I been down here?"

"His body was found in his home."

"How?"

"We're not sure yet. The sheriff believes he died from natural causes, but I'm not willing to rule anything out yet, and I believe someone else is still pulling the strings from behind the scenes, and it certainly isn't O'Shannon."

"Then who?"

Suddenly they heard the crowbar scrape across the metal as someone removed it, and then the cellar doors flew open, bathing the musty, dark basement in light as footsteps descended the creaky steps. Liddy clutched Hayley's arm as Boyd marched forward, scowling. Behind him was Rufus's sweet, innocent, waiflike granddaughter Ellie.

Only now she didn't look so innocent.

She had a sick, twisted smile on her face.

And she held a gun in her hand.

Chapter 32

"I figured Boyd wasn't smart enough to do all this by himself so there had to be some kind of mastermind behind the scenes," Hayley said, eyeing Ellie warily as she slipped out from behind Boyd to take center stage.

Boyd smiled at her dumbly, a big grin on his simple face, still madly and hopelessly head-over-heels in love.

"You figured right," Ellie said, not a trace of the wide-eyed purity left in her now hardened, stern demeanor. "It's a pity. You should have left Salmon Cove when you had the chance."

"How long did you know the truth about your grandfather?" Hayley asked.

"Since I was about fifteen or sixteen. I was up one night watching one of those late-night true crime shows on Discovery Channel or something, and there he was, my grandfather, on TV in old news footage, a mafia crime boss! Can you imagine the shock?"

"You must have been devastated," Liddy whispered, trying desperately to stay calm.

"Devastated? Hardly! Actually, I thought it was pretty cool. I was invisible at school, didn't have many friends, nobody really cared to hang out with me or get to know me. I was just the awkward, lost little girl who lived with her soused grandfather. But now I had this huge, amazing secret that made me special. I'll never forget Granddaddy's face when I confronted him about knowing everything! Even that he lied about my father having died in a plane crash when he was in reality wasting away in prison for the rest of his life! I thought Granddaddy was going to keel over right then and there. He thought I was just this sweet, innocent young thing who was far too fragile to handle the truth, but he was wrong . . ."

"It turns out you take after him in more ways than one," Hayley said pointedly, eliciting a small pout from Ellie.

"Yes, I suppose so," she said haughtily. "I told him his secret was safe with me, and I never breathed a word to anyone."

"And everything was hunky-dory until Jackson Young showed up in town," Hayley said.

Ellie nodded. "Granddaddy spent most days at the Starfish Lounge downing his whiskeys, without a care in the world, but I was obsessed with getting caught. He was getting sloppy and careless, and so I spent every day constantly online reading up on the FBI's search for him and all the fame-whore journalists trying to beat them to it for a scoop, so Conner Higgins was on my radar long before he brazenly arrived in town pretending to be a travel writer. I pegged him right away!"

"You knew Boyd was in love with you and would do anything for you, and was easily susceptible to manipulation. So you convinced him that the alien invasions he was so obsessed reading about in his comic books were real, and that was how you got him to do your bidding."

Boyd, only half listening, just gazed happily at Ellie. "She loves me."

"Yes, I do, Boyd, very much," she said, gently stroking the side of his face. "Now do me a favor and go find a shovel. I think I saw one in the garage propped up against the tractor."

"What do you want me to do with it?"

"I want you to dig two holes out back near the edge of the woods, okay? Can you do that for me, sweetheart?"

"Anything for you," Boyd said as she leaned in and lightly kissed him on the cheek.

Liddy was near tears, her whole body shaking, while Hayley fought hard to keep her cool and try to figure a way out of this. Her best option at the moment was to just keep Ellie talking.

Boyd lumbered up the steps and outside, leaving Ellie playfully tapping the barrel of her pistol against the side of her leg.

"I couldn't stomach the thought of that obnoxious reporter writing some tell-all, splashy article in *Vanity Fair* or *Rolling Stone*, using my beloved granddaddy to get his Pulitzer . . ."

"So you told Boyd he was part of the alien invasion, and you had him strangle Higgins to death on the beach at the clambake when no one was around. You thought that was the end of it, but then when you came to the bar to pick up Rufus a couple of nights ago you saw Liddy snapping photos of her car tires and a few of them happened to catch your grandfather in the background so you had him try to steal her camera at our cabin, and when that didn't work, he just snatched her off the street. Did Rufus have any idea what was going on?"

"I kept him informed every step of the way. It was his idea to keep your friend down here for a while, at least until all the brouhaha over Jackson Young's death died down, when we could take care of her properly so she would never be found."

"That's why he lied to me at the bar about seeing Liddy drive out of town," Hayley said. "He was aware of what you were up to and was doing whatever he could to help you cover your tracks and make it look like Liddy left on her own accord."

Liddy, panicked, threw herself at Ellie, who stepped back, raising her gun to keep her at bay. "Please, Ellie, Rufus is gone now! There is no reason to be afraid of him getting arrested or going to trial! The whole nightmare of hiding is over! So just let us go. I swear we won't say anything to anyone!"

"I wish I could believe you, I really do, but I'm much smarter than you give me credit for. There is no way you won't tell someone about all this. I was going to eventually pin everything on Boyd, let him go down for the Conner Higgins murder, I even planned on attending his trial, and testifying as a character witness, but he would obviously lose in court and be put away forever, and I would give him a tearful good-bye, make my lips quiver just so, and lie and tell him I would wait for him. I would send him off believing I was still behind him one hundred percent and then just be done with the big dumb goon!"

"You're a regular Meryl Streep," Hayley said, disgusted.

"You have to be a good actress when you're hiding from the feds," Ellie said with a crooked half smile.

"Please, I'm begging you, Ellie, don't kill us!" Liddy wailed.

"Stop whining! You're really starting to irritate me," Ellie shouted.

"Think about it, Ellie. Sue already knows the truth about Rufus, as well as the entire FBI, and it's only a matter of time before they round you up for questioning, it makes no sense to harm us at this point."

"You said it yourself, Hayley. I'm a regular Meryl Streep. I think I can still deliver one more good performance as the adoring, well-mannered, but hopelessly naïve granddaughter, who was totally in the dark about her family history, and will need the support of her loyal townsfolk to help her get over the shock and trauma. Yeah, I can totally pull that off!"

"But what about us?" Liddy cried.

"What a shame about you two, everybody thought you left town to avoid having to go to trial for all that breaking and entering and tampering with evidence business! What an awful mess you were in! I would run away too! But when all of your family and friends report you missing, the sad truth emerges that you were just the poor, unsuspecting victims of a deluded nutcase who actually thought aliens were running around Salmon Cove! I can hear people buzzing about it at the Starfish Lounge now. 'Can you believe that crazy boy killed *three* people? I heard they found those poor women buried in his backyard! Such a tragedy!'"

"Ellie, you can't be serious—!" Hayley said.

Ellie turned her head and called up the cellar stairs. "How are you doing up there, Boyd?"

They could hear him yelling back faintly from a distance. "Just about done! Two big holes!"

Liddy fell against Hayley, about to faint dead away, as Hayley grabbed her by the shoulders to keep her from collapsing to the ground.

Chapter 33

"After you, ladies," Ellie said, gesturing for them to head up the stairs with the gun in her hand.

"No! You're going to shoot us and bury us in those holes!" Liddy cried, hugging Hayley.

"I can just as easily shoot you down here, it honestly doesn't make any difference to me. I'm just trying to save Boyd the trouble of having to lug your bodies up those flimsy old stairs and I don't want him straining his back!"

"You're so cold, Ellie," Hayley whispered, shaking her head.

"You said it yourself, Hayley. I take after my grandfather. Now move," she seethed, losing her patience.

"Come on, Liddy," Hayley said soberly, leading her by the arm past Ellie, who kept her gun trained on them, and up the stairs to the outside of the cellar.

When they reached ground level, both Hayley and Liddy squinted from the blazing sun and covered their eyes, after being trapped in a dark basement.

Ellie looked around for Boyd, but there was no sign of him.

"Boyd?" she hollered. "Boyd, honey, where are you?"

They noticed the two holes that had been freshly dug

on the far side of the property near a thicket of trees but the shovel had been left lying on the ground.

"Boyd!" Ellie yelled, slightly nervous.

A couple of small birds rustled some tree branches as they flapped their wings and flew away, and then there was stillness again.

Hayley saw Ellie gripping her gun tighter as her eyes darted around, suddenly suspicious.

And then they heard a low, even voice directly behind Ellie.

"Put the gun down."

It was Sheriff Daphne Wilkes, and she held her own standard-issue police pistol, pointing it right between Ellie's shoulder blades.

Ellie hesitated, her mind racing.

"I'm not going to tell you again, Ellie. Do it now," Sheriff Daphne said.

She wasn't kidding.

She was fully prepared to shoot.

And Ellie knew it.

She slowly bent down, set the gun on the ground, and then raised her hands in the air.

Within seconds Daphne had her weapon holstered and Ellie's hands cuffed behind her back.

Sheriff Daphne's squad car was parked in front of the main house. Hayley could see Boyd locked in the backseat, his own hands cuffed behind him, a subdued, sad look on his face. Mona and Corey were positioned behind the car, out of harm's way, undoubtedly at the behest of the Salmon Cove sheriff, who clearly didn't want to endanger them until both suspects were safely in custody.

Ellie appeared to be in a trancelike state, emotionally shut down, as Sheriff Daphne escorted her over to the squad car. After all her herculean efforts to keep a lid on her family's secret, she just couldn't believe her single-minded mission had failed so miserably and spectacularly.

Once Ellie was placed in the back of the squad car with Boyd, Sheriff Daphne gave Mona and Corey the all clear, and they raced over to Hayley and Liddy, who was still a little light-headed and wobbly from the entire ordeal so Hayley kept her hands clasped firmly onto her shoulders to keep her steady.

"So my call to you got through! Thank you, Jesus!" Hayley cried.

"At first we thought you had just accidentally butt dialed me, but then we heard Boyd and Ellie talking and put two and two together, and that's when we called the sheriff, jumped in Corey's truck, and raced right over here to meet her," Mona said.

"If you had gotten here just a few minutes later, it might have been too late," Hayley said, glancing at Liddy, whose eyes were heavy, like she was in a state of shock.

"Well, I got to say, I know we've had a few run-ins with that sheriff, but she arrived on the scene before we did, and let me tell you, that woman is fearless. I bet she can kick some serious ass!" Mona said, impressed.

"Are you okay, Liddy?" Hayley asked, still holding her up.

Liddy nodded, forcing a smile on her face. "Yes, I'm fine."

"Really? Because you look a little pale," Hayley said.

"No, seriously, I'm good," Liddy said.

"I'm going to let go of you now, okay?"

Liddy nodded again, and Hayley slowly removed her hands from Liddy's shoulders. Her eyes rolled up in the back of her head and she promptly fainted and dropped to the ground in a heap.

Corey rushed in and scooped her up in his arms. "I'll take her over to my truck. Sadie's waiting in the back and that dog is real good at waking people up with a lot of sloppy wet licks to the face."

Corey carried her off like some romantic hero from a Nicholas Sparks novel.

Hayley turned to Mona. "He's a really good guy."

"I know," Mona finally admitted.

Sheriff Daphne ambled over to them.

"Sheriff Wilkes, I just want to say—" Hayley said.

Daphne held up her hand. "There's no need to say anything. I acted irresponsibly and unprofessionally, and that's on me. I just want you ladies to know I'm going to drop the breaking and entering charges."

"Thank you," Hayley said, smiling.

"But you still have to pay the parking tickets," she said, not cracking a smile.

Mona opened her mouth to protest, but Hayley elbowed her in the rib cage and she shut it again.

"So I guess everything's all wrapped up now," Hayley said.

"Not quite," Daphne said. "We know Ellie hoodwinked Boyd into strangling that journalist at the clambake, but there is still the matter of Rufus, or as we now know him, Enos O'Shannon."

"Wait, you said you believe he died of natural causes," Hayley said.

"I did. In fact, I was sure of it, but Sue pressured me into shipping the body to the county coroner's office for an autopsy, and I did just to prove her wrong so she'd stop hassling me. They just called me with the results," Daphne said, pausing, not for dramatic effect, but because she was ashamed she had been so adamant and yet so wrong. "He was poisoned."

Hayley gasped. "Poisoned?"

"By a pretty hefty dose of it too. Someone was really determined to knock him off," Daphne said.

"How did they get it into his system?" Hayley asked.

"I asked myself the same thing, and so I asked the doctor to list all of the stomach contents that were in his report, and he told me that all he found was traces of blueberry pie."

"Blueberry pie?" Mona asked.

"Polly Roper," Hayley said in disbelief.

"What about her?" Daphne asked.

"She told me she regularly baked blueberry pies for Rufus because he loved them so much," Hayley said. "But why? What motive could she possibly have to murder Rufus? Unless . . ."

"Unless what?" Mona and Daphne both said at the same time.

"Polly was somehow aware of Rufus's true identity, that he was in fact Enos O'Shannon, and you can be sure a violent and murderous mafia crime boss like O'Shannon has a long history of ruining people's lives along the way, and there has to be more than a few of them who might be willing to do anything to exact revenge."

Chapter 34

"Something sure smells good," Hayley said as she entered Polly Roper's kitchen to find her bent over and taking a baking pan out of the oven while wearing oven mitts with pictures of little lobsters on them.

"I'm making chocolate chip cookies with nuts and raisins for the fifth-grade class at the Salmon Cove Elementary school," Polly said as she carefully set the pan down on a cooling rack.

She picked up a green ceramic bowl and started vigorously stirring it with a wooden spoon. "This batch is without nuts because little Stevie Harrison is allergic."

Hayley nodded and smiled.

"Go ahead, help yourself," Polly said.

"No, thanks," Hayley said, a bit too abruptly, which caused Polly to look up from her cookie batter.

"Seriously?"

"Yes, I'm good."

"Hayley, I've read enough of your columns to know you have a bigger sweet tooth than I do!"

What was she going to say? *No, I'm not going to eat one of your cookies because I'm afraid they're laced with poison!*

Polly reached for a Saran Wrapped–covered plate on the counter, pulled back the plastic, and then walked over to personally offer her one.

Hayley didn't have much of a choice.

She picked up a small one off the plate, took a tiny bite, and chewed it, hoping Polly didn't have a nefarious plan to poison the entire fifth-grade class of Salmon Cove Elementary.

"Delicious!" Hayley said, swallowing quickly.

"Is anything wrong?" Polly asked, setting the plate of cookies down on the counter and looking at Hayley sideways as she folded the plastic wrap over it again.

Hayley fought to keep her cool. She was still reeling from the information she had uncovered, and didn't know how she was going to go about bringing it up with Polly. Her only option at this point was to just plow ahead.

"I'm sure you've already heard the police solved that journalist's murder?" Hayley asked, as casually as she could manage.

"Yes, I did!" Polly gasped. "I could not believe it! I've known Boyd for years and he always struck me as such a gentle boy, granted not too bright, but hardly capable of harming anyone let alone strangling a poor man to death!"

"I guess when you are so hopelessly in love and impressionable like he was, you can see how he could have been easily manipulated," Hayley said.

"By Ellie, of all people! Honestly, she's the last person in town I would ever suspect of having such a devious, murderous mind! She came across as so sweet and innocent!" Polly said as she lined a new baking pan with tin foil.

"She played the part perfectly. I suppose she had to because she couldn't risk anyone finding out about her grandfather Rufus."

"Now that's a wild story! A mafia don hiding out right

here in Salmon Cove! If that were the plot of a Hollywood movie, I would call it too over the top and utterly ridiculous to be believable!" she said, shaking her head, eyes focused on her baking pan as she poured dollops of cookie batter from the ceramic bowl onto the pan to form a fresh batch of cookies.

"I guess you just never know what kind of secrets people are hiding," Hayley said, a sharp, pointed tone in her voice.

Polly didn't flinch. She just flattened the three rows of cookie dough into round shapes, not looking up.

Hayley took a deep breath. "I'm sure a few more will bubble to the surface now that the police have ruled Rufus's death a homicide."

Polly finally looked up from her cookie dough. "Excuse me?"

"Someone murdered him."

"But I heard he died of natural causes, I mean, let's be frank, the man was well into his eighties and a heavy drinker!"

"That would make sense if they hadn't found poison in his system."

"Poison? Really?"

"Yes, not to mention traces of blueberry pie."

Polly stiffened. "What are you implying, Hayley?"

"The poison had to get into his system somehow."

"So you believe I put poison in one of the blueberry pies I gave him? That's preposterous, Hayley! What possible motive would I have to kill him?"

"Because you knew that his true identity was Enos O'Shannon."

"How could I know about all that? I'm just like you, a small-town wannabe chef with a cooking column in my local paper! Hardly someone with connections to a big-city mob boss! I'm sure that man made plenty of enemies in his line of work! The police should be chasing after them!"

"But none of those enemies tracked him down here four years ago, set up stakes here in town, and plotted their revenge!"

"I'm sure I don't know what you are talking about!" Polly said, shoving the baking pan with the cookie dough into the oven and accidentally burning her finger on the oven rack. She yelped and licked her red finger with her lips. She was rattled, and Hayley knew it.

"Just like Ellie, you played your part well. Your name isn't Polly Roper, is it? It's Janice Fields."

Polly flinched for the first time. She slowly withdrew her burnt finger from her lips and stared at Hayley.

"You are the daughter of Joe Fields, a restaurant owner in South Boston who refused to pay protection money to Enos so he shot him in cold blood. The police knew it, you knew it, but there just wasn't enough evidence to convict him so he got away with it. And shortly after that, O'Shannon disappeared, never to be heard from again. The idea of him being out there, free to live his life, ate you up inside, until you somehow found him here."

Polly's eyes welled up with tears, her mouth agape, as Hayley nailed her to the wall with the truth.

"How did you do it? How did you find him when all the resources of the FBI couldn't do it?"

"It was a complete accident—" Polly said, shaking. "I came here on a lark, a summer vacation, I love seafood and hiking and I read about this place in a travel magazine and it just seemed so perfect. And on my first day here, literally hours after I arrived, I passed him on the street. It was like a sign! I was meant to find him!"

"But instead of alerting the authorities, you decided to take matters into your own hands."

"How could I allow that ruthless, cowardly killer to be put back in the public eye like some celebrity? The press would have turned him into a legend, the crime boss who eluded the feds for so long! I couldn't stomach the thought of seeing his smug face on TV every day, books being written about him, it was just too much to bear!"

"So you quietly moved here and told everybody you were Polly Roper, an aspiring chef and food writer, got a job at the paper, made friends with all the locals, played to their love of sweets, discovered Rufus was a fan of blueberry pie, and waited for the right moment."

"I didn't want to knock him off too soon after I got here because I wanted to become a part of the community to avoid any unnecessary suspicion. I wanted to wait a few years, and I honestly didn't plan to do it when I did, but when that investigative journalist was killed at the clambake, and suddenly there was all this attention focused on Salmon Cove, I knew I had to act fast before someone else recognized Rufus so I made my usual blueberry pie delivery to his house, this one with my extra little ingredient added in the pie filling, and waited for him to get hungry!"

"And because of his advanced age, you thought people would just assume he died of natural causes, except Sue didn't, which led her to push for an autopsy."

"I certainly didn't choose a fast-acting poison. I wanted him to suffer a slow, painful death, and I am happy to report he did. I hope as he was sprawled out on the floor dying, he thought about every life he took, every life he ruined!"

"But the sad result of all your efforts is you also ruined your own life," Hayley said.

"What do you mean?"

"Enos O'Shannon was a horrible man whose past was littered with all sorts of heinous crimes, but that doesn't give you the right to kill him. Now you're going to have to pay for it!"

Polly noticed a sharp butcher knife lying on the counter, wrapped her fingers around the handle, and slowly raised it. "I don't see why we can't keep this little secret between us, right, Hayley? After all, we're friends! I bailed you and your buddies out of jail!"

"And I appreciate that, but the problem is, the secret isn't just between us anymore!"

"I don't understand—"

Hayley pulled up her shirt a bit to show her cell phone stuffed behind her belt. A red button on the screen indicated she was recording the entire conversation.

Polly stepped forward, gripping the knife, and said, "Give me the phone, Hayley."

"It won't do you any good, Polly, because I wasn't foolish enough to come here alone."

Sheriff Daphne Wilkes suddenly swept into the kitchen, gun drawn, and pointed it at Polly, who dropped the butcher knife. It clattered to the floor. She slowly raised her hands in the air and started to weep softly.

"I'm sorry, Polly, but you are under arrest for murder," Daphne said as she stepped forward and kicked the knife to the other side of the kitchen, safely out of her reach, and turned her around.

As Daphne passed Hayley, she gave her a little wink, acknowledging she was proud of how she had handled the situation.

Hayley was taken aback. Praise from her former adversary was unexpected. But it made her feel good inside. Maybe, just maybe, these two could wind up as friends.

As Daphne read Polly her rights while patting her down, Hayley surreptitiously moved over to the pan of cookies on the cooling rack. Now that she was certain they were safe for consumption, she plucked one from the plate and popped it in her mouth.

Chapter 35

"I'm sure going to miss this place," Mona said as she, Hayley, and Liddy did one last look around her uncle's cabin to make sure they hadn't forgotten to pack anything.

"Mona, you can't be serious," Liddy scoffed.

"I don't know, being here brings back a lot of childhood memories when it was such a simpler time and I had my whole life ahead me, and I didn't have an inkling I would end up marrying my deadbeat husband, Dennis, and get stuck with a wild, uncontrollable bunch of brats . . ." she said, eyeing Hayley's and Liddy's judgmental faces, before quickly adding, ". . . all of whom I love unconditionally!"

"I think we're good," Hayley said. "We've certainly left the cabin cleaner than when we found it."

As they headed out to the car, Mona stopped to lock the front door with a key. A white pickup truck rolled up, and Sadie jumped out of the back, tail wagging, and ran over to Mona, panting. She warmly petted the top of her head.

Corey slid out of the driver's seat, looking impossibly

sexy in a pair of tight jeans and a plaid work shirt with the sleeves rolled up.

"Thought I'd swing by and say good-bye one more time before you left," he said with a sad smile.

It was obvious he didn't want Mona to leave.

Mona kept her focus on Sadie, and was now down on her knees scratching underneath the dog's chin, avoiding eye contact with Corey.

Undeterred, he ambled over to her. "It was sure nice seeing you again, Mona."

"Yeah, it was," Mona said as casually as she could, and then she rubbed noses with Sadie. "It was nice meeting you, too! You're a good girl, yes you are, a good girl!"

"I'm hoping you'll come see me again sometime," he said.

"Well, you know I got my lobster business to run, and my kids are quite a handful as I'm sure I've told you, and—"

"Come here, Sadie," Corey called, slapping the side of his leg.

Sadie licked Mona's face and then obediently returned to her master, leaving Mona no choice but to finally look up at Corey.

Her eyes were brimming with tears, and her face, if not full of regret for what might have been, certainly betrayed a fondness and warmth for the man in front of her, and the strong, deep connection that had been reignited.

Mona hastily wiped away her tears and bit her quivering lip.

Corey stepped forward and gently hugged her.

She clasped her arms around him, holding him tightly, enjoying their last moments together.

When he pulled away, he took her by the shoulders, stared into her eyes, and then moved in for a kiss. She turned her head so his lips would land on her cheek, but he anticipated it, and lifted one hand, using his index finger to turn her head back to face him, in a perfect position for a lip lock.

Mona half struggled, certainly not forcefully, and then, she melted into it, and just let it happen.

Liddy audibly sighed, caught up in the romance of it all, even though it wasn't happening to her.

And then, Corey Guildford brushed the side of Mona's cheek with his hand one more time, and turned and strolled back to his truck with Sadie chasing after him.

"I'm married, you know!" Mona yelled.

"I know, you told me! That's why I did it!" he called back, not turning around.

"What are you talking about?"

"I figured if I had one last chance to kiss you before you went home, I sure as hell was going to make it count!"

He opened the driver's-side door of his truck, allowing Sadie to jump in first and settle into the passenger's seat, and then he climbed in and rode away.

Hayley, Mona, and Liddy stood in front of the cabin, in silence, watching the truck speed down the road, kicking up dust as it disappeared in the distance.

"Well, I know one thing," Hayley said. "I really need a vacation after this vacation!"

"Please, can we finally go home now?" Liddy begged, pressing a button on her remote to unlock her Mercedes.

Mona foraged through her luggage in the trunk, grabbed a paper bag, and pulled out a banana, which she began to peel before Liddy snatched it out of her hand.

"No eating in the car, Mona!"

Mona grumbled before slamming the trunk shut and crawling in the back.

Hayley relaxed into the plush leather passenger seat.

With Liddy behind the wheel, they backed up, allowing Mona to steal one last look at her childhood camp, and then they zipped down the dirt road to the main highway.

They were only five minutes into the ride home when Liddy glanced up at her rearview mirror.

"You have got to be kidding me!"

They all turned around to see a police car on their tail, blue lights flashing.

"It can't be!" Mona barked.

"Yes, I think it is," Hayley said, sighing.

Liddy pulled the Mercedes to the side of the road and the police car pulled up behind them, so close their bumpers nearly touched.

Sheriff Daphne Wilkes got out, those intimidating sunglasses covering her eyes, her whole face tight and serious.

"I swear I wasn't speeding!" Liddy declared, before turning to Hayley. "Was I?"

Hayley shrugged. "I wasn't looking at the speedometer."

Daphne circled around to the driver's-side window and leaned down to get a good look inside the car as Liddy pressed the button to lower the window.

"Good afternoon, Sheriff," Liddy said, with as much respect as she could muster.

"Ladies," Sheriff Daphne said, glancing around for any illegal substances that might be lying around. "You out for a joy ride?"

"No, we're heading out of town," Liddy said, her voice cracking just a little. "As much as we've enjoyed our stay in Salmon Cove, it is finally time to go home!"

"I see," she said, nodding. "Tell you what, why don't I give you a police escort to the edge of town?"

"You don't have to do that," Liddy said.

"I insist."

Daphne stood up and walked back to her car, hopped in, and then pulled out in front of them, blue lights still flashing.

Left with no choice, Liddy followed her.

"A police escort, really?" Liddy laughed. "That's a little over the top, but a nice gesture, I guess."

"There's nothing nice about it," Hayley said. "She wants to make sure we cross the county line and don't come back!"

Island Food & Spirits
by
Hayley Powell

I was flipping through my old card file of recipes the other day and happened upon one of my favorites—Lobster Mac & Cheese. This particular recipe reminded me of a promise I had made just about a year ago when my girlfriends and I found ourselves embroiled in some big trouble while vacationing Down East in Salmon Cove because we'd met a man who happened to love lobster.

Well, after a tragic turn of events and a situation that spiraled out of our control that is too exhausting to recount here, let's just say the girls and I found ourselves in quite a jam. Okay, to be honest, we found ourselves in jail, and this nice woman named Polly, whom I had met earlier, was kind enough to bail us out.

Anyway, I promised to pay her back by giving her one of my recipes, but sadly I never got the chance, as she was unexpectedly forced to leave town. Okay, full disclosure, she was whisked off to serve time in the state pen for murder, but that's another story.

Still, a promise is a promise, and so I decided to test the Lobster Mac & Cheese recipe to see if it was as good as I had remembered. As luck would have it, I already had some cooked lobster meat from Mona in the freezer as well as a hunk of amazing gouda cheese that Liddy had given me after she'd raided our favorite wine and cheese shop in town, House of Wines, a few weeks prior, but then decided she needed to preserve her delicate waistline after the purchase, so she got rid of the cheese and I was the happy beneficiary. She kept the wine for herself, however, because, in her words, "If I'm going to stick to my diet, I'm going to need a lot of wine to help me get through it!"

So, with my necessary ingredients, I prepared the Lobster Mac & Cheese and used my brother's husband, Sergio, as my guinea pig! As Randy and Sergio both used their forks to scrape the bottom of the casserole dish for every last piece of melted cheese, I knew my recipe was a hit! Now I had to try to find a way to get it to Polly! I wrote her a sweet note, apologizing for the amount of time it took me to fulfill my promise, but when I called the state prison to get her exact address, they told me she had already been paroled, and they did not have any forwarding information.

I was stunned. How did she get out so early? Where did she go? Did she move back to Salmon Cove?

I called the only person I knew who might have some answers.

Sheriff Daphne Wilkes in Salmon Cove.

When Sheriff Wilkes answered the phone, she was all business as usual with no time for small talk. She informed me that after a trial that ended with a dead-locked jury, the prosecutors, given the violent criminal past of the victim, feared they would never get a murder one conviction so they offered Polly a plea of manslaughter plus time served, which she accepted. After a year of good behavior, Polly was released and was now working in a bakery in South Portland. Sheriff Daphne gave me the name of the bakery, and before I had a chance to thank her, she abruptly hung up. Like I said, all business.

I mailed off the recipe to Polly. I never heard from her, and I had no idea if she'd even received it, but my guess was she probably wanted to put that whole sordid chapter of her life in Salmon Cove behind her, so I was not the least bit offended by her lack of response.

About a month or so later, I was home watching my imaginary boyfriend Mark Harmon on *NCIS* when the phone rang. When I picked it up, I was stunned to hear the voice of Sheriff Daphne Wilkes. Only this time she wasn't gruff and distant and all business. I could tell she was crying, and as she spoke, I listened in utter disbelief. When she finished with her news, I immediately hung up the phone, jumped in my car, and drove as fast as I could to Mona's lobster shop, where I knew she would be.

Screeching to a halt, I could see Mona through the open door standing behind her cash register, staring into a bubbling tank of live lobsters. I hurried inside the shop. She looked up at me with tears in her eyes and then collapsed in my arms sobbing uncontrollably.

Sadly, the reason Sheriff Wilkes called me was to get Mona's phone number. They may not have been great friends, but they did have something in common, and that was their close friendship with Corey Guildford.

Sheriff Wilkes called to break the news that Corey Wilkes had died that day on the ocean that he loved, doing what he loved most, in a freak lobstering accident.

Mona, Liddy, and I canceled our annual summer getaway plans and drove to Salmon Cove to attend Corey's funeral. It was a somber affair; the people of Salmon Cove adored Corey, he was a local fixture along with his truck and beloved dog, Sadie.

Sadie.

What was to become of Sadie, Corey's golden retriever, his constant sidekick and faithful companion?

According to Sheriff Wilkes, Sadie ran off when she showed up at Corey's house after the accident, and was probably out looking for her master. There had been a few spottings by locals, but no one had managed to catch her. When they tried to get her in a car or on a leash, she would take off running again.

On our way out of town after the burial, Mona requested we stop one last time at the cemetery so she could have a private good-bye with her friend and first love. Liddy and I sat in the car, tears streaming down our faces as we watched Mona kneel down on the ground in front of Corey's grave. That's when Sadie suddenly appeared out of nowhere and began licking away Mona's tears. She put her arm around the dog, and we all took it as a sign that Mona should be the one to give Sadie a new home and a fresh start. In her heart, Mona felt that's what Corey would have wanted. So we had one more in the car as we drove back to Bar Harbor.

Today I'm sharing my mouth-watering, addictive Lobster Mac & Cheese recipe, and Polly, if you are reading this, I will always be grateful for your friendship and kindness when we most needed it!

I enjoy a nice dry red wine with my Lobster Mac & Cheese, but if you would like to fancy it up a bit, here is an easy Red Wine Spritzer recipe to enjoy beforehand.

Red Wine Spritzer

<u>Ingredients</u>
Bottle of your favorite red wine
Carbonated water
A few raspberries (or your favorite
    berry), for garnish

Fill a tall glass half full with ice and
then fill the glass halfway with your red
wine. Top off the glass with carbonated
water and add a few berries for garnish on
top. Easy but oh so refreshing.

Luscious Lobster
Mac & Cheese

<u>Ingredients</u>
16-ounce box pasta shells (or your
    favorite pasta)
¼ cup flour
3 cups milk
1 cup shredded sharp white cheddar
    cheese
1 cup shredded gruyere cheese
1 cup shredded fontina cheese
1 teaspoon each: salt, ground black
    pepper, garlic powder
2 cups crushed Ritz crackers

Cook your pasta to almost al dente
according to the directions on the box.
Drain and set aside.

While your pasta is cooking, melt 3 tablespoons of the butter in a saucepan over medium heat. Whisk in the flour, then slowly add your milk. Whisk until it begins to thicken a bit, add your cheeses, and keep stirring until they are melted. Remove from heat and add your salt, pepper, and garlic.

In a large bowl add your pasta, chopped lobster, and cheese sauce. Stir to combine, making sure all the pasta is evenly coated in the cheese sauce. Pour into a greased 13x9 baking dish.

In a small saucepan melt the remaining 3 tablespoons butter and mix with the cracker crumbs. Sprinkle evenly over the top of the lobster and pasta.

Bake in a preheated 375 degree oven for 25 to 30 minutes until hot and bubbly and cracker crumbs are golden brown. Remove from oven and let the dish sit for at least 10 minutes before digging in! Bon appetit!

Index of Recipes

Dear Reader:

We hope you enjoyed *Death of a Lobster Lover*, the latest installment in the Hayley Powell Food & Cocktails Mystery series. This was a particularly fun book to write because it's always a joy to explore the bond between Hayley and her pals Liddy and Mona, her two best friends since childhood. And a fun girls' weekend road trip story seemed the perfect way to do that.

Hayley will return next year in *Death of a Cookbook Author*, a brand new mystery, which finds our intrepid heroine faced with a real head scratching puzzle. It all starts when Hayley excitedly attends a Meet the Author event at her local bookstore featuring her idol Penelope Janice, a mega successful cookbook author, who it turns out is also an admirer of Hayley's recipes in the Island Times. Penelope is hosting a celebrity potluck at her fancy seaside estate in Seal Harbor during the long Fourth of July weekend. It's an annual tradition. Penelope invites all her favorite famous chef friends to gather at her home and prepare their signature dishes in a friendly competition. Much to Hayley's shock, Penelope invites her to participate, and even offers her a room in the main house so she has full access to Penelope's state of the art kitchen and full-time staff. It's a dream come true for an amateur cook!

But on the very first night, Hayley gorges on a batch of spoiled mussels and later suffers from a nasty bout of food poisoning. Disoriented and nauseous, she wanders about lost in the mansion late at night in search of a bathroom and accidentally overhears two guests conspiring against their hostess Penelope. The next day, no one seriously believes Hayley's wild tale of a murder plot especially given her fevered state at the time, but then a dead body is discovered on the rocks below the cliffside estate, and it suddenly becomes clear to everyone that something sinister is definitely afoot. Now it's up to Hayley Powell to whip up some answers in what promises to be her most twisty, toe-curling suspense-filled adventure yet!

Please be sure to check our website LeeHollis Mysteries.com for the release date of Hayley's next mystery and visit us on Facebook for more information and mouthwatering recipes by typing in Lee Hollis.

Sincerely Yours,

Lee Hollis

Connect with

Visit us online at
KensingtonBooks.com
to read more from your favorite authors, see books
by series, view reading group guides, and more.

for sneak peeks, chances to win books and prize packs,
and to share your thoughts with other readers.

facebook.com/kensingtonpublishing
twitter.com/kensingtonbooks

Tell us what you think!

To share your thoughts, submit a review,
or sign up for our eNewsletters, please visit:
KensingtonBooks.com/TellUs.